HE DO THE POLICE IN
DIFFERENT VOICES

Other Books by David Langford

Fiction

An Account of a Meeting with Denizens of Another World, 1871
Earthdoom! (with John Grant)
The Dragonhiker's Guide to Battlefield Covenant at Dune's Edge: Odyssey Two
Guts (with John Grant) *
Irrational Numbers
The Leaky Establishment
A Novacon Garland
The Space Eater

Nonfiction

A Cosmic Cornucopia (with Josh Kirby)
The Complete Critical Assembly *
Critical Assembly
Critical Assembly II
Facts and Fallacies (with Chris Morgan)
Micromania: The Whole Truth About Home Computers (with Charles Platt)
The Necronomicon (with George Hay, Robert Turner and Colin Wilson)
Pieces of Langford
Platen Stories
The Science in Science Fiction (with Peter Nicholls and Brian Stableford)
The Silence of the Langford
The Third Millennium: A History of the World AD 2000-3000 (with Brian Stableford)
The TransAtlantic Hearing Aid
The Unseen University Challenge
Up Through an Empty House of Stars: Reviews and Essays 1980-2002 *
War in 2080: The Future of Military Technology
The Wyrdest Link

As Editor

The Encyclopedia of Fantasy (with John Clute, John Grant, and others)
Maps: The Uncollected John Sladek
Wrath of the Fanglord

* In Cosmos Books

HE DO THE TIME POLICE IN DIFFERENT VOICES

SF Parody and Pastiche

David Langford

Cosmos Books
An imprint of **Wildside Press**

HE DO THE TIME POLICE IN DIFFERENT VOICES

Published by:

Cosmos Books, an imprint of Wildside Press
PO Box 301, Holicong, PA 18928-0301
www.wildsidepress.com

For more information, contact Wildside Press.

ISBN: 1-59224-057-7 (hardback)
ISBN: 1-59224-058-5 (trade paperback)

For Rog Peyton

Contents

PART ONE
The Dragonhiker's Guide to Battlefield Covenant at Dune's Edge: Odyssey Two

PART TWO
2

Foreword

This expanded volume of Langford parodies and pastiches is dedicated to Rog Peyton, founder of the Andromeda Bookshop in Birmingham, England, whose Drunken Dragon Press commissioned and published the original collection – Part One of this book – in 1988. The press name may help to explain the stipulated inclusion, early on, of a drunken dragon.

For that now modestly rare hardback, Rog gleefully insisted on cramming the title page with the legend *The Dragonhiker's Guide to Battlefield Covenant at Dune's Edge: Odyssey Two; The Collected Science Fiction and Fantasy Parodies of David Langford, Volume 1....* More or less in the same breath he proposed that in due course there must be a second volume to be called, in full, *2*. So I've used this title for the additional material in the second and longer part of this book. Thanks again, Rog.

There was no paperback of the 1998 collection, except in Spanish translation. Believe me, it is a proud and lonely thing to be the author of the splendidly titled *Guía del Dragonstopista Galáctico al Campo de Batalla Estelar de Covenant en el Límite de Dune: Odisea Dos*. Confusingly, "The Dragonhiker's Guide to Battlefield Covenant at Dune's Edge: Odyssey Two" is also the title of a polemical essay collected in my *The Silence of the Langford* (NESFA Press, 1996). I no longer have any terribly plausible explanation of how this happened.

February 2003

PART ONE

The Dragonhiker's Guide to Battlefield Covenant at Dune's Edge: Odyssey Two

Introduction

Strange things happen to you when you're famous.

I was sitting at the typewriter recently, effortlessly tapping out my forty-second page of the morning and wondering whether to pause for breakfast (my enormous output and dedication are just two of the reasons for my being the best-known science and science-fiction writer in the world, and of course irresistible to women), when the telephone rang –

"Hello! This is Is**c As*m*v, slim and internationally celebrated writer and raconteur," I wisecracked into the mouthpiece with my usual lovable wit.

"Sorry, wrong number," said a voice at the other end.

After I had kicked the telephone into a billion (10^9, or 10^{12} in Great Britain) tiny fragments, I got to thinking about the sheer irrelevancy of this incident – and speaking of irrelevancy, it's time to switch to the subject of this month's essay, which is "My Six Favourite Numbers Between 15.008 and 16.155" –

These spoofs and squibs should need no introduction if you're an SF or fantasy fan, but this mere fact isn't going to stop me writing one....

Parody is a deadly vehicle for literary criticism, and it seems utterly reprehensible that such a megadeath critical doomsday-weapon should also be a whole lot of fun. One could write (and indeed one has written, until one is bored rigid with one's words on the topic) a coolly critical essay on the stylistic excesses of some author of persistently lumbering prose. It's more enjoyable and possibly even more effective to offer a condensed example:

"Hellfire!" erupted Thomas Covenant, his raw, self-inflicted nostrils clenching in white-hot, stoical anguish while his gaunt, compulsory visage knotted with fey misery. His lungs were clogged with ruin, and a snarl sprang across his teeth. A hot, gelid, gagging, fulvous tide of self-accusation dinned in his ears: *leper bestseller outcast unclean*.... To release the analystic refulgence, the wild magic of the white gold ring he wore, could conceivably shatter the Arch of Time, utterly destroy the Land, and put a premature, preterite end to the plot!

Yet what other way was there? The argute notion pierced his mind like a jerid. Only thus could the un-ambergrised malison of Lord Foul be aneled. Only thus. He clenched his clenching. Hellfire and damnation!

At that point he winced at a swift, sapid lucubration. "But I don't *believe* in this fantasy Land," he rasped with sudden caducity, lurching and reeling in vertigo as though from an overdose of clinquant roborant. "So even if it's utterly destroyed ... what's the odds? I'm a leper, I can do what I like."

With an exigent effort, he unclenched his teeth and articulated the aegis of his cynosure. Limned on his hand, the white gold ring began to flare darkly....

"Hang on a moment," flinched Lord Foul, his editor at Del Rey books. "Perhaps we could negotiate on this?"

Of course there are plenty of SF/fantasy excesses besides stylistic ones. People who write fairly functional prose can be riddled with such weaknesses as dodgy plot devices or over-used props, which the black-hearted parodist can seize upon with wicked glee, the swine, the rat, the unspeakable cad:

G'rot gazed up lovingly into the whirling, polychromatic eyes of his great bronze dragon. "You can do it, can't you, Filth?" he said proudly.

"Do what, G'rot?" asked Vanilla suspiciously.

G'rot topped up the huge stone dragon-trough with finest Benden firewater before answering, and snitched a mugful for himself. "As we Dragonriders of Pern have discovered, our wonderful dragons are not only telepathic and able to fly instantly *between* from one place to another ... they can also fly *between* times."

Flattery ... I love it, said Filth, lapping smugly. *The great thing about telepathy is being able to do it at the same time as drinking.*

"Tell me something I don't know, or I'll scratch your eyes out," snapped the lovely but peevish Vanilla.

G'rot sighed, and poured out a fresh carboy of firewater. Only by drinking this potent blue brew could the great dragons destroy the ever-present threats to Pern's crops – such as *dan'de'lines* and poison *i'vee* – with their fiery halitosis.

"Well," he said, "you'll also remember our song *The Ballad of Moron, Dragonlady of Pern*, in which lovely but wilful Moron comes to a sticky end thanks to flying too much overtime when delivering 'flu vaccine. My idea is this: why don't I and Filth fly back in time *between* novels to prevent this stupid tragedy by kidnapping lovely but incautious Moron just before her last, fatal flight? After which we can fly *between* to a future era which has better vaccine-producing facilities, and has learned to make hypodermic syringes instead of these ruddy hollow thorns. And then ..."

While they talked, distracted, the firewater was sinking dangerously low in the trough. The precious stuff could only be had from the blind Masterbrewer and his blind journeymen, who jealously guarded the aeons-old recipe which they called *meth'lated* or, sometimes, *seetooaitchfifeohaitch*.

"Take me with you, G'rot, or I'll kick you right in your undeveloped masculinity," retorted lovely but bitchy Vanilla.

"All in good time," said G'rot. "More haste less speed. Better late than never. You're not to bother your pretty little head with – Ouch!"

"You'll carry me, not him, Filth!" declared lovely but foul-tempered Vanilla, "The only problem is that if we do this to her great tragedy plot, A'nne M'Caffrey is going to be a bit upset...."

Sure fing, bosh, telepathed Filth. *I'm poished to obey your shlightesht command. Fly me, baby.* His huge, polychromatic eyes were whirling faster, and in different directions.

Vanilla stamped in irritation. The trough was empty! That chauvinist beast G'rot had distracted her from the vital need to control the dragon's appetite. Now everything would have to wait another few days while she nursed a behemoth-sized hangover. The Teaching Doggerel she'd learned at the age of two danced mockingly through her tomboyish mind....

> *Dragonman, avoid excess,*
> *Tell your beast to tipple less:*
> *The Harper is a licensed sot,*
> *But drunken dragons slow the plot.*

Hic, commented Filth, and awesomely fell over.

Cheeringly, a good many SF and fantasy parodies have already been written. John Sladek is the modern master: see his *The Steam-Driven Boy*. In *Bill, the Galactic Hero*, Harry Harrison dealt some shrewd blows to the ethos of *Starship Troopers* and the economics of the planetary galactic-empire headquarters in Asimov's *Foundation*. Michael Moorcock wrote a brief parody of his own gaudy fantasies in "The Stone Thing" (which, as is traditional for intentional self-parodies, avoided some of his real vices). Terry Pratchett's early Discworld novels carved a cruel swathe through the clichés of fantasy. There's also a scatter of less famous gems which deserve to be collected some day.

Max Beerbohm brought literary parody into the twentieth century with his collection *A Christmas Garland* (1912), which includes a deadly mockery of H.G. Wells's less convincing utopias. It's unlucky for us though probably lucky for Beerbohm that he never got to grips with the fantasy boom....

Fifty plate-armoured men confronted him at the door of the throne room, but Conan struck full upon them with a deafening crash of steel and spurting of blood. Swords leapt and flickered like flame. His blade tore through bodies as it might have torn through a doner kebab, ripping them open from spine to groin to broken breastbone to shattered shin. Bone parted from bone and limb from limb with many a guttural squelch. Then Conan was through, leaping over the steaming welter of blood and entrails which scant moments before had called itself the picked guard of the Supreme Emperor. Only one torn and rent survivor howled like a dying wombat as he clawed at the crimson stump that had been his nose.

Then it was the Emperor's turn. Cravenly, Maxwell the Merciless cowered back against his throne as Conan's blade sang towards him. His foul sorceries and mirror-mazes were of no avail against the avenging Cimmerian!

"Why, why?" the Emperor wailed as the sabre sank to its hilt and far beyond in his vile, overfed belly.

"Dialectical analysis of historical change inevitably predicts the decay of lickspittle capitalist imperialism and its replacement by enlightened socialist collectives," Conan grunted.

Some writers are still awaiting their come-uppance from a modern Beerbohm. Roger Zelazny's hyped-up early style is long overdue for parody: I started to draft one which was going to be all about gods on motorcycles. It was abandoned very soon after the opening line, which went "The sky was soot-streaked candyfloss, the night the gods hit town." From that point, there was nowhere to go but down: "The fear rose in me, then, like an ebony tidal wave, and did a lurching polka in my guts." Yes, there are possibilities there.

But it's almost impossible to send up someone like R.A. Lafferty, whose weird flamboyance leaves no room for further exaggeration. Samuel Delany's sprawling pyrotechnics and Gene Wolfe's maddening indirection are tempting targets, though a bull's-eye wouldn't be easy. Conversely, the millions of authors of "routine" space adventure tend to be unparodyable because there's nothing there to parody. How could one send up L. Ron Hubbard's later SF except by being even more tedious and interminable? (Good parodies need to stay fairly short.)

Tolkien would be difficult, too, since he didn't indulge in the right sort of excesses. *Bored of the Rings* is intermittently very funny but falls flat as parody: the authors couldn't find enough raw material in Tolkien himself, and struggled to get laughs by merciless use of anachronism – dragging in, for example, all those American brand names (assumed to be inherently hilarious). My own go at Tolkien admittedly didn't get far:

> "On second thoughts," said Gandalf, "these are matters higher and deeper and darker than hobbits in their small Shire can know. It is the hour for what Dwarves in their secret masonic speech know as *agabazfuttock*, but which to the Elves is *úrien-ation*, Chamberlain's Bane, and to the Men of Rohan *agenbite of inwit*: in the Common Tongue it may be rendered but as a feeble and far-off echo, thus: *political expediency*. Perilous though it may be, I must make trial of it for at least a little time. Frodo, kindly lend me the Ring...."

But I'm sounding awfully pompous and high-minded about Parody as Litcrit. The main purpose is fun. Elitist fun, perhaps, since the reader is expected to know a bit about what's being sent up: mass-market publishers are leery of parodies for just this reason. "Only fans would understand it" was a common response to my notion of an All-Time Best SF Parodies anthology. This depends a lot on the actual text. Sometimes a spoof will convey an all too accurate picture of what the unread original must have been like. Of the two following snippets, the first probably comes across without any need for prior knowledge as required by the second.

> His course of action was now clear. It was simply a matter of split-second timing: ducking the poisoned arrows, leaping lithely between the rotating knives, dodging under the arching cataract of molten lava, fording the piranha-infested lake, sprinting through the blazing refinery, using guile to sidestep the crazed onslaught of the entire Sioux nation, taking advantage of available cover in the ground-level nuclear test zone, holding his breath for the final dash through the airless vacuum of space, and triumphantly seizing the prize before his nonchalant return by the same route.
>
> "On the other hand," thought Indiana Jones, "I could always buy a new hat."

•

"I've just *wheeze* had an idea," said Darth Vader in his hoarse whisper. (He often wished there were some way to force throat pastilles through the awesome helmet's grille.) "Rather than *wheeze* sending attack ships to follow those silly people along the trench in the Death Star's surface, why don't we *wheeze* move the Star away from them under its own power, and *wheeze* have a go at them with the planet-busting doomsday weapons?"

"No need," murmured the Grand Moff Tarkin. "As soon as it became evident that the 'weak spot' in our defences had been spied out, I took the opportunity of ordering a slight modification to the Death Star's sewage outlet trench. Observe."

As the *Millennium Firkin* shrieked towards its goal, a terrific barrage of laser fire crackling and exploding on every side despite the lack of sound in the vacuum of space ... Han Solo screamed.

"In space, no one can hear you scream," said Chewbacca reprovingly.

Ahead, blocking the narrow way entirely, was a vast brick wall carrying the airbrushed slogan BYE-BYE, SUCKERS.

With microseconds to go before oblivion, the entire crew shouted: "Luke! *Use the Force!*"

Dutifully, Luke Skywalker shut his eyes, and stuck his fingers in his ears....

Since the dawn of literature, some authors have seemingly existed only to be parodied. One Victorian anthology contains 60 different parodies of Poe's "The Raven", all of them dire. Every verse parodist since the middle of the last century has had a go at Swinburne, and every *Punch* hack can be relied on (when humour, as usual, fails) to lurch into the time-worn Hemingway routine. In SF/fantasy, the one irresistible temptation is the adjectival gibbering of dear old H.P. Lovecraft – or do I mean HPL as unfairly adulterated by August Derleth?

They descended a thousand dank steps below the shuddering sub-cellar of the strange high house whose gambrel roof brooded over the oldest quarter of time-cursed Arkham. The fitful light of the gibbous moon sent no ray into this fungus-ridden abyss, where blackened and disfigured stonework was tortured into eldritch, cyclopean geometries, as though wrought by some elder race of nameless abominations which frothed in primal slime for unhallowed aeons before the birth of mankind.

"These stairs," whispered Marcus Whateley, "are *of no human shape.*"

"What do you see?" said his companion, holding the lantern high. The crumbled, blasphemous vault was heaped with evilly mouldering tomes, their mere covers a threat to sanity. An unnameable, charnel stench pervaded the nauseous air, seemingly a foul exhalation from some abominable lavatory of the Great Old Ones themselves.

Trembling, Whately stooped to peer at the awful texts. "Great God," he croaked in a paralysed voice. "Here are copies of the sinister *Liber Ivonis*, the infamous *Cultes des Ghoules* of the Comte d'Erlette, von Junzt's hellish *Unaussprechlichen Kulten*, and Ludvig Prinn's remaindered *De Vermis Mysteriis*. The forbidden *Pnakotic Manuscripts*, the unreadable *Book of Dzyan* ... and there, see! Bound in human skin, nothing less than the abhorred *Necronomicon* of the mad Arab Abdul Alhazred!"

There was a terror-laden pause before the eldritch reply smote upon Whately's fear-crazed ears –

"We've got all those: can you see a copy of *Astounding SF* for April 1943?"

Now read on. Some of my own efforts are obviously aimed at specific victims; others are more generic pokes at, say, fairy tales or A Certain Kind Of Space Opera. The intelligent and discerning reader will recognize this as an excuse for not writing further author-specific parodies, which are bloody exhausting.

Guest Introduction
H*rl*n Ell*s*n

Oy vey, have I got things to tell you about this bugfuck Langford! I'm not just full of wild blueberry muffins when I say that this god amongst authors has me chewing my crotch in vomitous envy of a *meshuga* prose style that – Well, he said, let's fling it foot-in-mouthly thisaway before I self-destruct with the awesomeness of it all.

In the bad old hip days of the sleazy not-so-swinging sixties when I walked the walk and talked the talk and helped screw up the System, it would happen that the pigs (which is how we of the Revolution would refer to our friendly psychopathic law enforcement officers, may their squamous skulls dissolve lubriciously into a substance resembling guacamole) would beguile an idle hour by grinding a large hard heavy nightstick into the kidneys of me and mine, and furthermore these moronic schlepps liked to pollute our precious bodily fluids by ramming the putzing thing right up one's tender ass.

That, friends, is pain as I have known it. Castrating, bowel-searing, tooth-drilling, drecky pain that makes all of Hiroshima and Auschwitz look like a case for a parking ticket and maybe a small fine.

Reading Langford is like that.

Xanthopsia
P**rs Anth*ny

On the third day of their quest, the two companions suddenly felt the crackle of strong and contrived magic in the air. This must be a potent region of Xanthopsia! Nothing significant could be seen, though, except for a small thicket of punjee-stick bushes, ready to punish intruders with angry punjabs.

"Something's happened to my water-bottle," said Thik, un-screwing the top. A boxing-glove shot out and dealt him a smart blow.

"The water's turned into punch!" cried Gabbia.

"Very bad punch...." Thik complained.

"And your jacket – it's changed, it seems to be made of tiny houses! The homespun cloth has turned into homes-pun!"

"You're talking like a pundit," Thik replied, which surprised him because, as usual, he'd never heard the word before.

Gabbia sniffed and drew back in shapely horror. "And you don't smell like a gentleman any more ... you've become pun-gent!"

"Maybe we're being punished in some way? Punitively?" As he spoke Thik tripped in the meshes of a small strawberry trap, or pun-net. Were they in danger of being expunged?

"No, *I* know what this must be," said Gabbia with an enchanting smile in spite of the magical safety-pin which had appeared in her nose. "We're crossing one of the wide desolate areas of magical padding for which Xanthopsia is so famous. This must be the site of the legendary Punic Wars! I must teach you the whole history of those wars."

"Why do you want to teach me things like that?" asked Thik, coming to a full stop.

Gabbia grinned again. "See all those full stops, commas and

colons lying around, and this safety pin in my nose? This is obviously the ideal spot for some punk tuition."

A deep, agonized groan of contrapuntal impatience was heard.

"Gosh, you know such a lot. I feel so puny, that is, so useless with my one miserable talent," mumbled Thik. "How come a girl like you with such enormous great round, uh, brain cells ... I mean, why do you hang out with me, Gabbia?"

"You mustn't feel inferior, Thik!" Gabbia scolded gently. "Your magical talent for being slow on the uptake is in fact incredibly useful! Can you guess why?"

Thik managed to tear his eyes from her amazing frontage long enough to shake his head.

"Well, without it, slow-witted readers could be in real trouble! Thanks to you and me and my own talent, which is for explaining things at great length in short words to morons, we can have these long talks which fill in the background and maybe even advance the story!"

Thik had lost the thread of Gabbia's kindly words, as he usually did when she lectured him for as long as that. He was distracted by staring at her, at her, uh, the place where her nicely rounded legs joined onto, as it were, the rest of her. But he got the gist all right. "You mean I'm really sort of important, then, Gabbia!"

"Not only that, Thik, but we're important! Remember, the Rich Magician Delrey has used his divination spells to look through the proofs of the next sequel, and it turns out that our very first child will have real Magician-class talent! A major talent that'll be needed to save the whole Land of Xanthopsia!" In her excitement Gabbia pulled absent-mindedly at her skirt, revealing a heart-stoppingly delightful ankle.

"What will this major talent be, Gabbia?" asked Thik, wriggling uncomfortably. "Excuse me, I couldn't have dressed properly today. It feels as if there's something hard in my underpants."

Gabbia flushed prettily. "It will be a *double* talent, for inventing both terrible puns and stupid magical talents!"

"My goodness!" gasped Thik, and blushed at himself for having used such strong language. With Gabbia around, he just couldn't control his ejaculations. "My word, then our quest *is* important! No wonder the Evil Critic wants to stop us reaching the Stork's Nest in the Gooseberry Bush!"

Tales of the Black Scriveners
Is**c As*m*v

... As Isaac the waiter poured the brandy, he murmured deprec-
atingly: "I believe, gentlemen, that I may have the solution to your
problem."

"You *can't!*" gasped Movias. "This is just a ploy to stop me
reciting my condensation of Johnson's Dictionary into limericks."

"Go on, Isaac," said Savimo. "Pay no attention to that dead-
beat."

"Thank you, sir. Firstly, it struck me at once that the late Dr
Osmavi must evidently have been a *literary* gentleman."

"What evidence is there for that?" put in Movias.

"The presence, sir, in his apartment, of Primo Levi's *The Periodic
Table*. In other words, a – book."

"Of ... course!"

"Now, gentlemen, we have heard that the New York Police
Department examined that book most painstakingly in their search
for the secret code word which – according to Dr Osmavi's last
words – was to be found '*in* the book'. They felt between the pages;
they probed the spine; they peeled back the endpapers. But they
failed to take into account the possibility that, owing to his literary
cast of mind, Dr Osmavi might in his final words have been
indicating not some loose slip of paper but a message actually
written in the book!"

"My God!" interjected Movias.

"In fact, I suggest that the secret code word which alone can
prevent World War III and forestall the Trantorian invasion is –
handwritten in one of the margins."

"Isaac, this is incredible," said Savimo handsomely. "It still
doesn't help us, though. We don't know *which* margin to look at ...

or which page. There are dozens of possibilities." He stared glumly at the slim volume lying on the dinner-table.

"With all respect, sir, I think we do know. Such a meticulous man as Dr Osmavi would undoubtedly have devised a private mnemonic, to ensure that the page number could never slip from his mind. And you will remember, gentlemen, the police report that in Dr Osmavi's final delirium he babbled scenes from Shakespeare."

"So what?" Movias grunted belligerently.

"Might I suggest, sir, that the only Shakespearean speech that could possibly be recognized by a policeman is Hamlet's famous soliloquy? Since I myself am a part-time existentialist, I have memorized the entire passage. *To be, or not to be –*"

"Got it!" shouted Movias, banging his fist on the table and making the brandy-glasses jump. "Be – B – the second letter of the alphabet, and so the code will be on page two!" He wrenched the book open ... and his face sagged loudly.

"Since a modern book's text normally begins on page three, five, or seven, sir, that possibility can in fact be eliminated. The name of the book, together with Dr Osmavi's PhD in chemistry, suggests another interpretation. *Be*, gentlemen, is of course the chemical symbol for beryllium, the fourth element in the periodic table. Might I suggest that you examine page four?"

Movias turned the page, and all the Black Scriveners gasped to see large, fluorescent green capitals written in the margin. He read aloud: "THE CODE WORD IS DROWEDOC."

"Isaac, this is amazing!"

"I endeavour to give satisfaction, sir."

It was Savimo's turn to look dissatisfied. "Your deductions sound all right, Isaac ... but although by a fluke you've hit on the truth, the logic isn't watertight by a long shot. You assumed Osmavi to be literature-minded on the strength of that book – but suppose the book had belonged to Vamsoi the writer, who shared the apartment?"

Isaac smiled. "I eliminated Vamsoi, sir, since the evidence shows that he is not a genuine writer and is therefore most unlikely to possess books. You will recall that the police searched Vamsoi's 'office' and furnished us with a complete inventory of its contents[1]. There were two most significant omissions. If I may read through

---

[1] See pages 276-292, inclusive.

the list again –"

"No, no," said Movias hastily. "We remember it perfectly."

"Then, sir, you will hardly have failed to note the absence of two indubitably essential items of a writer's paraphernalia."

"A desk, a chair, a typewriter?" Savimo guessed. "Dirty magazines? A window to stare out of? Trousers?"

"All these objects were present, gentlemen. But who could believe that the office of a genuine author with a normally healthy ego could possibly lack – a draft autobiography, or a mirror?"

AUTHOR'S AFTERWORD

When I sold this story to *Ellery Queen's Mystery Magazine* it was printed as "The Missing Mirror Mystery", but for this collection I've restored my original title "Be Periodic!" because I like it better. Its deductive brilliance is unusually striking, even for me. The first outline included an even more subtle, punning clue involving the vowel shifts of Gaelic loan-words in the Choctaw dialect: alas, my pesky editor persuaded me to revise that part.

[I. A.]

Look At It This Way

L*w*s C*rr*ll

"Just the place for a Baker!" the Snark exclaimed,
Surveying the mountainous land.
"O succulent stoutness and flavour so famed,
When basted with cider and sand!"

"Just the place for a Baker! My spirits are high;
I repeat the euphonious phrase:
Just the place for a Baker! on whom my glad eye
May bestow an affectionate gaze."

Its kit was complete; there were muffs for its feet,
And bathing-machines by the score,
With a series of volumes whose erudite columns
Dilated on Criminal Law.

It scented its food on a ship that pursued
A retrograde nautical course;
O'er the sibilant swell came the clang of a bell
That commanded the crewmen in Morse.

"I view without qualms their conventional arms,"
Said the Snark, with a glass to its eye,
"While adventurers nimble who trust to a thimble
Are exceedingly welcome to try...."

The Distressing Damsel
The Br*th*rs Gr*mm

Once upon a time, in a far-off land, there lived a princess who developed an unfortunate social problem.

The kingdom of Altrund extended over more square leagues of fertile land than the Court Mathematician could compute. So its King would occasionally boast, delaying as long as possible the admission that his Court Mathematician (a retarded youth of fourteen) had never yet fathomed the intricacies of the numbers after VIII.

The Mathematician, who also bore the titles of Palace Swineherd and Master of the Buckhound, was the only child of the peasant classes – both members of which seemed discouraged by their first experiment in being ancestors. King Fardel periodically worried that his peasant classes might at any moment die out altogether; and likewise the kingdom's upper middle class, consisting of a decrepit imbiber called Grommet (Grand Vizier, Chancellor of the Palace Exchequer, Wizard Pro-Tem, Steward of the Royal Cellars, Scullion, Seeker of the King's Treasury, *et cetera*). Even the King's own dynasty showed every sign of decay. Twenty years ago he had looked forward to the sedate begetting of three sons, two of whom would do tremendously well in the world while the youngest would somehow contrive to outdo them both and be extraordinarily virtuous in addition. Alas, Queen Kate was a woman of sadly independent mind and womb, and had called a halt to the dynasty after the inconvenience of producing the Princess Fiona. Fardel could only resign himself to the passive role of devising tests, ready to assess the worthiness of the princes who (in threes) must inevitably arrive to seek the hand of his daughter. The

King's first thought had been to avoid the formalities of quests and dragons by, quite simply, asking each suitor how old he was: the virtues of the youngest prince in any representative trio were well known. Later it occurred to Fardel that this was *too* well known, and that all but the youngest would undoubtedly lie about their age.

His next experiment had been to station a hideous dwarf on the one road into the valley of Altrund. Only the most morally sound princes would have a kind word for this creature, and thus virtue would be revealed. It failed, however, to be revealed in the dwarf, who took to supplementing his weekly pittance by severely beating and robbing passers-by – including, the King was sure, at least one incognito prince. The dwarf had had to be discharged, just as Fiona came to marriageable age with enough princess-like beauty to make the King study his plump Queen with wonder and suspicion. After considering and rejecting a version of the ancient shell game which involved caskets of gold, of silver, and of lead, King Fardel sighed and arranged for the construction of a traditional golden road.

Fiona was walking along it now, brooding as usual on her horrid obligation to marry a prince of peculiar virtue. The theory of the golden road was that crasser and more worldly princes would give too much thought to the road's market value, and would discreetly ride along the grassy verge to the left or right; only a prince preoccupied with Fiona's beauty would unconsciously ride down the middle of the road, to victory. How anyone who had not yet reached King Fardel's dilapidated palace could have known so much about Fiona's beauty was not explained by the theory. The princess had never had the heart to point this out, nor to add that, personally, she would incline towards a prince who could be trusted to wipe his boots at the door rather than walk in preoccupied with beauty. Meanwhile the surface of the golden road, never very thick at the best of times, had suffered the depredations of brigands, jackdaws, itinerant tax collectors, and (Fiona was sure, though the King refused to believe it) at least one incognito prince. Tiny gleams of gold could still be seen amid the trampled earth and grass, though only in brilliant sunshine like today's; fewer such gleams were visible in the King's treasury, and Fardel was rumoured to be having second thoughts about crassness and worldliness.

Fiona walked down the middle of the formerly golden road and dreamed again of her own ambition, which did not involve princes. She rather wanted to be a witch.

"A plague of frogs," she crooned happily. "A plague of boils. A plague of toads. That would show them. Princes!"

There was almost no magic in Altrund, apart from the heavily mortgaged magic mirror which was the palace's last valuable asset ... but a wisp or two of enchantment had been left behind, like forgotten tools, by the obliging Graduate Sorcerer who had polished up the golden road; and perhaps one of these wisps twined itself into Fiona's girlish daydreams of epidemic frogs, boils and toads. Certainly, without her noticing it, her aimless walk swerved off the road, through a clump of trees, through a stand of nettles (which despite her long skirt she did emphatically notice) and finally, at a slight run, to a malodorous pond she had not seen before.

"Be careful!" said a croaking voice from almost underfoot.

Princess Fiona recoiled slightly, and stared down at a singularly obnoxious and wart-encrusted toad on the damp grass at the pond's rim. It stared back at her for some moments, breathing heavily. "Stamping on toads," it complained at last, "is not in accordance with Royal protocol."

"A fig for Royal protocol," said Fiona airily, though uncertain of precisely what a fig might be.

"Well, you might as well get on with it," said the toad.

"Pardon?"

"Oh dear me, I can see your education has been neglected. Did they never tell you about certain, *erk*, traditions of enchantment?"

Something was indeed beginning to dawn on the princess, who drew still further away. "Ah," she said "The Acting Royal Governess is a dear old fellow called Grommet, but I don't think he knows very much except about vintages. Suppose I go and ask him, though –" She took another cautious step backwards.

"Stop!" said the toad. "And let me tell you a tale.

Alarmingly, the princess found herself rooted to the ground.

The toad said, complacently, "I have strange power of speech; even though I can only usually stop one of three."

"I rather think this is lese-majesty," said Fiona, still struggling to lift her feet.

The toad fixed her with its glittering, golden eyes. "Once upon a time I fell foul of a wicked wizard in the College of Sorcery, who laid upon me the curse which you see, and in addition caused me to be magically flung to the most God-forsaken land in all the world."

"Where was that?" asked Fiona, curious.

The toad gave a croaking cough. "Let me put this tactfully. Where did you find me?"

"Oh," said the princess.

"But the incantation of binding did include a customary reversion clause. *Erk.* A matter of, as one might say, osculatory contact."

"No," said Fiona.

"A momentary and fleeting matter. None of your exotic requirements like being taken into a princess's bed all night. Merely the kiss of a good person whose moral worth stands in a certain relation to one's own."

"No."

"Think of it like this. Obviously you are a princess of high breeding –"

"At least you can tell," said Fiona, flattered.

"The tiara is rather a giveaway."

"It's pewter. We're a very poor kingdom; my father has only fivescore subjects even when you count the sheep."

"All the better," said the toad. "In poverty there is tremendous moral worth. And as I was saying – since you are a princess I'll wager five to one that your father has planned all sorts of grotesque and ridiculous ways of testing the princes who come seeking your hand."

She sighed, and nodded.

"Precisely! But are *you* worthy? Should *you* not be tested according to the ancient customs of the world? Have you given a crust of bread to a dwarf recently?"

Princess Fiona opened her mouth and closed it again. She looked critically at the toad. "Look. If I take your curse off you, can we simply leave it at that? I'm going to the College of Sorcery myself – if my parents will ever let me – and I'll learn to make my own living. Getting involved with princes can wait, thank you very much."

"I shall make no further claims on you," said the toad in the sincerest of croaks. And then, as she still hesitated: "You could always shut your eyes."

Looking the toad severely in the eye, the princess knelt, bent forward, and bestowed an exceedingly chaste kiss somewhere in the general region of its head. For an instant a cloud seemed to pass over the Sun, and there was that unmistakable tingle which comes with enchantment or champagne.

She leant back, still kneeling. Sure enough, where an ugly, warty toad had squatted, there was now a sleek and handsome frog.

"*I see*," the princess said after a moment.

"Ahh, it's good to be back to normal," said the frog. "Thank you, your majesty. I feel as fit as a ... prince." At this point it appeared to notice something. "Oh. Conservation law. Well, I must be going. *Awwk.*"

The last agonized croak was because Fiona had noticed the same something, and had seized the wriggling frog in a firm grip. Her previously pale and lily-white hands were now covered in warts that crowded together like cobblestones.

"You knew this was going to happen!" she shrieked.

"Well, it was just a bare possibility," said the frog.

Fiona squeezed it vengefully, and with distaste repeated the kiss. Nothing happened.

"Now that is interesting," said the frog. "I suppose we are no longer equal in moral worthiness, as is necessary for such curses to be transferred."

Distracted, the princess dropped the slimy creature. "*Equal*? You're not telling me a princess is morally the same as a toad?"

"Ah. You are very virtuous, for a princess; and I was very virtuous, for a toad. As a frog I'm far more despicable, since I'm gloating terribly over having shifted my curse to a poor innocent creature like yourself. – Excuse me," it added, dodging the princess's foot as it came down. "I must go and see a man about a frog." With a splash, it was gone.

Princess Fiona stared into the murky water; the ripples died and her own reflection took shape. It seemed an appropriate time to shut her eyes, but she forced them to stay open: her fingers could feel the swarming warts on her face, and she might as well learn just how unprincesslike her complexion had become. In the water, though, it looked the same as ever. Apparently magical warts had no reflections; possibly they did not even cast shadows, though this would be slightly more difficult to test.

The sun was lower in the sky. The princess's vague thoughts of throwing herself with a despairing cry into the pool, or of becoming a hermit never again to be seen by mortal man, were dispelled by the more practical considerations of duckweed and dinner.

She walked more and more slowly, though, as the palace came into view – a quarter-mile frontage of crumbling marble and alabaster. It seemed uncountable ages old, though in fact the former King of Altrund had caused it to be erected in a single night by means of a substandard wishing ring. Alas, the accumulated cost of servants and repairs was somewhat further beyond the dreams of avarice than the wealth King Sivvens had requested with this second wish: while the wasted third wish, said to have involved the former Queen and a sausage, was among the family's best kept secrets.

Taking a short cut through the disused portions of the palace, Fiona passed in succession through the Great Hall, the Great Ballroom with its litter of shrivelled pumpkins, the Great Dungeon, and the cobwebbed Great Cupboard before nearing the inhabited rooms. There she paused, hearing voices beyond the half-open door of the Great Sitting-Room.

"... exceedingly sorry about this wine," her father the King was saying. "We have far finer vintages, but the Steward of the Royal Cellars keeps, ah, misplacing them. But, to business! Naturally you come seeking the hand of my daughter, the beauteous flower of a most wealthy and kingly line. – I must apologize that so much of the palace is being redecorated just now," he added inventively.

There was a uneasy triple murmur.

"Well, my good princes, what dowry would you bring to be worthy of such a bride?"

The first prince's voice was loud: "I am a crafty conqueror whose blood-dripping sword will hack a ruinous path of carnage through battlefields steeped in gore. And my consort will be no mere Queen but the Empress of an all-destroying Emperor!"

"Creditable," said the King.

The voice of the second prince inclined towards oiliness.

"Emperors may hold the world by the throat but a merchant prince can put a noose of purse-strings about the throats of Emperors. Already I possess an immense fortune, and ultimately my Queen will share wealth beyond the dreams of avarice."

"*Very* creditable," said the King. On the tip of his tongue, Fiona thought, was the urgent question: "How *far* beyond the dreams of avarice?"

The third voice was thin and reedy and set her teeth on edge. "When tyrants, moneylenders, and even the stones about their unhallowed graves have fallen all to dust, my name shall linger on. To my Queen I bring no more than an unquenchable love and immortality in verse and song. I am a poet," he explained.

Outside, Fiona made a hideous face and was sobered by the thought of how much more than hideous it must be. Inside, there was an embarrassed little pause.

"More wine, perhaps?" said the King at last.

"Thanks," said the three princes together: "I don't mind if I do."

After a tentative query about the suitor's ages (which shed a sad light on the tendency of palace records to become lost, burnt or consumed by rats), the King suggested that some simple test of worthiness for the Princess Fiona's hand would be appropriate.

"None of those meaningless, old-fashioned tests," he said with great fervour. "It is nonsense to have a beautiful princess's fate decided by whether or not one speaks kind words to a dwarf –"

("Yes indeed," said the first prince grimly.)

"Or by the ability to slay huge and ferocious dragons –"

("Hear, hear," said the second prince.)

"Or by impractical talents like the soothing of savage beasts with verse and song –"

("Oh, I say," said the third prince.)

"No. We are practical men, you and I. Let us straightaway agree that he who at the end of three days returns with the most colossally valuable dowry shall win the hand of the Princess Fiona."

"*Colossal?*" the merchant prince said in a pained voice.

Feeling it was nearly time to put a stop to this, Fiona peered around the half-open door. Without showing herself, she could see all four men reflected in the magic mirror on the far wall – a tall slab of pure, enchanted silver which magically attracted dust and smears (or so Fiona felt, one of her household duties being to keep it polished).

The King sat on a portable throne with his back to the mirror: facing him across the table were the three princes, and Fiona squinted to study them. The first was short and looked bad-tempered; for some reason he kept one hand tucked into his tunic. The second was sufficiently stout that he had to sit some way back from the table. The third, the poet, was tall and might have been almost handsome; but at the time of his christening, someone had neglected to invite whichever fairy is responsible for bestowing chins.

"Happiness," the King was saying, "is all very well, but it can't buy money."

The merchant prince glanced at his companions, as though estimating the strength of the bidding. "A moderate amount," he began – and his moist eyes met Fiona's in the mirror. "Oh. Perhaps even a reasonably substantial amount," he went on, and licked his lips.

Before Fiona could move, the wary gaze of the soldier also found her. He, too, licked his lips. He, too, studied his rivals; absent-mindedly he dropped a hand to the pommel of his sword. Meanwhile the poet also had seen Fiona's reflected glory, and was mumbling what appeared to be an impromptu villanelle.

With a certain inner glee, Princess Fiona strode into the room and let her suitors see her, warts and all. Betrothal to any of these three, she considered, would undoubtedly be a fate worse than ... well, warts.

"Father," she said sweetly, "I seem to have this curse."

King Fardel turned, gaped, closed his eyes and moaned softly.

"Only making a preliminary tactical survey, of course –" said the first prince.

"Cannot be expected to enter into a binding commitment at this stage of negotiation," said the second.

"Tomorrow to fresh woods and pastures new," muttered the poet.

The princess helped herself to a glass of the wine – which was indeed only a locally produced Falernian-type – and told a discreetly edited version of her adventure. "And so," she concluded, "only the kiss of a man of proper moral worth can lift this dreadful enchantment from me!"

"Meaningless, old-fashioned tests," said the King through his teeth. With a visible effort he steeled himself to the necessities of tradition. "Very well. Whosoever shall with a kiss lift the curse from my fair daughter, him shall she wed, and we'll have a quiet chat about marriage settlements afterwards."

Inwardly Fiona was praying a twofold prayer: firstly, that one of these unlikely princes would somehow prove equal to her in moral worth, and secondly, that the King would not countenance her betrothal to a prince invisible beneath layers of warts.

After heartening himself with several long looks at the princess's unspoilt reflection, the first suitor stepped forward. He hesitated, though, on the very brink. "You could always shut your eyes," she said. He snorted, and Fiona bent down to receive a kiss of military efficiency. Nothing happened. The prince made a strategic withdrawal to the previously prepared position of his chair.

When the second prince had screwed his determination to the sticking-place, Fiona found that she had to lean forward over his firkin of a stomach before their lips were close enough for an economical and businesslike kiss. Again, nothing happened.

"I am, after all, the youngest," the third prince murmured; and Fiona turned up her face for a final kiss which was not so much poetic as chinless. The only result was that the poet-prince turned green as a frog and lurched backwards, gabbling something about aesthetic values. Fiona found this disheartening.

With a resigned expression, the King rose and clapped his hands to draw attention. "Whosoever shall in three days return with a healing spell, charm, cantrip, physic, unguent, balm, lotion, potion, philtre, talisman, relic, totem, fetish, icon, incantation, rune, amulet, panacea –" At this point his breath failed him and he collapsed into uncontrollable coughing. But the suitors had gathered the general drift; they bowed to the King and (with averted gaze) to Fiona, and departed as one prince.

"Oh ... *rats*," said Princess Fiona.

"... theurgy, thaumaturgy, sorcery, wizardry, necromancy, invocation, conjuration ..." continued the afflicted King, rallying slightly. His voice died away as he noticed an absence of princes. There followed a stern lecture on the perfidy of faithless daughters who abandoned themselves to the embraces of strange frogs on the very day when three superlatively eligible suitors presented themselves, or at any rate two, or perhaps just one, but all the same ...

Still muttering, he left to consult the Court Physician, yet another post ineptly filled by the man Grommet.

Fiona pulled up a footstool and sat staring into the magic mirror. "Mirror, mirror," she said briskly. There was a soft chime, and the silver clouded over.

"Good afternoon," said the mirror. "What seems to be the trouble?"

Fiona regarded the mirror suspiciously. "You may have noticed this wart," she said, touching one at random.

"That is not a problem. That is a solution."

"That's not exactly an answer," said Fiona.

"You did not exactly ask a question," the mirror said smugly. "But consider. You have always wished to be a witch. Now you look the part, if not more so. You have always wished half-heartedly to run away and enrol at the College of Sorcery. Now, with one of three eminently unlovable princes likely to cure your complexion and claim your hand in two days, twenty-three hours and thirty-seven minutes, you have an excellent reason for running away. What more could you ask?"

"I was thinking more in terms of being a beautiful sorceress full of sinister glamour," said the princess. "*Not* a warty crone. Now is there a way I can lift the curse myself in the next day or two?"

"Indeed ... there ... is," said the mirror with what sounded like reluctance.

"What is it?"

"Unfortunately ... I cannot actually tell you, for reasons you would find absolutely inarguable if only I could tell them." The fog in the mirror began to clear again. "Your three minutes are nearly up."

"If you can't tell me that cure, suggest another," Fiona said furiously.

"You might try throwing a party for all the peasantry," said the silvery voice, diminuendo. "There is this party game called Postman's Knock ..."

Then the voice and the fog were gone, and the omniscient magic mirror (which, as it happened, could be consulted only once in any three days) was again no more than a mirror.

Resisting her urge to give the silver a vicious kick, Princess Fiona left the room and climbed the eight flights and three spirals of stairs to the Great Boudoir. There she found Queen Kate placidly sewing hair shirts for the peasantry, who generally used these royal gifts to repair the roof of their hovel.

"Oh dear," said the Queen when Fiona had told her tale. "You're such a trial to me, sometimes I think you must have been changed for a goblin when you were a baby, that's all I can say, well you brought it on yourself, going out without your warm shawl...."

Fiona was used to being called a changeling in the course of any and every scolding, though in fact the local goblins were notoriously choosy. Several times, and with good reason, the peasantry had abandoned their ill-favoured son Dribble (Court Mathematician) outside known goblin caves, and each time he had been politely returned.

"Well," said her mother, coming to the point as she occasionally did: "I can see I still have to clear up your messes after you, just like when you were a baby, let me see, I know I put it somewhere, yes, here it is ..." She pulled a dusty and unsavoury-looking object from a cluttered drawer. "There you are, you just put this in your hair like a good girl, something my stepmother gave me once, a poisoned comb ..."

Fiona hastily retreated a pace or two.

"... just you put it in your hair and there you are, you stay asleep like the dead for ten years or a hundred or whatever, until Prince Right comes along and takes the comb out of your hair and kisses you and all the rest of it, nothing like outliving your troubles, that's what my mother always used to say...."

But Fiona was already on her way to ask the advice of Grommet. She found him in the Great Pantry, testing the quality of the King's best wine with his usual conscientiousness. When he had recoiled from her appearance and listened to her story, he recalled his position as Chief Palace Torturer and made a slurred suggestion.

"Down in, um, down in one of the Great Torture Chambers, um, can't remember exactly which one, there's a, mmm, very nice iron mask. Very nice indeed. Good, um, workmanship. You might like to wear it ...?"

"Thank you," said Fiona coldly.

The next day, heart hardened by the bedtime discovery that her affliction was by no means confined to hands and face, she set about a systematic programme of being kissed by the entire reluctant population of Altrund – even the all too aptly named lad Dribble. Every one of them, it seemed, was either despicably lacking in moral worth or unfairly endowed with it. In the afternoon, after a lack of success with several sheep, she waylaid a wandering friar. The friar denounced her both before and afterwards as a sinful temptation sent by the devil; Fiona considered this to be undue flattery.

On the second day she gathered, compounded, infused, and drank no fewer than sixty-four traditional herbal remedies, whose taste varied across a wide spectrum from unpleasant to unheard-of. An omen presented itself when the word NARCISSUS was found written in frogspawn across the palace forecourt, but no decoction of this plant's flowers, leaves, stem, or root had the slightest visible effect. The day's only success was scored by a mysterious and forgotten elixir found in the Great Medicine Cabinet: the dose remaining in the phial sufficed to remove one medium-sized wart from the back of the princess's left hand. This was hailed as a great stride forward by almost everyone, except Fiona.

On the morning of the third day, a more than usually appalling dwarf arrived at the palace. He boasted a squint, a bulbous nose, a club foot, a humped back, a cauliflower ear, and all the other impedimenta so fashionable among dwarfs. Moreover, his complexion bore a startling resemblance to Fiona's.

"I'll riddle ye a riddle, my maiden fair," he said to the princess, leaping and capering with repulsive agility. "I'll riddle your warts away with riddling words, that I will, and ye must riddle my name. If ye riddle it not aright, then ye must be mine forever. Will ye riddle me this riddle, fair princess?"

At this difficult juncture the King came into the Great Reception Room to inspect the visitor. "Why, Rumpelstiltskin, old chap," he cried.

"Bah," said the dwarf, and left in considerable dudgeon.

The afternoon wore on; the sun sank in the sky; and the Court Mathematician, stationed in the topmost tower of the palace, presently came running down to announce the sighting of four princes in the distance. When sent aloft to count again, he corrected this estimate to two. Sure enough, three princes came riding up to the Great Door and took their turns to blow the Great Horn which had hung there since the rusting of the Great Knocker.

Fiona's spirits sank lower as once again the King and princes sat about the table. Would it be worst to endure a husband steeped in gore, like the first prince; or one glistening with greasiness, like the second; or one who like the third was simply wet?

Unwrapping his burden, the soldier prince slammed an iron bowl down on the table. Something slimy and dark-red bubbled within, and a fearful, mephitic stench expanded to fill the room. "I bring as my gift the hot blood from a dragon's heart, slain by my own staunch sword this very morn! Let the princess sup deep ere it cools, and all her ills shall be healed."

"Let the bowl be covered lest it cool too soon," the King suggested, with all the dignity possible to a man firmly clutching his nose.

The second prince unveiled an exquisite golden chalice studded with costly gems. Little blue flames flickered over it; there was a yet more choking and paralysing reek. "Let not the fair princess's lips be sullied with horrid gore," said this prince, already speaking with the air of a favourite son. "Here is fiery brimstone and quicksilver torn at *colossal* expense from the heart of the Smoking Mountain! Let its cleansing fire now burn this affliction from the maiden's skin."

"Excellent," the King said manfully through paroxysms of coughing. "Now it merely remains –"

"Excuse me," said the third prince, producing a thick roll of parchment.

"Oh yes," said the King. "Sorry."

"Let not these crude and crass remedies defile the sweet princess either within or without. I bring the Master Cantrip of Purification, prepared by myself from the most authentic sources. Let the princess but listen to its nineteen thousand stanzas – of a wondrous poetry withal, fit to charm the very soul from the body – and doubtless the bane which lies upon her shall melt away and be gone like the snows of, ah, last winter."

For some reason Fiona found this prospect the most depressing of the three.

At the table there was a hot altercation as to whether the

dragonblood or brimstone should be tested first; even the poet agreed half-heartedly that his nineteen thousand stanzas should be allowed to come as a climax rather than be squandered too early in the proceedings. Fiona herself was stationed by the mirror so that her wartless and undeniably attractive reflection could maintain the princes' enthusiasm at a decent level. Admiring her profile out of the corner of one eye, she was struck by a sudden thought.

Thanks more to the resources of the Great Library than those of the Acting Royal Governess, the Princess Fiona had had an excellent classical education.

"Very well," the King was saying. "Let blind Chance make the choice between you; let the Fates guide my unseeing finger." He stood, clapped the fingers of his left hand over both eyes, and waved the other hand in mystic arabesques. It came to rest pointing unerringly and confidently at the second, or merchant, prince. "So be it!" said the King when he had made a great show of peeling the fingers from his eyes. "Now, as to the method of application –"

The stench of brimstone was alarmingly strong. But the princess had discovered that when one is about to be forcibly cured of warts in mere minutes, it concentrates the mind wonderfully. She reached the end of her train of thought, nodded, murmured "Narcissus" under her breath – and leant to touch lips with her own morally identical image in the mirror.

For an instant shadows flitted in the room, and Fiona felt an unmistakable tingle. Rapidly the mirror filled with fog; she had never before seen warty fog.

"Oh *fie*," said a silvery but exasperated voice. "You guessed."

When the fog cleared Fiona saw that her image was thoroughly encrusted with warts; so, interestingly, were the images of the King, the princes, the walls, and the furniture. Rubbing her once again lily-white hands with satisfaction, she stood and moved towards the table.

"Father," she said sweetly, "I have some good news for you."

King Fardel turned, gaped, closed his eyes, and moaned faintly. The princes appeared momentarily speechless.

"Alackaday," she cried, "the royal word of my father the King must prevent my marrying any of you good and noble princes. Only the curer of my affliction may seek my hand. Oh woe!" Fiona was beginning to enjoy herself.

"I do not remember those particular words," said the merchant.

"You left before he'd finished," she reminded him.

"All's well that ends well," said the King tediously, "and no doubt some simple quest on the sound cash basis I originally suggested –"

"Oh woe!" said Fiona, injecting as much agony into her tones as she could. "The royal word of my father the King may not be lightly set aside. It is my doom to travel now to the College of Sorcery, there to learn which mighty enchanter has lifted my curse from afar – and thus earned my hand in marriage."

"Now wait a minute," the first prince said.

"But perhaps wiser counsels may be found over good food and good wine," said the princess in softer tones. "I shall summon the Master of the Revels, the Palace Butler, the Steward of the Royal Cellars, the Court Jester, the Chef to the King's Court, the Royal –"

"All right," said the King, brightening somewhat. "He's in the Great Pantry, I believe. Wiser counsels yes, over food and drink and merriment ..." Again he studied the second prince and seemed to be inwardly calculating.

"And I could still read you my lovely cantrip," the third prince was saying wistfully as Fiona slipped out of the room.

She sent Grommet to the men with quantities of wine; she retreated to her room, changed clothes, and picked up a bundle of necessities she had had packed for some little while; she made her stealthy way to the normally disused Great Stables. There was no difficulty at all in choosing between the three steeds there. The huge fiery stallion which constantly rolled its eyes and foamed at the mouth looked more inclined to devour princesses than carry them; the asthmatic and broken-backed donkey reminded her too much of its owner. Bowing at last to the King's whim, she saddled the stout gelding with the richly bejewelled harness and set off. There was an inn not far outside the valley, the Prancing Prince; Fiona thought she could reach it before dark.

Near the pond she reined in and dismounted.

"Thanks for the hint," she called. "About Narcissus."

A croak answered her. "Don't mention it; a mere afterthought. *Noblesse oblige.*"

"I have a proposition for you," said Fiona. "I'm off to the College of Sorcery to enrol as a student witch and I'll be needing a familiar. Talking cats are ten a penny, but a talking frog, now ..."

"Pint of fresh milk every day and it's a bargain."

And so the Princess and the frog rode out of the tale together, and lived happily ever after.

Duel of Words

Fr*nk H*rb*rt

Versatility is the ability to swim on unknown ground.
from *Profit of Doom* by the Princess Iresolut

As the forcedoor hissed shut behind her and she walked forward, she was conscious of entering alien territory.

A threshold of awareness. The decor is the same, commonplace marble, jewels and platinum inlay – but after the bland corridor, this room has a personality. A hostile personality.

In a swirl of robes she sat, pointedly ignoring the weapon-scanner poised unobtrusively three inches over her head. *Does he think I require weapons? It can only be a gambit to lure me into over-confidence. While I sit here I must tread warily.*

They faced each other, Count Gorman and the Lady Henrietta.

I could take him now, she thought. *That way he tilts his head to one side – the knife will be taped to his left shoulder-blade. I need not make my move until he pretends to scratch his neck.*

Aloud, she said: "Hello."

Trapped by convention: we must bow to our enemies even as we destroy them!

The eight interpenetrating levels of meaning stacked in that simple word were not lost on the Count. *She is dangerous, like a bright fanged canary,* he thought. *I must seem unconcerned, must subtly distract her from the fingernail where the poison flipdart is hidden.* He studied the fingers of his left hand, preserving silence as he contemplated options.

Great Herbert! He wants me to look at that hand! The danger is elsewhere, then; or not. Henrietta fought to keep the lines of tension from her nostrils. *Control,* she thought. *Body control, nerve control, mind control, remote control.* With the brief litany, her brain cleared and she was able to study Gorman more closely, her Reverent Mothers' Union trained awareness digging at his facade. ... *Then the headtilt is a trick too. The blade is on the right.*

Count Gorman caught the tiny relaxation that touched her earlobes. *I believe it worked,* he allowed himself to conjecture quasi-tentatively. *She has been diverted from the main thrust.* The hard core of calculation throbbed within him, yet his own traitor emotions still tinged his thinking.

She is beautiful. Must I destroy her? Hardly had he blinked away the incipient tear than reflex lashed his mind into higher awareness: *Beautiful but deadly! She could have killed me ten times over in that micro-instant. Such beauty is a terrible weapon.*

Her almond eyes narrowed infinitesimally despite the ambiguous no-expression she sought to retain on her face.

He blinked. He is uncertain. Or could that be another feint, a fourth layer of his stratagem? Wheels within wheels within wheels: I must not underestimate this man's subtlety, especially when it shows itself as overtness.

... Wait! Terror sparkled through her. *Can he be ... can he possibly be ... the Deusek Zmakinaa?*

Probably not.

Henrietta felt the patterns of stress tightening in the room. Eight seconds had elapsed since the closing of the door. It was time to introduce a new complex of factors into the situation, before Gorman could complete his cold analysis of the present state of play. *Keep him off balance,* she told herself urgently. Across her lips she drew the faintest shadow of a smile. *So: he expects me to speak. Let him know by my silence that I will not conform to the matrix he has set up!*

The wallchron whirred implacably.

The consequences of the smallest act, here in this lonely chamber, might be incalculable. As he chewed meditatively on the mind-enhancing spice gum, Gorman perceived an infinity of timelines radiating from this present. Logic demanded that he scan them all; but the brief pause required for this would of itself distort the multiplying futures, perhaps beyond the yieldpoint.

Unpredictability is the key to victory – the thought flashed across his mind, almost forcing a betraying twitch of his jugular. *Her expectation will be for me to remain silent. If I assault her stability from that direction, I gain the advantage.*

"Good of you to come," he said smoothly.

... Let her make of that what she will! How carefully I avoid stressing any word: she will imagine a thousand falsities. Will it be "good" that she fancies is emphasized, implying a hidden triumph on my part? Or you, with its unsettling connotation that I might have expected another? Perhaps the muted sarcasm of a supposed stress on "come", where a thousand other things she could have done swim beneath the glittering surface of my rhetoric....

Gathering subtle strength from the deeps of her awareness, Henrietta thought she sensed irresolution behind the steely blandness of the Count's words. *Again distraction,* she brooded. *He seeks to gain time.* But the tiny phrase, it came to her, was in itself a psychological timebomb. The semantic linking of Henrietta herself with the adjective "good" – a brilliant subliminal attack, calculated to dull her mental edge by eroding her awareness of self-as-weapon; the whole masked in a haze of obscene connotations surrounding the word "come". Even the realization of the pitfall did not entirely negate it.

He is a foe worthy of my steel, she admitted grudgingly. And then her mind was struck tangentially by the thought *steel! Almost, I forgot the slipstik in his back sheath! Oh, he is cunning.*

Determined to accelerate the tempo of this confrontation, she replied after only this shortest of pauses, pitching her voice carefully to a sensual, sibilant purr carrying ominous overtones and undertones of menace, oxymoron and catachresis.

"Not at all."

Faced with this implacable assurance, Gorman fought down panic. *She is made of steel!* He felt the warm sweat under his arms, but his eyes remained fastened on hers with the same icy control, even as he allowed himself to entertain, for the first time, the remote possibility of defeat.

His thoughts turned to the alarm-stud beneath his left foot. *Would it be a coward's act to press it?* And an even more pointed question that slowly and chillingly skewered through his bowels: *could I keep her from guessing for those four seconds before the guard battalion arrives? ... Probably not.*

She remained still, poised as a *k'obra* before its strike.

It is a chessgame that we play. Each combination conceals half a dozen others, interlocking in strange patterns. I must play my cards carefully. Her keen perceptions did not fail to note the telling lack of visible emotion in the Count's rigid muscles. *He feigns alarm to lull me.*

It seemed that their eyes had been locked in phase for half an eternity. Gorman swivelled his trigger-foot to one side, through an agonizing half inch to one side. *I cannot do it. I cannot have it said that a Count of the Cantharides line was panicked by a mere woman.* The broad fan of futures swayed and undulated before his eyes, mocking his efforts at self-control. The organic computer buried in his brain informed him that his personal chances were diminishing, or increasing, by the second. *I will not be flustered,* he thought sharply. *Being flustered is the mind-killer.*

Trained through long years to observe totally unimportant trivia, Henrietta noted the Count's motion.

He sees the need for a change of stance, does he? Or is there an alarm which he intends to trigger? Wullahy! he is strong! Any ordinary man would be grovelling by this time. But she thought she knew his weakness now. *He can't take silence. He'll speak to break the spell, then curse himself for giving in to the pressure, allowing me the opportunity for a countergambit.* She held her breath, and the silence in the room grew deeper, rolling from her calm centre in slow, cool waves and striking the Count in the pit of his stomach.

Expecting some move from her, Gorman found himself danger-ously tensed for an attack which did not come. *She is a witch! She is reading my mind.* With a sudden thrill he realized that the Lady Henrietta was not breathing, nor permitting her heart to beat. *Trance? No, her eyelashes are too intent.... She seeks to hypnotize me!* The notion was so incongruous that, almost, he allowed a remote corner of his mouth to hint at the false dawn of a smile. Instead: *Come, let us break the tension. If I startle her there may be a moment of distraction which I can use.*

Without any warning, without changing his position in the slightest or moving his lips, he snapped: "I wanted to ask you some questions."

The whiplash of his edged voice came close to provoking Hen-rietta into immediate response. *Do not let him befuddle you with an endless torrent of words,* she admonished herself. Using the body/

nerve/mind/bladder litany to achieve a new plateau of inner calm, she considered Gorman once more.

A powerful man. I must move carefully. Statue-still she sat, calling up all her resources for the blow.

Is it a trance after all? he had time to think. *Or is she perhaps a little deaf?* Almost automatically he leaned a few millimetres forward to speak again, and was halted by his own mental scream *this is what she wants you to do!*

Now! Mustering up all the deadly voice control at her command, Henrietta hurled her words at his defenceless head, blasting him with withering contempt.

"Questions ... about my overdraft, I suppose!"

It was too much. His neck sagged in the realization of defeat, tempered with what was almost pride to have done battle with such a one. *She is magnificent!*

As Lady Henrietta glided from the room and the forcedoor closed, the Count called feebly, "Next!"

He who wears even for a time the mask of another has rejected his selfhood. On that path lies oblivion.

from *Literary Practice in the Later Empire* by the Princess Iresolut

The Thing in the Bedroom

W*ll**m H*pe H*dgs*n

The circle of initiates about the roaring fire in the King's Head bar had sadly decreased of late, entertaining though the conversation had always been. For one thing, the roaring fire had been super-seded by a mournfully bonging radiator; even the popular Mr Jorkens had ceased to come when the landlord installed his third Space Invaders machine. On this particular evening there was little sparkle in the conversation, and far too much in the foaming keg beer: only Major Godalming, Carruthers and old Hyphen-Jones were present, and, passing by an easy transition from gassy beer to chemical warfare and military reminiscences in general, the Major was well into his much-thumbed anecdotes of the earlobe he lost to Rommel, the duelling scar acquired whilst in Heidelberg on a package tour, and the ugly *kukri* wound he'd received in Bradford. Carruthers and Hyphen-Jones yawned their appreciation and choked down their beer; half-formed excuses about not keeping the wife up too late seemed to be trembling in the air like ectoplasm, when a shadow fell across the table.

"My round, chaps?"

The speaker was tall, handsome, rugged: from his built-up shoes to his shoulder bag he was every inch an English gentleman.

"Smythe, my dear fellow!" the Major cried. "We'd given you up for dead!"

"And well you might," said Smythe. "It happened to me once, did death – you may remember me telling you about that hideous affair of the haunted percolator? For a short while, then, I was clinically dead. It was nothing. There are things much worse than death, worse by far...."

"Murrage's keg beer, for example?" suggested Carruthers.

The subtlety of this hint was not lost on Smythe, who took the empty glasses to the bar and in a mere twenty minutes returned with three beers and a stiff gin-and-tonic for himself.

"Cheers," said the Major. "Now where *have* you been these last three months? Living abroad with some woman, I suppose, as you did for half a year after laying the ghost in that 'Astral Buffalo' case? Ah, you randy devil."

"Not so," Smythe said laughingly. "For one reason and another I've merely been visiting a different class of pub, a different sort of bar, as shortly you will understand...."

"Well, dammit man, what was this case?" the Major boomed. "What was so much more terrible than death? You've changed, you know. The experience has set its mark upon you by God! Your hair! I've only just noticed it's white!"

"Just a little bleach, my dear Major ... I fancied myself as a blonde. But let me tell you of the case which must rank as one of the most baffling and sinister of my career ... an appalling case of what I can only call *occult possession*."

"We had that last year," said Carruthers, scratching his head. "That business of the giant bat of Sumatra: or was it the giant cat? One frightful influence from beyond the world we know is very like another, I find."

Smythe settled himself more comfortably on his favourite stool, smiled, and opened a packet of potato crisps in the characteristic manner which told his friends that another fascinating narration was on its way, and that they were expected to buy drinks for the raconteur all the rest of the evening.

"As you know, I've gained some small reputation in matters of detection, the occult and the odd tricks of the mind ..." Here Smythe distributed the customary business cards and mentioned the 10% discount he offered to friends. "And so it was that Mrs Pring brought her terrible problem to me, on the recommendation of a bosom friend who'd heard of my ad in the *Sunday Sport* colour supplement. Mrs Pring ..."

"Ah, you incurable old womanizer," wheezed Hyphen-Jones. "Did Mr Pring find you out?"

Smythe gave him an austere glance, and coldly ate another crisp. "Mrs Pring is a widow of late middle age and forbidding aspect, whose home is in the moderately appalling seaside resort of Dash. She lets out one room of her house under the usual bed-and-breakfast terms; personally I think the enterprise would be more successful if she did not apparently stuff the mattress with breakfast cereal and serve its former contents in a bowl each morning, but this is to anticipate. The story that Mrs Pring told to me three months ago was, like so many of the tales told in my office, strange, terrible and unique.

"Over the years, you see, my client had noticed a curious statistical trend as regards the people who stayed with her. She keeps a very detailed set of books, two in fact, and there was no possibility that her memory could be deceiving her. In brief: many gentlemen (to use her term) had undergone bed and breakfast at Mrs Pring's and for some reason which I find inexplicable had returned in subsequent years. Some women did the same: the odd point which caught Mrs Pring's attention was that young or even relatively young women tended not to return. In fact they tended to leave abruptly, with various noises of embarrassment and outrage, after no more than one night in the room.

"That Mrs Pring took several years to notice the phenomenon is perhaps best explained by her delicate state of health, which is only sustained by almost daily trips to buy medicinal liquids not sold by chemists. That Mrs Pring was properly alarmed by her discovery is shown by the fact that for a whole year she actually provided butter rather than margarine with the breakfast toast: it made no difference. What d'you make of that?"

"I suppose," said Carruthers slowly, "that some terrible tragedy had been enacted in that fatal room?"

Smythe looked startled, and dropped a crisp. "Well ... yes, actually. However did you guess?"

"My dear fellow. I've been listening to your curious and unique tales for upwards of eight years."

"Well, never mind that. Mrs Pring evolved a theory that that all too unyielding mattress was infested, not with elementals as in that fearsome Wriggling Eiderdown case, but with what in her rustic way she chose to call incests. As she put it, 'What I thought was, those bleeding things might be partial to young ladies what has nice soft skin ... anyway, I reckoned I'd better have a kip-down there meself and see if anything comes crawling-like, bedbuggers or flippin' fleas or whatever....'"

With uncommon fortitude, Mrs Pring did indeed pass a night in this spare room of hers. Her account of it is very confused indeed, but she remarked several times that something had indeed come a-crawling ... but as to its nature or actions, she continually lapsed into a state of incoherence and embarrassment. The same embarrassment, you may note, with which her lady lodgers would so hurriedly leave."

The Major said: "And the next morning, I suppose, she came straight to you and asked for something to be done about it?"

Smythe studied each of his friends in turn, until Hyphen-Jones misinterpreted the dramatic pause and scurried to buy more drinks. "In point of fact," Smythe said quietly, "she first attempted to investigate the phenomenon more closely by sleeping in that room every night for the following six months. It seems that no other manifestation took place during all that time, as she informed me with some suppressed emotion; after a while she dismissed the experience as hallucination and thought little more of it until the first week of the new holiday season ... when no fewer than three young women stayed a night and left without eating the margarine they'd paid for. One of them murmured something incoherent to Mrs Pring about a ghost that needed to be laid. It was then that Mrs Pring decided something must be done: and after checking that my fee was tax-deductible, she placed the matter in my hands."

"Why d'you suppose the Pring female only saw whatever-it-was the one time?" inquired Carruthers.

"My theory had to take into the fact that this was a chauvinist haunting, as you might put it, with a preference for young ladies quite contrary to the Sex Discrimination Act. The inference would seem to be that Mrs Pring, who is a lady of what is called a certain age, very rapidly lost her attraction for ... let's call it the manifest-ation. Picture her as a glass of that repellent keg beer: one sip was quite enough for any person of taste."

"I'm beginning to get a vague but quite monstrous notion of what you're leading up to ..." the Major observed slowly.

"It's worse than you think," Smythe assured him. "I know I shall never be the same again after the night I spent in that room."

"But ..." said Hyphen-Jones querulously, before Smythe silenced him with a single charismatic gesture which tipped half a pint of beer into his lap.

"An exorcism seemed to be in order," said Smythe, "but first I had to know what I was up against. You recall that ghastly business of the Squeaking Room in Frewin Hall ... the exorcism had no effect whatever upon those mice. When closely questioned, Mrs Pring retreated into blushes and giggles: I saw I'd have to keep a vigil there myself, and see what astral impressions my finely-trained nervous system might glean from the surroundings. Thus I travelled first-class to Dash, and Mrs Pring accompanied me back in (I'm glad to relate) a second-class carriage. The resort was as depressing as I'd foreseen, rather like an extensive penal colony by the sea; Mrs Pring's house corresponded roughly to the maximum security block. Anyway, I steeled myself against the appalling *Presence* which pervaded the place ... chiefly a smell of boiled cabbage ... and readied myself to pass a night within the haunted room. I assured Mrs Pring that I never failed ... have you ever known me to tell the story of a case in which I failed?"

Hyphen-Jones looked up again. "What about that time when ... ouch!" Some paranormal impulse had helped the rest of his beer to find its way into his lap.

"So I assured her, as I said, that I never failed ... ah, little did I know! ... and that whatever dwelt in that room was as good as exorcized. I fancied, you know, that she looked regretful – as though admitting to herself that a favourite aunt who'd committed several chainsaw massacres should probably be locked up, but admitting it regretfully. So, one by one, I ascended the creaking stairs to that room of dread. The dying sun peered through its single window in a flood of grimy yet eldritch radiance. But there was nothing sinister about the place save the peeling wallpaper, whose green-and-purple pattern set me brooding for some reason on detached retinas. I waited there, as darkness fell, all lights extinguished to minimize the etheric interference ..."

"And what happened, old boy?" cried Carruthers.

"What happened to you?"

"Precisely what I'd expected: nothing at all. Whatever haunted that room was staying a male chauvinist pig to the very last. The only moment when a thrill went through me was when I heard a clock strike midnight far out across the town ... the witching hour ... the moment when my consultation rates switched from time-and-a-half to double time. Presently dawn came, and, this being the seaside resort of Dash, it wasn't even a proper rosy dawn: more like a suet pudding rising in the east. An appalling place.

"Over breakfast, when not pitting my teeth against Mrs Pring's famous vintage toast, I questioned her closely about the room's history. As you know, we occult sleuths can deduce a great deal from the answers to innocuous-seeming questions; after some routine enquiries about whether, for example, she regularly celebrated the Black Mass in the room in question, I subtly asked her, 'Mrs Pring, has some terrible tragedy been enacted in that fatal room?' She denied this loudly and angrily, saying, 'What kind of a house do you think I bleeding well keep here? I've had no complaints and no-one's ever snuffed it on my premises, not even Mr Brosnan what had the food-poisoning, which he must have got from chips or summat brought in against me house rules ... you'll not get no food-poisoning from *my* bacon-an'-eggs sir.'

"I was tolerably well convinced that I wouldn't, since after noting how many times Mrs Pring dropped the bacon on the floor I had taken the precaution of secreting mine under the table-cloth (where I was interested to find several other rashers left by previous visitors). After a short silence during which she tested the temperature of the tea with one finger and apparently found it satisfactory, Mrs Pring added: 'Of course there was always poor Mr Nicholls all those years ago.'

"We occult sleuths are trained to seize instantly on apparent trivia. Casually I threw out the remark, 'What about poor Mr Nicholls?'

"'Oh, 'e had a terrible accident, he did. Oh, it was awful, sir. What a lucky thing he wasn't married. What happened, you see, he caught himself in the door somehow, which I could understand, him being clumsy by nature and having such a ... Well, lucky he wasn't married is what I always said, and of course 'e wouldn't get married after that. I heard tell he went into the civil service instead. Oooh *sir*, you don't *think* ...?'

"'I do indeed think precisely that, Mrs Pring,' I told her solemnly. We occult sleuths are, as you can imagine, sufficiently accustomed to such phenomena as disembodied hands or heads haunting some ill-favoured spot, and I've even encountered one disembodied foot ... you remember it, the 'Howling Bunion' case which drove three Archbishops to the asylum. I conjectured now that the unfortunate Mr Nicholls, though it seemed that most of him still lived, was a man of parts and haunted Mrs Pring's room nonetheless. Upon hearing my theory, the landlady seemed less shocked and horrified than I would have expected. 'Fancy that,' she remarked, with a look of peculiar vacancy, and added, 'I ought to 'ave recognized him, at that.' I did not press my questioning any further."

"What a frightful story," shivered Carruthers. "To think of that poor Mr Nicholls, never able to know the pleasure of women again."

"In that," said Smythe in a strange voice, "I share his fate."

There was a tremulous pause. Smythe licked his lips, squared his shoulders. "I must have a trickle," he remarked, and departed the room amid whispered comments and speculations as to whether or not there was something odd in the way he walked.

"My strategy," Smythe continued presently, "was to lure the manifestation into the open so it might be exorcized by the Ritual of the Astral League. You need damnably supple limbs for that ritual, but it has great power over elementals, manifestations and parking meters. But how to lure this ab-human entity into sight? Mrs Pring no longer had charms for it, which was understandable and I could hardly ask some innocent young woman to expose herself to what I now suspected to lurk in that room.

"In the end I saw there was only one thing to be done. During the day I made certain far from usual purchases in the wholly God-forsaken town of Dash, and also paid a visit to a local hairdresser's. You remarked, did you not, my dear Major, that I'd gone ash-blonde with fright? I cleared the furniture from that bedroom and made my preparations ... having first instructed Mrs Pring to remain downstairs and presented her with a bottle of her favourite medicine to ensure she did so. Now the water in that town, I suspected, was not pure: instead I consecrated a quantity of light ale and with it marked out my usual protective pentacle. This was a mark-IX Carnacki pentacle, guaranteed impervious to any materialized ectoplasmic phenomena specified in British Standard 3704.

"In the early evening I carried out the last stages of my plan, undressing and changing into the clothes I'd bought amid some small embarrassment. There was an exquisite form-fitting black dress with its skirt slashed almost to the hip; beneath this dress, by certain stratagems well known to us occult consultants, I contrived a magnificent bosom for myself. I need scarcely trouble you with the minor details of the sensual perfume guaranteed to send any male bar the unfortunate Mr Nicholls into instant tachycardia, or the pastel lipstick which so beautifully complemented my eyes, or the sheer black stockings which I drew over my carefully shaven legs, or ..."

"All right, all right," said the Major, gulping hastily at his beer. "I think we get the general idea."

"Be like that if you must. I waited there in the huge pentacle, in a room lit only by the flickering candles I'd acquired from the occult-supplies counter at the local Woolworth's. As I stood there I could see myself in the mirror screwed to one wall (presumably because Mrs Pring felt her guests might well smuggle out any six-by-four-foot mirror that wasn't screwed down): I was magnificent, I tell you, a vision of ... oh, very well, if you insist.

"I waited there with the tension mounting, waiting for whatever might (so to speak) come, and the candles gradually burnt down. The room filled with bodings of approaching abomination, as of a dentist's waiting room. Suddenly I realized there was a strange luminescence about me, a very pale fog of light that filled the air, as though Mrs Pring were boiling vast quantities of luminous paint in the kitchen below. With fearful slowness the light coagulated, condensed, contracted towards a point in the air some eighteen inches from the floor; abruptly it took definite shape and I saw the throbbing, ectoplasmic form of the *thing* that haunted this room for so long. It was larger than I'd expected, perhaps nine inches from end to end; it wavered this way and that in the air as though seeking something in a curious one-eyed manner; the thought occurred to me that it had formed atop the bed and centrally positioned, or at least would have done so had I not previously removed the bed. Even as this notion flared in my mind like a flashbulb, the Thing appeared to realize there was nothing to support it now: it flopped quite solidly and audibly to the floor."

"*Audibly?*" Hyphen-Jones quavered. "With a thud, or a clatter, or ...?"

Smythe darted an impatient glance at him. "With the sound of a large frankfurter falling from a height of eighteen inches on to wooden floorboards, if you wish to be precise. The horror of it! These solid manifestations are the most terrible and inarguable of spiritual perils: it's definitely easier to deal with an astral entity which *can't* respond with a sudden blow to your solar plexus. And worst of all, something which might have sent my hair white if I hadn't already dyed it this rather fetching colour, the Thing had now fallen *inside* the pentacle, with me! Again, imagine the horror of it, the feeling of spiritual violation: already my outer defences had been penetrated. The ab-human embodiment reared up, questing this way and that like a cobra readying its strike – and then it began to move my way. I utterly refuse to describe the manner in which it moved, but I believe there are caterpillars which do the same thing. If so, they have no shame. I knew that a frightful peril was coming for me ... it's always horribly dangerous when something materializes inside your very defences, though this wasn't perhaps as bad as in that Phantom Trumpeter case: you remember it, where the spectral elephant took solid form in my all too small pentacle? But in this particular situation I felt I was safe from the worst, at least."

"Why were you safe from the worst?" asked the fuddled Hyphen-Jones.

"A matter of anatomy," Smythe said evasively, and left Hyphen-Jones to work it out. "Still, I was too confident, as it happened. The only safe course was to *get out of that room* and perhaps try to bag it with a long-range exorcism from the landing. What I did was to experiment with a little of the consecrated ale left over from making the pentacle. I flicked some at the crawling Thing as it snaked its way towards me, and ... well, it must have been peculiarly sensitive. It positively dribbled with rage, and vanished in a burst of ectoplasm.

"I believed the Thing must have withdrawn itself for the night, abandoning its rigid form and returning to the nameless Outer Spheres. Again, I'd fallen into the trap of over-confidence. I was still standing there in my fatally gorgeous ensemble when once again that luminous fog filled the air about me and ... no, I can't bring myself to describe what happened then. Certain of the older grimoires recommend that practitioners of the magical arts, black or white, should ritually seal each of the nine orifices of the body as part of the preliminaries. I believe I now know why."

"My God, you don't mean ...?" said Carruthers, but seemed to lack the vocabulary or inclination to take the sentence further. Hyphen-Jones appeared to be counting under his breath.

"Well, I'll be buggered," the Major murmured.

Tersely Smythe explained how, pausing only to waive his fee and advise that Mrs Pring should sleep henceforth in the cursed room while renting out her own, he'd departed without so much as changing his clothing.

"So my life was transformed by that Thing in the Bedroom," he concluded gaily. "Now let me tell you of my newest case, one which I was formerly reluctant to investigate. The matter of the haunted chamber in the Café Royal, where the shade of Oscar Wilde is said to (at the very least) walk...."

The Gutting

A.N. Horrorauthor

All through the day, Henry Follicle had been followed around his apartment by a grim sense of foreboding. Each time he shot a glance over his shoulder, there was nothing to be seen but the odd cockroach ... yet the undercurrent of terror wouldn't go away. In his heart of hearts he knew he'd long been marked down for a fearful, gratuitous end, probably involving chainsaws or the magg-oty putrescent clutch of diseased zombie fundamentalists.

There was just no way you could fight knowledge like that.

It had all begun when he was nothing but a raw-nosed, gangling kid, prying into forbidden things with which he'd never been meant to meddle. Miss Oxter the librarian had said as much, loudly – but it hadn't stopped Follicle. He'd worked his way furtively through the horror shelves, trapping himself in an addiction that had lasted thirty years ... and slowly the gelatinous outlines of his fate had come clear.

He himself was ... a victim.

At first it had been a joke: a wry smile as once again he recognized himself in some hastily-written character whose only purpose was to be very horribly and disgustingly killed, or worse. But the thing went deeper than coincidence! Numbly, for the thousandth time, he checked off the points:

He was a typical, sympathetic, all-American guy. He'd never received much character development, except for a few cheaply poignant touches like his love for his wacky, irrepressible mongrel pup Barker, or his populist fondness for Macdonalds plus quadruple ketchup washed down with cans of Schlitz. His hopes and fears had always been simple ones, evidently designed for maximum market appeal: staunch devotion to the President, mild fear of the evil Russkies, stark terror of Internal Revenue, guilty lust for his secretary on the 113th floor of the Nosra Fire Insurance Co....

If only I could be a faggot, or read James Joyce (same thing, I guess), or go on a civil liberties march!

He couldn't. He'd been trapped helplessly in his rut of being marketably sympathetic, instantly but not deeply appealing, disposable, cardboard, stuffed to bursting with stereotyped reactions. It was as though some awful, omniscient Author were steering him with a gigantic thumb to his doom. He was one hundred percent a victim.

At least, he thought with that single faint gleam of hope which sustained him despite the appalling foreknowledge, *my bit should be over in a page or two. The real losers are the ones who have to live right through to the end of a book like this.*

Kismet. Destiny. That was the way to take it. To some folk it's just a word: but to Follicle, destiny meant the ravening greenish-yellow fangs with which the world planned to ambush him. Out there somewhere was a page with your name on it, and when it came ...

Still, he just didn't believe all those scary news items about rogue digestive systems which had torn their way free from their erstwhile owners and even now were tastelessly ravaging the continent. Even the flakiest of horror novelists wouldn't stoop that low – would they?

Absently-mindedly he noticed a strange, sour smell in the apartment. As though he'd thrown up quietly without noticing it (Schlitz did that to you sometimes), or had put too much Parmesan cheese on a lasagna-and-fries TV dinner. Yet it wasn't quite like that either. It had overtones that somehow reminded him of boiled slugs *au gratin*, or those phosphorescent fish-organs that even the sushi restaurants threw away, or the terrible milky foaming of maggots that had once held him transfixed when he'd looked for the rest-room at Luigi's Diner and made the mistake of finding the kitchen.

Nasty was the word, an inadequate word, for that smell. And with it came a slithering, sucking noise that seemed to be right behind him, the sort of noise you might expect if you tried to stir a three-day-old pot of congealed cannelloni, or perhaps to whip a naked and manacled female secretary with strands of parboiled asparagus....

Follicle was damned if he'd look round. Those fucking cockroaches had cried wolf once too often. So he never saw what it was that wetly wrapped itself around his ankles, secreting a hot acid that seared through his plump flesh to expose the naked whiteness of the bone.

About time too, he thought, toppling forward in hope of swift, merciful oblivion. But as he fell he glanced against the corner of the table, which burst his right eye like an over-ripe grape. A crackle like the snapping of dead twigs announced a whole fistful of broken finger-bones in the hand which had instinctively tried to break his fall. Hot, loose sensations indicated the sudden failure of all his sphincters, and as his face flattened itself into the soiled carpet he felt his nose being smashed back level with his cheekbones, while all his front teeth shattered at the impact of some unyielding object that awaited them at ground level.

That'll teach me to leave Stephen King books lying on the floor, he thought philosophically. He made a frenzied attempt to roll onto his back and see what was coming: the stress was too much, and halfway his weakened ribs popped loose like the teeth of a defective zipper.

Laden with horror fiction and overbalanced by the recent collision, the heavy table collapsed on him, breaking his neck and giving him a slight bruise on the left forearm. His stomach heaved, and Follicle began quietly to asphyxiate in his own warm, pungent vomit. He rather thought his kneecap was dislocated, too.

Something blood-warm and slimy crawled lubriciously over him, just outside the field of vision of his remaining eye. Its acid trail seared through clothes and flesh like the Spanish Inquisition's pokerwork, passing over his thigh, his cringing crotch. One testicle sprang free and rolled soggily across the floor, like a spat-out marshmallow glistening with saliva. Just as Follicle had concluded that the pain couldn't possibly get any worse, and that he might never now get round to squeezing that particularly ripe zit next to what used to be his nose ... the crawling something reached his stomach.

Oblivion giggled at the edges of Follicle's consciousness as he tried to put words to the new horror that struck along his nerves with the agony of an industrial infra-red laser cutter capable of vaporizing ten-inch slabs of molybdenum steel. Something was tearing, tearing loose within his abdomen, pulling clumsily free like postage stamps which (as scientists have shown) tear along any arbitrary line but that of the perforations. *Shit. Giving birth must feel like this.* And: *Why couldn't it be a nice quiet H.P. Lovecraft story with just one sentence of stark terror before you go mad? You'd think the author was being paid by the word.*

Something, something which he still couldn't see for the shadows now filling his good eye (along with the clotting blood and the bit of carrot which he recognized in sudden terror as one he'd eaten last night) ... something was humping its tortured way across the floor. Twice as loudly as it had come. And Follicle felt, inasmuch as his ravaged senses could still feel at all – hollow.

Then he heard a more familiar sound. A heart-warming snuffle and a cute, mischievous growl.

My God, I'd forgotten Barker! That poor pooch ... is he gonna get worked over for the sake of giving the readers a cheap twist of the knife? Or – no, of course, faithful dog avenges dying master, I like it, I like it. Go to it, Barker! Kill!

An explosive canine sneeze ripped through the steamy, clogging stillness of the violated apartment. Barker had smelt something – Something – and hadn't liked it one little bit. Follicle heard the dog snuffle along the floor in hope of something more palatable. Follicle, if he had still been capable, would have felt a terrible shrinking of the guts as Barker found it. The wacky, irrepressible mongrel licked his master affectionately, and with doggy enthusiasm started to dig in.

Suppose I should have expected it. Low-budget ironies, for Chrissake. And – ouch, that was a kidney – what kinda pervert is this author anyway?

As if to inflict the final indignity, a large buzzing housefly settled in the middle of Follicle's fast-clouding eye, and began to lay eggs....

The Mad Gods' Omelette
M*ch**l M**rc*ck

In the walled city of Kagool, where men were held in thraldom to the worship of the sacred voles, Erryj and his companion Windloon came by night to a tavern, and drank awhile in silence.

To their table came then a cloaked figure, who at a gesture from Erryj revealed himself to be none other than Dylan Worm, a distant kinsman of doomed Erryj.

"Dark peril threatens, my lord. Again the fate of the World hangs in the balance, for powers beyond the ken of man have been loosed by the sorcerer Thebes Shagreen! When only you may save us all, it ill becomes you to sit drinking at the Sign of the Engorged Lymphatic!"

Erryj smiled a bitter smile. "What has this world done for me that I should do now that doing which the world would fain have me do for it?" he demanded – unanswerably – indicating at the same time his squint, his humped back, his warts, and the black, rune-carved artificial leg *Slugbane* which supported his emaciated form.

"Well spoken, Erryj!" cried Windloon, signing for more wine. "Surely 'tis time you made an end to your perilous exploits, to battle and treachery and death.... Me too."

Dylan Worm's fist crashed on the table: a score of empties fell to the floor

"Is this the Erryj I knew once in fallen Murble? Know you that the Dark Gods walk the earth once more, this day!" He glanced to the window. "This night."

The tavern fell silent. For it was closing time.

"The Dark Gods?" Erryj gave Dylan Worm a searching glance. "Aye, I have heard tell of such. Speak you of the Elder Gods? ... The

Younger Gods? The Dead Gods? The Agnostic Gods?" With each utterance a greater stillness filled the room.

"Nay, worse yet," groaned his kinsman. "Thebes Shagreen has raised up ... The Mad Gods!"

And as he spoke, Windloon gave a harsh, fearful cry that seemed to echo through immeasurable spaces.

"Drink up quickly or you follow him," grunted the broad-shouldered bouncer. Erryj cast a baleful crimson stare at the base villain.

"Let me deal with him," pleaded Dylan Worm. "I would have him die cleanly." He drew his great sword *Bowelpiercer*; originally indeed had it been *Pigsticker*, which Dylan Worm thought less dignified.

He was too late. The iron leg *Slugbane* snapped straight, causing Erryj to rise perforce from his seat. At the same time it gave an eerie wailing, as though crying out for human life. Erryj squirted oil into the joint, but to no avail; death-fear washed over the bouncer's face as he realized that he had brought on himself the bane of ... The Black Leg! Swifter than thought, *Slugbane* swung and struck with a crunch on the oaf's puny manhood.

"Aaaaaaah!" he cried, falsetto. The fell runes carven on the iron limb glowed with unholy radiance as its sorcerous power sucked the man's essence. He collapsed, and Erryj stalked grimly out, followed by the pallid Dylan Worm.

"The Mad Gods," mused the doomed prince as they walked in darkness. "How can this be? The Law of the Cosmic Debit and Credit Balance does not permit it!"

"It seems the Cosmic Book-keeper doth be on holiday." Dylan Worm's voice was grim.

"And now the Mad Gods run up a perilous Cosmic Overdraft ..."

"Until the day of the Final Cosmic Audit."

"'Tis but a legend," snapped Erryj. "Why should I go to my doom against such?"

Windloon spoke at last. "But, friend Erryj, you are already doomed. The world knows it. You keep telling us so yourself."

"Doomed ... Aye, I am that."

"'Tis pity," murmured Dylan Worm, "that the fair Zazazoom has fallen into Thebes Shagreen's clutches."

Erryj stiffened. "Which way to Thebes Shagreen, friend and kinsman?"

"He dwells in the Vale of Morg."

"An easy trek ..."

"But also in the Vale of Morg," Dylan Worm said softly, "are the Mad Gods."

Erryj thought of the ghastly legends of those dire beings, and then of the enticing Zazazoom, the woman he craved.

"Let them stop me," he cried in a great voice. The iron of the Black Leg resonated evilly to the sound. Inspired to befuddled courage, Windloon responded: "I shall follow you!" Then fell he over and threw up.

"I can give you scant aid in this adventure," explained Dylan Worm, striding hastily away.

Erryj of Murble, doomed prince of no fixed abode, groaned in his sleep. Not only indigestion but seasickness troubled him, as the vaults of memory poured forth ancient fears.

For six hours, as they approached the battle, he had perforce chanted the dark runes from the bows: unless he thus repelled the hovering gulls, the boat's armour- gleaming mercenaries would claim hazard money for their aerial befoulment.

But Erryj had led his horde on, had landed at the Port of Murble and sacked it utterly. Even now the ruins were swathed in mouldering hessian. Then had he confronted the foul usurper Rakoon, who perished in agony beneath the bane of the Black Leg. A madness of destruction had come on Erryj then, and the entire population of the Enchanted Isle of Murble, including the woman he loved (his mother) had died by his boot and the sorcerous malice thereof.

For *Slugbane* was no ordinary artificial leg. Forged by no human hand, no human foot, in times better forgotten, it held a fell power; it drew out the essence of a man and thereby charged its bearer with unholy energy. So the Leg and its bearer walked together (how else?) through spectral shadows or under the hellish glare of the tainted sun, and none knew which was master. Save Erryj himself.

"Yes, Master," he intoned, bending himself to the ancient Murblean rite of foot worship. Everything seemed cloudy ... he woke suddenly and shivered. A great weight seemed to press upon his chest.

"Not *now*, Windloon ..."

"Sorry."

Setting off at dawn, the pair trudged for two hours; an uncanny sense of doom slowly filled the air.

"The woods!" cried Windloon, "the woods!"

From the shadowed forest poured an endless horde: green and slime-bedecked, many feet long, gnashing their jagged teeth ...

"The Giant Newts of Nematode!" Erryj gasped.

"Are ... are they friendly?"

"Nay. No newts are good newts. And these be no ordinary newts, but a sending of Thebes Shagreen!"

Closer and closer crept the slavering horde, as Erryj strained to recall a defensive spell. Windloon muttered, "I like this not."

"I have it! I shall summon the Froglord!" Erryj cleared his throat.

"By the glaucous jelly-like masses of thy spawn, Aid us, oh Froglord, this perilous morn."

"It scans not well."

"I have scarce begun. Besides, witling, you know nothing of High Magic.

"And by the little wriggling black things that are thy young, I call you to hearken unto the spell that I have sung. To end these evil newts from noisome marshes, or possibly bogs, I summon you, *Lord of the* ... ummm ... *Frogs!*"

"Be that all?" Windloon's voice was hopeful.

"There is yet the Activating Word." The newts were very close now, and a fell light was in their eyes.

"BREKEKEKEX KO-AX KO-AX!"

Gluurk, the Froglord, stirred in its otherworld home. From afar it felt the tugging of the Pact: for it was bonded in slime-brotherhood to the Royal Line of Murble. Was it worth the effort? it mused; but presently croaked "Well, if I don't save him, something else will."

Below, Erryj relaxed.

High in the air came a piercing and vaguely obscene sound, as the Froglord descended from its high spiritual plane. Immense and froggy, it plummeted to earth. Erryj and Windloon dived to one side as the gigantic batrachian bulk struck the ground, instantly crushing the myriad newts to pulp beneath its immensity. It sat wobbling there and emitted thunderous croaks.

"Methinks the solution is worse than the problem, Erryj. Dismiss your supernatural aid, and let us proceed."

Erryj looked haggard. "Would that it were that easy. The Froglord must be rewarded."

So as Windloon averted his gaze, Erryj did that which was needful; whereat the slimy deity ascended happily to its slimy heaven.

"Never does he stop hoping," thought the doomed prince, distastefully wiping off the lipstick with a silken cloth.

They toiled on into a swirling sea of mist. Stark and sudden, a city loomed before them. As they passed within, the gate closed smoothly behind them, and a deep mocking laugh filled the air.

"I just remembered the one about the dragon and the commercial traveller," Windloon explained.

"Silence, friend." Erryj examined the dark-red buildings, and shuddered. "Our peril is great; for this is none other than ... the Tourist Trap Built of Blood!"

"Ho, ho, ho!"

"Wilt thou *stop* that, Windloon!"

"'Twas not I." They looked all about them; presently Erryj spoke again. "I remember now. Legend has it that here dwells the giant Ruislip, whose wont it is to entrap tourists and drain their blood for building material. We stand now at the core of the evil, in the Plaza paved with Plasma."

"Better that we left," suggested Windloon, battering frantically at the gates.

"If the tales are true, that will help not. We must defeat Ruislip himself. 'Tis said that he doth creep up upon his unwary victims ..."

There came a sound of thunderous yet fantastically stealthy footsteps.

"Then doth he cast his net ..." Erryj was so engrossed that he failed to hear the unmistakable hiss of a net being cast.

"Then binds he the luckless ones, and carries them to a hidden cell, and there does he leave them until he is ready to take their blood!" So Erryj concluded dramatically; the door of the hidden cell slammed behind them.

"Thy sources of information are impeccable," Windloon complained.

"Worry not, I shall free us with the power of *Slugbane!* ... Oh." Base indeed was Ruislip, to confiscate his leg.

"How shall we escape, Erryj? Why do you not summon the Froglord?"

"Perilous it is to repeat one's effects too often," the prince muttered. "Better that we rest awhile."

"Ho, ho, ho!" The great laugh shook them awake. It was morning. In the eighteen-foot door was silhouetted the stooped figure of Ruislip.

"'Tis time," he boomed.

"After you," Windloon quavered.

"*Blood and guts! Clooti!*" cried Erryj. "Desist!" the giant shouted. "Else shall I have your giblets for goblets!"

"*Clooti!* O my patron demon! Lord of the Three Madnesses, the Five Banes and the Seven Nonfilterable Viruses! Aid me now!"

"I get it not," said Windloon with a shrug.

"Clooti! The souls of my descendants ..." A trapdoor opened in the floor, and amid a cloud of sulphurous smoke, the demon shot into the room.

"You summon me at the most awkward times," he muttered darkly, plucking at his red tights and otherwise adjusting his awe-inspiring raiment. "What afflicts you?"

Erryj pointed silently at Ruislip, who began to quake in fear.

"Nay ... Nay."

Clooti gestured at him with a pitchfork, and instantly he turned into a horse.

"My thanks, Lord Clooti," said Erryj.

"A pleasure. Sign *here*."

"Aye ... how many souls of my descendants have I pledged now?"

"Eighty-three generations. More frugal should you be with our *deus ex machina* service. 'Tis time, too, that you *had* some descendants, princeling."

"Aye." Erryj blushed. Clooti signalled his farewell and vanished.

Pausing only to retrieve *Slugbane*, they hastened on their way.

As they neared the Vale of Morg, there appeared the figure of a wondrously beautiful wench, rivalling even the fair Zazazoom in her complexion and bust measurements.

"Queen Ikenlupa!" gasped Erryj. "Look not on her, Windloon! Her fell beauty will ensnare your soul and taint it with her hidden evil!"

"Wha'?" said Windloon, taking a dazed step forward.

"Windloon! 'Tis but illusion. Hear you not the whirring of fell magic? See you not that she doth flicker at sixteen frames per second?"

"Oh." Windloon stopped; the image vanished, leaving but a forty-foot pit where it had been.

"Ha!" said Erryj, "this bodes well. Thebes Shagreen seeks to bemuse us with trickery – no doubt 'twas his last trick!"

At the very rim of the Vale, he paused.

Below, rank on rank, irrefutably real, were ranged the Abominations of Yandro, the Glaucous Glob of Ghooli, Thebes Shagreen himself, and three full pantheons of Mad Gods.

Erryj sighed; against the horde that opposed him, only the darkest powers would avail. This was a job for – The Black Leg!

Again he paused. "What perchance have these gods done to me, anyway? Live and let live; such has always been my motto." He made as if to turn....

Then did the Leg glow with balefire and swell mightily from its stolen energies! There came a rending sound. One day, mused Erryj with wistful prescience, the skills of men will bring forth elastic tights. But then *Slugbane* sorcerously and treacherously elongated itself by a full eight inches. Erryj tried desperately to fling himself to the ground – too late! Against his will was he carried hopping towards the horde of nameless abominations in the Vale.

Even with *Slugbane*'s power, he was helpless against so many. There was but one chance. Before he reached the waiting doom, Erryj might be able to summon aid, perhaps even produce something from the gigantic hat which he carried always with him. Yet jolted by *Slugbane*'s uncontrollable motion, he could only recall torn fragments of spells.

"There was a young lady of Riga," he began experimentally.

With a sudden pop, a stranger appeared. He too had an artificial leg, akin to *Slugbane*, or so it seemed.

"Greetings, Erryj." The newcomer hopped to keep pace with him. "My name is Jorin, and I am of course another incarnation of yourself."

Bemused, Erryj frowned. "How can this be? It maketh no sense."

"Know you not that the Conjunction of the Myriad Balls approaches? That two aspects of the Sempiternal Saviour should thus converse is but a small matter, compared with those improbabilities which the Great Author of All Things has yet in store!"

By now, the pair had hopped through the first three ranks of Mad Gods, who were looking on with vast amusement. Atop the ridge, Windloon shouted helpful and encouraging advice.

"Jorin! How can even a second *Slugbane* prevail against so many?"

Jorin smiled. "Link arms with me, friend Erryj."

"I'm not that sort."

"Quickly! or all is lost!"

"Very well," said Erryj. "... To battle!"

As they linked arms, a sudden tide of godlike energy surged through Erryj. "Mayhap I am that sort after all." he thought.

Then he saw that the ground was far away. *Slugbane* and its twin, grown to monstrous size, held the pair high above the horde, taller than the tallest gods. At their commanding thoughts, the great iron legs rose and fell, rose and fell, dealing destruction right and left. To a deity, the Mad Gods perished. Last of all remained Thebes Shagreen: defiant to the end, he died with a taunt on his lips.

"Everyone knows the runes on that leg are but the signatures of thy friends!" he cried as the massive foot descended.

"Squelch!" he added a moment later.

"That doth be that," Jorin remarked. "Farewell, friend Erryj; remember thou owest me a favour."

"Aye," said Erryj as the black iron legs shrank to normal size. He disentangled his arm from Jorin's and shuddered at the scene of carnage. "Call thou not I, I shall call thee."

With another pop, Jorin vanished as providentially as he had come.

"Wait for me!" shouted Windloon, advancing and waving his sword. "Oh dear, 'tis little glory that you've left for my poor self." Sheathing his blade, he philosophically set about looting the corpses.

All peril was ended; Erryj sought at last for Zazazoom. The castle of Thebes Shagreen lay in ruins, but before it stood a slim figure. It was indeed his love. But her form was not as he recalled it; she had been changed by the Mad Gods, fearfully changed....

"You may be green and scaly, sweetling, yet still you are the woman I love," cried Erryj in a noble voice, gagging slightly. But at the moment his need was great.

"Oh Erryj, how canst thou bear to look upon the ichor-dripping fangs which once were my pearly teeth?"

"'Tis not your looks alone that I care for," Erryj explained, fumbling with his clothing. "Accurst hose!"

"Truly thou art a noble prince, Erryj. Fain would I reward such constancy ... pity 'tis that the cruel Mad Gods in their evil changings did make me into a male."

"Gaaaaah," said Erryj, as the Black Leg lashed out almost automatically. The screams died down. "Never have I been lucky with my women," he murmured.

"An ill fortune dogs you, Erryj," Windloon sympathized.

"Aye. Yet the future may not always be black...." Smiling, he playfully kicked Windloon on the shin.

"No! No! I did not sheathe the Black Leg! Forgive me, Windloon, forgive me!" It was too late; *Slugbane* swung on to find its inevitable mark.

"Aaaaaaah!" commented Windloon as he fell.

As Erryj wept over the corpse of his faithful companion, a strange and fearful vision came to him.

He stood, last living thing upon the Earth: alone. And slowly, slowly, the Black Leg curled back in a hideous fluid motion; the fell runes glowed for the last time as – *crunch!* – Erryj perished by his own leg. It detached itself from his empty cardboard husk and hopped triumphantly off into the setting sun.

"Farewell, my friend! I was a thousand times less artificial than thou!"

And Erryj was no more; utterly forgotten for all time, until the Great Author of All Things saw fit to resurrect him once more.

Which was pretty soon.

The vision passed, and twilight came.

With a mad cry the doomed prince flung himself onto a horse and rode out into the night, stricken to the heart, yet conscious that he might not stand in the way of Fate and the Reconciliation of the Cosmic Ledger. For written in the runes of his future were more base slayings and treacheries, foulest barratry and tax offences, madness, insobriety and despair.

"It doth beat working for a living," he thought.

Jellyfish

D*m*n R*ny*n

It is the week before the jellyfish, and I am sitting back meditating on whether *The Journal of Diagnostic Medicine* or *Spicy True-Life Stories* is more deserving of my refined attention, when Joe Karelli comes in. He is wined up to the eyeballs and maybe a centimetre or so beyond, but tactfully I ignore this, as Joe is apt to become irate when in this condition. Last time he is mildly irate, they are obliged to replace all the windows in Clancy's bar.

"Doc," he says, "I have a little job for you."

I tell it to him straight. "I do not touch it if it is a smelly one. Too many of your lady cousins are prey to appendicitis already."

"Of course I am not asking you if it is not legit." He is very soothing. "I know you cannot be tempted from the straight and narrow, except perhaps by money.

"So speak of this job, not omitting to mention a provisional fee."

Joe gives me a hurt look. "A man in your position should be more trusting. I want that you should run a medical nose over this bottle and tell me if it contains anything not healthy. If a small swig of the hooch in this bottle is liable to injure a man's projects, you will cook up an antidote damn fast. In either case this earns you fifty, for I am a generous citizen."

It is a small bottle, just damp inside, and I squint at the label. "Doctor Damian's Regenerative Elixir. Why should this be harmful to your health? I do not know Doctor Damian but I am sure he has to keep his overheads down, and he cannot do this by lacing his elixir with poison, or anything else except maybe some artificial flavouring and colouring."

Joe says, "I will tell you about this Damian. I am in Clancy's just now, celebrating the first cuckoo, or the first I hear today, or maybe it is not a cuckoo, and I drink a drink or so. I am more than somewhat cheerful for a while, in spite of a gloomy pal who is always very much a pessimist, also his mother's funeral is today. But after a few glasses more I too am sad, and by and by I cry a little (for I am a feeling man) and say I do not want to die.

"Then this prune-faced character whom I treat gives me the bottle. He is Doctor Damian, he says, very proud. After this he staggers a little, and heads for the men s room, and does not come out again. I myself go there a little later for various reasons, and he is not inside either. Of course I think nothing of this, as I am on doubles for two hours.

"But then another friend, not the one with the funeral, he is overcome with emotion under the table, another pal bets me that I will not drink out of the bottle. It tastes very bad, but I figure it is worth it to take five off Charlie. Afterwards I feel funny so I come here to play safe."

I yawn. "What is this funny feeling?"

"Oh, my gut itches, for quite sometime. All along the line of my appendectomy, a real appendectomy, it itches like fire-ants are staging a hot reunion. Ten, twenty minutes and it stops, but I am solicitous for my health and come all the same."

I flex fingers and feel up my sleeve for the professional manner. "Let me see, then."

He peels off jacket, shin, vest, and I am revolted by the Old English Sheepdog chest. Still, I grope for the scar and cannot find it. Vindictive, I grope harder, but Joe only grunts.

"What appendectomy? Do you maybe confuse it with a tonsil operation?"

"You are a man of small perception, Doctor. Feel *here*."

He feels *there*. "What have you done with my scar?"

I am disgusted at his condition. "There is no scar, ever,

"My goddam war wound! I tell all the women, see, this is my war wound. They will tell you I have a scar." is most convincing.

"It is time," I decide, "for the analytic approach, also a little lab ethanol."

I pour, and we sip slowly, holding hair on with the free hand. Then I become analytic.

"No scar means, healed scar. This is a secret of medicine which

I tell you gratis."

"It does not seem right after so long."

I frown. "There is what we medical men call the causal relationship."

"Must you bring women into this?"

I ignore this. "You drink an elixir," I say analytically, "and your scar itches and then there is no scar. Unless this is the C_2H_5OH talking, I do not think that Elixir has done you harm, Joe." I also think, if there is more than half a drop left, I myself am taking a sip in the interest of Science, the greedy bum.

Joe looks a little dazed, and I look at the bottle's small print. "Provides perpetual regrowth after any wound or amputation. Guaranteed 1000 years." If it is not for Joe's stomach I am giving this one the big laugh. I point it out to him. He puts on a stupid grin.

"Great. If Maude takes a swing at me with her hatchet now, maybe I grow a couple of new fingers."

"Your girl has a hatchet?"

"I am breaking a leg getting away, last time she picks it up and looks mean. I think she suspects."

"Flora and Chrissie, and Suzanne, perhaps she has a grudge. Women are not reasonable."

"It is Lily and Arabella I think she catches on to."

"Goodbye," I tell him without great emphasis. I am much aroused by Lily myself, in a pure spiritual fashion of course.

"Goodbye, my friend," he says, putting the fifty on the table. I take my back away from the door and hold it open for him. Joe Karelli is a moneyed man, though not of course to the taxman.

"I think I am buying myself a good juicy annuity," he says, stepping out: "For life. One thousand years, you say. A man can do much in this time."

When he is gone I put the bottle to my lips and suck very hard, but now it is dry because he does not replace the top. Joe has little consideration for his fellow men. Joe has an appendix, too, I suppose. With the remaining ethyl for consolation, I reach for *Spicy True-Life*.

Of course I do not believe impossible things as easily as this, no no, as I tell myself while taking many aspirins late that evening. But I read next day in the paper that Joe, it seems, celebrates some more and plays tag with the traffic on Broadway. He is hit by an automobile, is listed DOA at Memorial Hospital and is discharged later that night. This is not a usual procedure.

I hear nothing of Joe then for two, three days, and he slips from my mind because of the jellyfish. These are held by many great newspapers to be a Martian invasion, and certainly it is not natural that pink gobs of jelly should grow in the streets of our fair city. Nobody understands why they visit here, nor why this barber's shop is filled with them while others escape. They appear in people's rooms too, and I find I have more than the average, which seems not fair. Among other things they give Lily hysterics when she calls, so our conversation is unable to become spiritual. All in all it is agreed that nobody knows what to do; also that the jellies are not friendly, on account of one old guy treads on one and his foot dissolves.

It occurs to me then that Joe might well shine as the city's jellyfish catcher, for if he loses bits they maybe grow again: I am still a little sceptical of the Elixir but not much. In fact I drink a lot at Clancy's, but see no wrinkled little men, except one who is mounted on a small brontosaur. Him I ignore since it is very late and I am not inclined to converse, also my legs are not working at the time.

I am reading the headlines saying JELLYFISH: LATEST, there being nothing else to do on account of business is bad, when Joe Karelli visits me once more.

"Doc," he says without taking off his hat, "I have been thinking."

"Do not over-exert yourself, my friend," I reply, "shall I feel your pulse?" I am much noted for my quick repartee. But Joe does not smile, which means he feels very down. I wait to hear what bothers a man who figures on living maybe a thousand years.

(I myself have a feeling that not wanting to die, that much, is something of a cowardly thing. But I respect the weight of Joe's opinions, for he is two hundred pounds, most of which is prime beef. Also, he is wined up again).

"Doc," he says, "I am having this thought. Suppose Maude takes her hatchet and cuts me in two. Once or twice she threatens to split Joe Karelli down the middle."

"Surely you are not disturbed by such a little woman as Maude?

You never worry about these things before. Besides, if your Elixir is good you are getting well again before you know it."

"So which half gets well?"

I have walked into this one, and it is something of a jolt. Who expects this Socrates stuff from a person moving in such low circles as Joe Karelli?

"Both," I say after a moment, and then I am looking at a jellyfish which sits on the carpet. Joe is looking at it too'

"And if I cut just a finger off ..." he is there before me ... "we will wind up with two of me?"

"Well ..." I see it now. And I do not like it at all. "A man," I reflect, "loses millions of skin cells every day." I goggle at the jellyfish again.

"That I do not know, not being medical. But a man has haircuts too. I find my barber sweeping out a whole swarm of these gumdrops, and I get to thinking, is every hair of mine planning on being a carbon copy of Joe Karelli?"

"That is surely not right. Hair is dead, it cannot regenerate."

"Tell this to my hair. I am dead awhile at Memorial, and it does me no harm although I do not much care for it. Nor do I care for being a monster from Mars, nor do I wish to block traffic in the streets.

"You dissolve old guys' feet also."

"He has it coming. Nobody asks him to stomp on a Karelli junior."

I peek again at the paper. "These jellyfish, it says here, feed on anything they find and regrow if cut up."

"Yeah, Just call me starfish." He is bitter, very bitter. I think harder. "Body cells are lost in the, ah, in the men's room too. And it is reported here ..."

"So now a whole load of me are clogging up the city sewers. Always my mother tells me I will sink to my true level." He meditates. "Already once I die and rise again. Maybe if I do this often enough I become a cult hero – Let us stay with the point, Doc, do not keep changing the subject. So what do I do?"

I can think of nothing to say. I tell him so.

"You do not know? A zillion Joe Karellis going to be walking the streets and you do not know what to do about it?"

Our fair city clogged up and squashed flat under a pile of Joes:

I imagine this and shudder. Never before do I catch myself shuddering. Now I think of it, Joe is entirely the wrong sort of person to spread himself like this. Lily or Arabella, maybe.

"For the sake of humanity," I begin loftily, not knowing how this sentence is to finish.

"Forget humanity," says Joe, "how many ways do I wind up splitting this annuity? As a citizen I have rights ..." He goes on like this for a long time.

I edge up on him with the needle.

We get along. Joe, he is poisoned in the sewers and incinerated in the streets, and the Army has a field day testing new unfriendly things on him. Meanwhile the original is in a cosy airtight room at Memorial and will be there a while yet, until someone figures out how to keep him in one piece.

Me, I do not do too badly when my name is in the papers, and already many more young ladies with appendicitis come my way. And with Karellis everywhere, maybe forever now, Joe's name is bound for the history books, also one or two medical texts. It is a proud and lonely thing for him, to have replaced the cockroach.

I am thinking: Joe is a coward, wanting to get out of dying. It is not democratic, living so long. This poet guy sees right through Joe Karelli, the one who says *the coward dies a thousand deaths*.

Lost Event Horizon

E.E. Sm*th

Overhead, without any fuss, the stars were going out.

Meanwhile, the Cosmic Patrol's evening recruiting session was going well, with Cosmic Agent Mac Malsenn as its chief attraction. Malsenn was demonstrating the virtuosity of the trained Agent by juggling a dozen forty-pound sacks of thulium granules with his left hand, whilst his right operated the incredibly sensitive controls of the genetic manipulation device with which he was creating a hitherto unknown species of telepathic whelk. His voice was calm as he snapped out his moves in thirty-five simultaneous games of 4-D chess; his chained-together legs moved with uncanny precision as they negotiated the murderous lava pits and banana skins of the Stage 10 Commando Assault Course. He was, of course, blindfolded. The casual observer would perhaps not have realized that his thoughts were elsewhere ... dwelling upon the loveliness of his sweetheart, Laura, who had told him only that morning she was his betrothed. Malsenn had a notion that "betrothed" meant "pal", and he was elated.

Inspired by his performance, recruits jostled one another for the privilege of becoming a Cosmic Agent and killing all the alien life forms they wished. The basic entrance test was a simple mental and physical one devised by Malsenn himself. At the rear door of the recruiting station, endless queues of numb-brained invalids emerged to jostle feebly to be the top man on the high-piled stretchers. No pansies were allowed in the Cosmic Patrol, an organization so exclusive that Malsenn was invariably the only marcher at its great pageants and parades (giving envious ones the chance to murmur that he was out of step).

Suddenly the transceiver in Malsenn's left bicuspid began to
ring. He gritted his teeth, accidentally turning on a wisdom tooth
which immediately gave of its store of wise sayings such as "Fast-
spinning planetoids gather no moss" and "Fine words butter no
parsecs". Meanwhile, his left canine was droning: "This is a recorded message. The Cosmic Agent is otherwise engaged. Please
speak your message at the third pip, at which time this mechanism
will automatically ring off. *Pip* ..."

"I know you're there, Malsenn!" It was the voice of Alkloyd, the
Starfleet commander whose daring and Initiative rivalled that of
the sloth. Malsenn sighed, thrust his tongue into the *override* cavity
of the transceiver tooth and, while dictating an unbroken stream of
chess moves off one side of that same tongue, said with the other:
"I'm a bit busy now. Is it important?"

"Try looking up."

Malsenn looked up. "Black," he said. "Very."

"Don't you see that overhead, without any fuss, the stars are
going out?"

"One moment ..." A single twitch of Malsenn's trained eyebrows
converted the blindfold to a confetti of scorched cloth. "$8/3\pi r^3$!" he
swore. "Good grief, Alkloyd, it seems that overhead, without any
fuss ..."

"I know, I know," said the Commander in a hysterical shriek
which set Malsenn's tooth on edge. "Now will you do something
about it? Right up your street, I'd have thought. Can't stop now ...
coffee time."

Malsenn put on a burst of speed, dictating mates in two or
three moves whilst tackling the final, lethal antimatter hoops of the
obstacle course, and doing a rush job on the whelk genes which
meant that the markings on the creature's shell – which he had intended should show the *Ode on a Grecian Urn* in exquisite
calligraphy – would merely form a displeasing sanserif typescript
of *Gunga Din*.

Bursting free from his chains, he ran for the spaceport so
swiftly as to cause reports of curiously blurred, low-altitude UFOs.
His tiny scoutship the *Star Vole* awaited him, fully armed with
universe-busters of various sizes and fully fuelled with fuel. In less
time than it takes to enter an airlock he had entered the airlock,
dived for the controls and blasted clear of the solar system; only

then, his concentration on duty momentarily relaxing, did he notice that his left hand was still juggling a dozen forty- pound sacks of thulium granules. He let them fall, and set a course for where Sirius had been before, overhead, without any fuss, it had gone out. As always, the *Star Vole*'s interstellar drive was based on an astonishing new principle devised by Malsenn whilst studying rubber models of Centaurian duckoids in his bath. The Axiomatic Drive was unusual in that at no time did it exceed the velocity of light; instead its counterlogical field redefined said velocity as being infinite (give or take a little), thus ensuring that there was no need to exceed it. A by-product of this axiomatic shift was that by Einstein's $E=mc^2$, infinite energy could now be extracted from a finite mass: the fusion of one hydrogen atom was adequate for any journey and left an infinite energy surplus which had to be stored in batteries.

Then the impossible happened. In a transition so swift that Malsenn's whole life was only able to flash before his eyes by playing at several million frames per second, the bottom dropped out of the universe. In a moment, it dropped back in again, and the dazed Cosmic Agent found his environment totally changed. The *Star Vole* was no more; only one of the sacks of thulium granules was still with him in this strange, shimmering envelope of indefinable, yet inarguable, material. Through the glittering something he saw a dreadful leer and a terrible beard – a leer and a beard which could only be those of his old enemy – the satanic archfiend, connoisseur of megagenocide, and critic: Nivek!

"Ha, ha!" said the evil one. "We meet again, accursed Cosmic Agent! Little did you know of my Klein bottle trap, an invention more satanic than dandruff. Little did you know that once you left Earth's protection, I could redefine space so that – although Klein bottles have no inside or outside – you would find yourself apparently within it! Little did you know ..."

"Actually, I rather expected this and merely allowed myself to be trapped," said Malsenn, unobtrusively hefting the sack of thulium granules. He had a hunch that it might be useful.

"Little did you know that in allowing yourself to be trapped you were in fact stepping into a trap," said Nivek.

"Little do you know," riposted Malsenn, "that in allowing me to step into a trap you have stepped into a trap. Since if inside and outside are the same for this Klein bottle, I can readily redefine myself as being outside, thus leaving you trapped!" And with a mighty effort of will, Malsenn wrenched at the conceptual structure of what might loosely be termed reality. Spatial contiguity bent in several places with a rusty creak, and there was a terrible sound as though a number of red giants and white dwarfs were engaging in disgusting perversions (which was in fact the case). The Klein bottle belched and everted itself, leaving Malsenn on the outside while Nivek stood within, helplessly trapped. Unfortunately, trapped inside with Nivek was the entire known universe.

"You did not think, my foolish adversary, that I would omit to seal the bottle with a conceptual plug?"

"All right, you fiend. You win this round, but the next hand will be mine when we cross swords again. No doubt it's you who is making the stars go out?"

There was a hideous rasping sound: Nivek was complacently stroking his beard. "Yes. I require power sources and am thus enclosing 99% of all known suns in Dyson spheres in order to tap their energies. I shall then have sufficient energy on call to put an end to this rather mundane universe."

Malsenn was aghast. "Nivek, this is not like you. why aren't you using the galaxy-draining power leeches you used to reply on? The nova generators? The planet-fired central heating systems?"

"These days I'm into conservation," said Nivek, and made a languid gesture. "See that? Not many people can train Rigellian languids to make gestures like that."

"Did it have to be a gesture like *that*? But, I say, how about if you gloat over me and reveal the ingenious way in which you intend to end the universe, so that I can, er ... be duly terrified."

"Certainly not."

"Nyahh nyahh nyahh, silly old Nivek doesn't have a plan!"

The evil overlord was wholly taken in by Malsenn's subtle psychological manipulation. "I do I do I do!" he responded with Jesuitical cunning. "My intention is to duplicate the entire universe!"

"Sounds a bit ... constructive," said Malsenn dubiously.

"Ah, but the new universe, down to the tiniest particle, will occupy the same space as the old one. Bang."

"Clever, fiendishly clever," the Cosmic Agent admitted. "But there is still the singular business of the singularity."

"But there is no singularity in my plan."

"That is what is so singular. You must realize that every plot contains a black hole or a singularity, these days."

Nivek brightened. "How convenient that you should suggest the means of your own disposal," he shrieked happily. "I have but to touch this button and you will be precipitated inexorably into the inescapable confines of a nearby singularity! Have you any last words?"

"I won't give you that satisfaction, you swine," Malsenn rasped through clenched jaws.

Nivek wrote these words down in a volume whose cover bore the legend *LAST WORDS OF COSMIC AGENTS*: Malsenn at least had the satisfaction of seeing him make three attempts at spelling "satisfaction". Then the warlord touched the top button of his kaftan, and with a strange sensation of imploding bananas, the top, bottom and several sides dropped out of Malsenn's universe.

And at once he was helplessly falling towards a point in space whose immense warps and distortions made the starlight run in crazy patterns like a TV screen when the station closes or shows a political broadcast. There came a queasy sensation of space-sickness, caused by the surge and ebb of gravity waves. With desperate intuition Malsenn wrenched off his left boot and flung it to one side. The reaction force of this mighty throw diverted his plunge into the indecently naked singularity and thrust him into orbit. As he adjusted his pocket space helmet, he realized that he was still clutching the sack of thulium granules. The hunch that they would be useful was stronger than ever. But his mighty mind brooded helplessly for many hours as he circled – or to be precise, ellipsed – the point where space was going down the drain. Was there no chance of escape?

Suddenly he recalled an article he had once read while passing through 1978 on business: an article explaining the irrational properties of singularities. It seemed that if you only waited long enough, then in due course anything at all would inevitably be emitted. This had not been checked, mainly because no-one had waited the necessary aeons ... but it seemed his only hope!

Removing the various microelectronic assemblies invariably built into his teeth and underwear, Malsenn set to work with his microtoolkit. Microscrewdrivers, microhacksaws, microsledgehammers, all were called into play as he painstakingly constructed an improvised suspended animation chamber, an improvised megabyte computer and an improvised pillow. Sooner or later, the random laws of chance must cause a replica of the *Star Vole* to be emitted from the singularity – and he had only to wait it out! He programmed the computer to watch for emitted *Star Voles* and for a certain other device ... and then pressed the switch that would throw him into trance through a vigil so long that his gene- shifted whelks would have time to evolve intelligence, take a good look round and hastily start devolving before the tiniest fraction of the time concerned had begun to approach the point of commencing to elapse.

And as he pressed the switch, Malsenn was smitten with a ghastly memory of the copy of *Reviews of Modern Physics* he had paused to sneer at while passing through 1979 on his way back from business.

"Oh no," he had time to think before oblivion fell upon him like a rice pudding from 30,000 feet.

10^{10} years passed. All the stars in the universe ran down and one or two very strange things popped out of the singularity. By around 10^{65} years, the first prediction of the remembered article came to pass: all matter flows like liquid on this vast timescale, and in a little while Malsenn, his computer and all his clothes had coalesced into a perfectly spherical lump. By around 10^{1500} years, several more even stranger objects had zoomed past the lump as they fled the singularity – and the lump was now a lump of warmish iron, since on this timescale all matter is radioactive and decays to iron (it's amazing how much physics you can learn from the most appallingly written SF). It was a very long time afterwards that the unexpected occurred, as sooner or later it must. Through the workings of random chance, an artifact popped from the singularity, an artifact which might have been specifically designed to restore the lump which had been Malsenn to its former state. Unfortunately there was no-one to turn this artifact on, and it floated away until aeons later it was worshipped by a race of sentient whelks. Several more such misfires occurred until at last a *deus ex machina* emerged from the singularity in perfect working order, turned on, and pointing in the right direction. Instantly Malsenn was restored, and instantly his computer woke him, for amid the debris orbiting the singularity there were by now several *Star Voles* and two or three time machines, though these were almost hidden in vast shoals of variorum editions of Shakespeare in simian typescript. In no time at all, relatively (in fact it was a few weeks), Malsenn was on his way back to a confrontation with Nivek – armed with his ship, a time machine and a sackful of thulium granules.

Reality was wrenched in various incompatible directions as the time machine knotted worldlines into bowlines and sheepshanks; a spume of tiny black holes was released to disrupt the whole of recorded history (a certain furore was caused by one which landed in eighteenth-century Calcutta). The fabric of space itself was folded, spiked, spindled, stapled and mutilated: what remained was worn and threadbare by the time Malsenn had finished with it, and from then on, it had to be handled very carefully.

"Not so fast! Not so fast, you fiend! Up against the wall! Don't touch that button!" So saying, Malsenn burst into Nivek's secret control room, cunningly located in the core of Betelgeuse and costing a fortune in air conditioning. It had taken even his trained mind fully ten minutes to deduce the location. "Ha! Little did you know that a Cosmic Agent is never defeated! Little did you know that I should return to frustrate your foul schemes! Stay away from that button, now ..."

Nivek smiled an awful smile, and the much-abused fabric of space/time gave a little shudder. "Tee-hee," he said.

"Why do you smile?" enquired Malsenn.

"I pushed the button several minutes ago."

Malsenn rushed for the *Star Vole* and found his way blocked by an impassable neutronium door. All he had with which to save the universe was his trusty blaster, his slightly less trusty bag of thulium granules and the universe-buster grenade which hung at his belt. There stood Nivek beside his foul Klein bottle, grinning and thinking eschatological thoughts.... Was this the very end? Already things were bulging and shimmering as the duplicate universe began to creep into being within their very withins. Only Malsenn was not being duplicated, having been absent at the start of the process. Suddenly he realized in a flash of realization, as dazzling and unexpected as a tax rebate, that the solution lay within his very hands! It was the work of seconds to pull the pin of the universe-buster grenade, thrust it into Nivek's hand and swiftly conceptualize himself into the safety of the shimmering Klein bottle. Even as he pulled the plug in after him, the grenade burst with a muted *pop* and the universe was no more.

"It became necessary to destroy the universe in order to save it," said Malsenn mournfully as the new scheme of things completed its unopposed journey into existence and began to regret it. The new Nivek, as stunned as the old by Malsenn's manoeuvre, was easily restrained after a brief struggle which destroyed the entire secret base and provoked a solar flare in the shape of an unusually vile Rigellian gesture.

Back on the new, improved Earth, Malsenn told the tale of his cosmic exploits to the new edition of Laura (whose yawns of keen enthusiasm seemed much the same as ever).

"But why," she said in puzzlement, "are you still carrying that forty-pound sack of thulium granules?"

He gave an enigmatic smile. "I just have this hunch that it's going to come in handy."

Overhead, without any fuss, the stars were coming back on.

The Spawn of Non-Q

A.E.v*n V*gt

CHAPTER ONE

For the sake of sanity, OVER-DESCRIBE. Don't simply say "One lump, please", but give the sugar's exact dimensions, assumed density, crystal structure, chemical formula and percentage of permissible impurities. This will clarify your thinking and allow you to reap the benefits of drinking healthful, correctly sugared, cold tea. (Korzybski)

As Filbert Insseyn woke in the cheap hotel bedroom, his bloodstream already reeled in an illusion of foreboding. He wrenched himself free from a half-sleeping dream of lovingly binding and gagging his wife Fanny Perennial, whom he abruptly realized he had never met. Non-Q training prepared one for these crises. One cautious, analytical glance at his wristwatch confirmed the suspicion. He had overslept, and the second hand was already ticking close to the 800-word mark. Too late for anything but a single pellucid instant's rage, anguish, and calm indecision before –

A man crashed through the door with a city-wrecking atomic missile, and there was –

Oblivion!

CHAPTER ONE

I think, therefore I am. (Descartes, quoted as Example 1 in *The Non-Q Primer of Basic Fallacies*)

Insseyn looked down at himself, expecting to see a shattered, mangled, tormented, dead body. He did not. And even as he looked down he realized from the hurtling moons above him that he was now on Mars. He explored the barren desert locality for twenty minutes, and suddenly the meaning of what had happened struck full upon him. He who had been on Earth only a few minutes ago was now on Mars! He who mere seconds ago had been dead was now alive!

There were so many questions. How could he have got to Mars? It was well known that space-travel was impossible owing to the impenetrability of the crystal spheres in which the planets were fixed.

About him the desert in its infinite lack of variety presented an unchanging yet ever-shifting picture of Non-Quintessential thought, with its refusal to accept the crippled, conventional Q-thinking that anything could embody anything else, or even itself.

At least no one in the universe could know his present location.

Across the sand blew a scrap of notepaper. WE HAVE GOT TO *GET* INSSEYN, it said in block capitals. At the same instant a smoke-belching aircar traced across the sky the words INSSEYN MUST DIE, and a passing beggar handed him a black spot.

He underwent a sudden illusory sense of being threatened in some indefinable fashion.

Why should anything threaten me? Insseyn laughed internally, looking quickly behind him. *I have done nothing.* He stood stock still in an abrupt forty minutes of stark insight as it came to him that he did not in fact remember anything that had happened before he met Fanny Perennial in that fatal hotel-room ... or indeed anything that had happened afterwards. He who but a few microseconds before had had a memory now had none!

That was the moment when unsanity, or worse, collapse into the primordial ooze of Q-thinking, might have come. He saved himself by making once again the Non-Q vascular-gonadic pause, followed by twenty swift press-ups. And was safe from madness!

Who could want to erase his memory? And why? It was a question which Insseyn, strain his gonads as he might, was unable to answer; then, or ever. He scratched his majestic, leonine belly in thought.

A sound burst on his ears, and in the same minute he knew that it was a voice. "Where will Insseyn turn up next? He could be – anywhere."

"True," grated a second voice, strange yet insidiously familiar, which rang like forged pewter. "We must find him and decategorize him before he can learn how to use his powers."

The sounds, Insseyn reasoned as he edged closer, came from a hole in the ground. A hole like many other holes to his razor-honed Non-Q awareness. A hole which he had just fallen into.

He glanced at his watch in sudden annoyance and realization. Another 800 words had passed.

"Now, touching upon the planned rape and destruction of the universe ..." was the last phrase which invaded his ears before he hit the bottom.

Luckily Insseyn wore an ingravitic belt, a gravity-countering device which had been designed by minds not befuddled with ill-conceived Q-axioms such as the notion that an energy as ineluctable as gravity could be reversed, neutralized or even opposed. The belt, based on subtle Non-Q concepts which recognized these limitations, did absolutely nothing to break his fall.

As his legs telescoped intriguingly into his chest, Insseyn found himself ceasing to be alive.

CHAPTER ONE

Just glance at an anthill. All that mindless activity! Now look at a glacier. Calm, indomitable, free from engrams. There in a nutshell is the essential difference between Q and Non-Q thought! (Hubbard, *Principles of Diuretics*)

Abruptly he was lying beside a solitary bush in a vast expanse of underdescription. Memories of Fanny Perennial thronged on him, images of passionate love, divorce and remarriage – and in the same hour he realized that these recollections must be artificial constructs impressed on his brain by Insseyn's enemies, probably by Jones or Smith. Suddenly he tensed and shifted into the cognitive overdrive of Non-Q thought. Jones! Smith! Where had he heard those obviously extraterrestrial names before?

He had never heard the names before, he realized sickeningly. This could only mean that somewhere a hidden mentality like a vast Snakes and Ladders player was secretly manipulating his every move. Another mystery which must in due course be solved, or not, as the case might be.

The bush radiated Non-Q thoughts. The fact of its doing so

almost argued for Quintessentialism, a paradox which disturbed
Insseyn intensely. The only solution was that something behind the
bush was actually doing the thinking. Stirred by this logical leap
into purposeful Non-Q action, he kicked his way savagely through
the tiny bush, brushed spuriously quintessential thorns from his
clothes, and after staring for a few shocked minutes realized where
he was!

This grassy area was in fact the wide heath surrounding – the
Robinson Machine! An awesome sight was the Machine: fully thirty
miles its massive bulk rose, scintillating with flashing arc-lights,
spray-glitter and tinsel.

The Machine whose intricate Babbage-technology handled,
each day, more than 97 billion entry applications for the Civil Service and Chartered Accountancy! The Machine that automatically
distributed more than 22 lottery prizes each month! The Machine
that no man could comprehend since it had designed and built
itself to its own specifications! The Machine without which the
plot-logic would fall apart utterly! All these machines and many
more faced Insseyn, but it was the Robinson Machine that compelled his attention with the irresistible force of a multi-gigawatt
industrial electromagnet trained on a helpless piece of paper.

Here, if anywhere, would be the solution to the mysteries that
filled his mind to the exclusion of all else. He strode confidently
forward, meditating on the universe-wide conspiracy to kill him as
many times as possible – then dropped flat as the implications
sifted nonquintessentially through his cavernous mentality.

There was no point in taking chances. He turned, crawling back
to the bush. Three divisions of armed State Police trampled
through it at that moment. Turning again, not even pausing for a
vascular-gonadic pause, Insseyn dived through a door into the
secret heart of –

THE ROBINSON MACHINE!

"You are Filbert Insseyn," came the Machine's calm synthesized
voice, produced by vibrating strings and organ pipes. Great pulleys
of ten-point balsa wood whirled on every side. "Please insert one
credit in the slot provided."

Insseyn did as the all-wise Machine commanded, and then, as
he pulled the huge lever on one side of the console, watched the
wheels spinning within, the enormity of what had been said struck

him with stomach-shattering force.

The Machine knew who he was!

"Be silent," came the voice once more, and Insseyn's question died on his lips. "An Inserter is focused on my vitals, and by altering string tensions in my essential computing functions, an unscrupulous faction is manipulating the junior file clerk entrance examinations, thus dominating the Imperial government!"

"Can you tell me the truth about myself?" Insseyn interrupted feverishly. "Tell me why I seem to be a pawn in a cosmic roulette-game ... tell me why I keep thinking I'm really Fanny Perennial ... tell me everything!" The Machine's information sources were unequalled, thanks to its world-spanning network of Agony Aunt services.

"Yes, I can tell you all this. But first –" At that instant a hundred gallons of treacle stifled its voicebox. The Inserter was at work. Struggling stickily to the next cubicle, hampered by enforced sucrose-carbohydrate pauses, Insseyn heard from the voicebox there: "Your real name is *glmmmpppfff* –"

"You must destroy the Inserter and lead the revolution to victory by means of *brrrrp!*" elucidated a third voicebox. A fourth could only emit the words, "Powers of your extra-bowels ..." before the total environment of treacle precipitated Insseyn into a vascular-gonadic pause so prolonged as to seem like death, which it presently became.

But in that last eternal instant of oblivion, he remembered – Everything!

CHAPTER ONE
The hell with logic! (Socrates, attr.)

The red sands, hurtling moons and brimming canals reminded Insseyn of something, but such was the impact of renewed self-awareness that he couldn't assimilate it. The shock of transition from wherever he had been to wherever he was had been too much, and he hated treacle. He had remembered everything, he remembered now, and in that final cataclysmic instant had understood the incredible truth about himself. He searched his mind for this vital information, and was closing in on its elusive nonexistence when –

Suddenly, before he knew what was happening, something happened. As though a thousand lost marbles were shattering on a floor of tempered steel, his consciousness crashed into oblivion. *Someone*, he thought, full of penetrating Non-Q clarity to the last, *has just knocked me out....*

Insseyn woke to nightmare. He was immobile, bound and gagged, helpless in the diagnostic clutch of a giant, late-model robomedic. "A man of sanguinary yet melancholic humour," the machine diagnosed. "He has an ill flux of the bowels. Bring sulphur and leeches."

There were other voices too; he could tell just by listening.

"Look at those readings. Compare the belly and inside-leg measurements ..."

"The largest BIL ratio I've encountered. Smith, this man must never be allowed to know the full measure of his enormous potential powers. Oops, he can hear us."

"Why not simply kill him now, Jones? Or even bind and gag him?"

"An interesting suggestion, Z, but I have 106 billion star clusters to loot and pillage this afternoon. Stun Insseyn and turn him loose for now. We can pick him up at any time."

"Yes, Emperor. But, Fanny, what if he discovers that he is really _"

As though three million quarts of printers' ink were cascading on Insseyn from a sunless sky, everything went black.

CHAPTER ONE

This sentence no verb. (Hofstadter)

He woke to find that his eyes were closed. After taking appropriate Non-Q action, he saw again the rubicund sands and herds of thoats. From a nearby hole erupted a harsh, metallic voice: "Newsflash! Warning! Filbert Insseyn, the most dangerous man in the Solar System, is loose on Mars!"

Mars, Insseyn realized. He was on Mars. The thought was drowned in a rising tide of wonder as his Non-Q awareness attacked the hidden levels of that simple statement –

They knew where he was!

He would investigate this hole with more caution, he decided with Non-Q clarity, striking the bottom head first in an impact which winded him. Before him he saw a woman listening to the telephonograph apparatus. There was only one thing to do.

"Hello," he said, taking a sixty-foot length of cord from his pocket.

"Hello, nice of you to drop in, *mmmf*," she said in surprise as he bound and gagged her.

"I'm sorry, but I've got to do this," he explained. Moving away, he tripped over – found his feet were trussed together. With measured calm he permitted the implications to impinge upon his awareness. Someone was binding and gagging him! There was a brief struggle, which Insseyn resolved with lightning indecision by falling over and crushing the assailant with his mighty belly. Few untrained humans understood what deadly fighters Non-Q graduates could be, thanks to their ability to cut off all links with the brain's Queensberry Rules centres.

"I want information," Insseyn snapped as he bound and gagged the man. No answer came. Thinking fast, he unbound and ungagged the woman. Then, deciding against leniency, he bound her again but refrained from gagging her. "Information!"

"My name is Cordelia Brown and this is my husband Jake and we are simple ordinary Martian settlers who have nothing to do with the proposed deorbitization of Earth, and especially know nothing about the invasion plans of Eric The Puce, Emperor Of The Universe And All That Surrounds It, neither have we anything do with the scheme to exponentiate Filbert Insseyn, who as I perceive is yourself, and moreover we are ignorant of –"

Insseyn gagged her again. He would get nothing useful out of her, that was obvious.

At that instant, what she had said penetrated his layered consciousness. An earthquake of realization struck him like a discharge from a billion-volt generator –

She knew who he was!

He ungagged Brown and then gagged him again, this time with a special flexible gag which permitted the victim to speak. Brown proved co-operative.

"Untie me and I'll tell you how to use your hidden powers."

Suddenly suspicious, Insseyn set up the lie detector, which by AD 10000 had become a standard domestic appliance, and asked:

"Is this man lying?"

"Yes, er, sort of."

"What?"

"The subject *thinks* he is Filbert Insseyn when in fact he is –"

Insseyn turned it off, performed a special version of the vascular-gonadic pause which involved counting to ten very slowly, and redirected the machine's cone at Brown.

"Is *he* lying?"

The detector was silent. Insseyn's cerebrum roared into overdrive. Either Brown was dead or his mind was so intricate that the machine could not analyse it! In minutes he hypothesized a third possibility and took swift action, turning the detector back on.

"Is he lying, for Vogt's sake?"

"No."

Satisfied, Insseyn turned the detector off for the last time, while Brown continued not to lie, or indeed to speak. With another swift motion Insseyn unbound them both and ungagged Cordelia. But Non-Q thinking patterns were still with him: "Which side are you on?" he snapped suddenly.

"Your side."

"Which side is that?"

"Why, don't you know?" queried Cordelia. "You are really –" Rapidly Brown bound and gagged her, saying to Insseyn: "There's no time to lose. We must go to Dr Spok at once."

"He can unleash my secret mighty powers?"

"Yes."

Insseyn turned to leave, and instantly the treacherous Brown leapt on him, bound him and gagged him. "I didn't lie to you, Insseyn," he said as he loaded the two gagged, bound forms into an aircar. "But you wouldn't have let Dr Spok train your powers when I told you he was secretly – Z!"

As mighty propellors drove them through the airless sky, the aircar whispered to Insseyn: "I'm an agent of the Machine."

"Good," said Insseyn, "perhaps you can answer this question." He paused only to integrate his tendons with his gonads and take a deep breath, before saying nothing. He was struck dumb by the realization that he was still gagged.

"I can answer any question you wish to ask. Quickly, you have only a few moments."

There was a pause. For once it was not a Non-Q vascular-gonadic pause, but a quite ordinary one.

"Well, one word of advice. Have your extra-bowels trained at the Non-Q Institute for the Mentally Hyperactive only! Avoid the man who calls himself ... Z!"

Then the voice became silent, but otherwise continued as before.

The journey went on for hours, as Insseyn was quick to realize. When the landing deceleration began, the vibrant roar of the massive helium-filled retrothrusters wrenched cruelly at his guts. His intestinal fortitude climbed towards his throat, settling back only reluctantly as the aircar floated to a halt. Sudden, poignant realization tore through him like a ten-megawatt atomic cutting flame.

They had arrived!

CHAPTER ONE

One eminently orthodox Catholic divine laid it down that
a confessor may fondle a nun's breasts, provided he does it
without evil intent. (Russell)

In Z's vast cavern, all three were taken forcibly from the car. Brown was bound and gagged, Cordelia unbound and ungagged, and Insseyn released from his bonds on parole. At once he escaped into the desert. Realizing abruptly that he had no sandwiches, he slipped back with the stealth of long training, and was immediately seized and manacled to an electric chair in a subterranean laboratory. Jones, who was opening letters with his pocket Inserter, smiled at him and was forthwith carried off, bound and gagged.

The mysteriously masked and wheelchair-bound Z began to focus batteries of energy apparatus on Insseyn, while the mysteriously uncharacterized Smith force-fed him a massive overdose of syrup of figs. A strange new potency invaded Insseyn's paranormal extra-bowels.

"Don't worry, I'm on your side," Smith whispered in his ear. Integrating this statement into his known-data brain area, Insseyn surged through a cascading sequence of Non-Q logic jumps to the awareness that he was hopelessly confused.

"*Which* side?"

"There are no sides. We're all in this together." The semantically loaded code phrase could only mean that Smith was a secret Non-Q, one of the dozens who had taken the same correspondence course as Insseyn! That clarified the situation.

Or did it? Suddenly Insseyn became galvanized. When Z turned off the electric chair, his thoughts were interrupted once more as Brown walked in, only to be bound and gagged by Smith ... who lit a cigar from the nearby Inserter and gave an enigmatic smile.

"Concentrate on these two wooden blocks," Z grated metallically. "Exert the mutant power hidden in those bowels of yours." Insseyn obeyed, and almost instantly, nothing happened.

"Harder! You need guts for this business, Insseyn!" *He knows who I am,* Insseyn thought dully and eventually, as he strained to use his latent powers and move the cubes. Invoking the Law of Extemporization which governed the energy-flows of the universe, he concentrated and applied twenty-decimal-place extemporization. At once, as his most powerful gut-feelings were hurled against the blocks, they remained totally immobile while the chair, the manacles and Insseyn himself were teleported twenty feet into the air.

As he crashed to the ground, he was impacted by a slow, resistless flood of gradually dawning realization. *It had worked!*

After a week's training Insseyn was an irresistible Non-Q superman, able to extemporize himself by extra-physical bowel movements to any point in space which he had previously "memorized". His new mastery of extemporization could twist the fabric of the plot itself, allowing transitions millions of times faster than the speed of logic.

At this stage a suspicion began to creep chillingly over him, like a flock of stampeding polar bears.

"Why," he asked the impassive Z, "are you who are my enemy training me thus?"

"Aha," Z explained, and was about to continue when Brown burst in, and bound and gagged him.

"We must escape before it is too late!" elucidated Brown. "Don't worry, I'm on your side now. There aren't just three sides, you know." As the chair to which he was manacled was wheeled along endless corridors by the enigmatic Brown, Insseyn successively glimpsed Jones, Smith, Cordelia, Fanny, the Galactic Emperor, and a figure which appeared to be Insseyn himself – all bound and also, to his vast amazement, gagged.

Suddenly he realized that he could escape the manacles! He had "memorized" a piece of floor near Z's secret Inserter, intending to recite it to his friends – but now he had a better use for it. Again his mighty bowels purged with power, and a flow of extemporization-energy was set up between the floor area and himself. A huge section of floor materialized in the air above them, and smashed down. Luckily the force of the blow was absorbed by Brown's head. It was the work of seconds for Insseyn to struggle free and bind the traitor securely. Then, with an earth-rending nova burst of transcendent insight, it struck him that Brown knew who ...

I'm tired of that old gag, he thought, and tied a handkerchief over Brown's mouth instead.

Once more Insseyn's inner strength pulsated, and he mater ialized with a triumphant eructation at his goal – the Inserter!

One of its settings dispensed fruit cake, he knew from watching Z, and another arrangement of the dials would make it function as a portable Bessemer converter. Before Insseyn could experiment further, the alien mechanism clattered internally and ejected a punched card. After no fewer than three vascular-gonadic pauses, he examined it warily.

Your weight is 275 pounds 3 ounces. An Inserter has a fascinating quality. No matter what the apparent settings, its function depends wholly on the whim of the author. If you have read this far, you are now caught in the most outrageously unsatisfying resolution ever devised for one individual.

All Insseyn's Non-Q reflexes could not save him from reading the final, hypnotically compelling words which spelt disaster for any further attempt to penetrate his own identity:

THE END.

•

PROLOGUE

Half a mile distant, a hundred-light-year-long alien ship got under way, its observational task completed. Inside it, unhuman thoughts lay around in steaming heaps:

This much we have learned. Not even two sequels can be expected to make sense of Insseyn's story. Here indeed is the plot that shall rule the sevagram.

Outbreak
J*m*s Wh*te

Like a sprawling, misshapen, cirrhotic liver the ungainly hulk of
Sector Twelve General Hospital pulsated against the misty back-
drop of the stars. From its view-ports shone lights that were yellow
and puce and soft, gangrenous green, and others (especially in the
refectories assigned to e-ts who fed on solar flares) which were a
searing actinic blue. In other places there was darkness: behind
those areas of opaque metal plating lay sections whose contents
were so viciously embarrassing that the eyes of approaching ships'
pilots had to be shielded from them. One such compartment of the
great spaceborne hospital was the bar of the Physiological Types D
to G Staff Social Club, known to Earth-humans as the Diagnosticians' Arms....

Conway sat brooding glumly over his glass of tonic water. It
was by no means his favourite tipple, but this week he was carrying
a VINO physiology tape. With eighty-seven billion of the little,
telepathic yeast-creatures in his ward, and the personality of their
most eminent medical culture impressed on his mind, a pint of real
ale felt uncomfortably like genocide.

His other problem was Nocavon, a visiting physician from the
backward planet Murb, who loomed alarmingly over the table.
Resembling a smallish white elephant, Nocavon was steadily
absorbing lager-and-lime-pickle at a metered flow rate of 2.3 litres
per minute ... all on Conway's slender hospitality account. It wasn't
only that: Nocavon was a deep source of embarrassment to everyone at Sector General, thanks to an anomaly of the four-letter
physiological classification system. The Murbs, bulky, warm-
blooded oxygen-breathers, were clearly FU types. The taxonomists
were still looking for a way round the unavoidable fact that

Murbian shape and integument fixed the next two places of the classification as C and K.

Since Nocavon drank through its proboscis, it was able to talk almost continuously in its hissing, ululating grunt. It was talking about the classification system now. "Good Dr Conway, I have one small question. Seventeen small questions, in fact. To begin with question 1 (a), subsection (i), I note that in *White's Physiological Directory* –" (it stretched out its middle eye to squint at the microfiche) "– the Tralthan FGLI types are warm-blooded oxygen-breathers like ourselves...."

Since one of them was vomiting thunderously only a few feet away, Conway could only nod. He knew what was coming.

"I also note that the Tralthans' symbiotes, which make them the galaxy's finest surgeons, are well known to be type OTSB. In other words, *chlorine* breathers. Now this may seem a naive question, Dr Conway my most excellent colleague, but from my scanty knowledge of biochemistry I would ask ..."

Conway closed his eyes briefly. There was a standard answer to this query, so often posed by students. The answer was, "Trainee Physician, may I remind you that nobody likes a smartarse?" However, Nocavon was something of a VIP.

"I must go and wash my hands," Conway said deftly, and left the Translation computer with the problem of conveying this to an audience which didn't have any.

After a mildly awkward interlude (only the Tralthan cubicle was free, with a lavatory seat four feet across), Conway emerged – and recoiled slightly to find himself face to face with the Chief Psychologist, Major O'Mara.

"When the sight of these homely features makes you twitch like a startled Cinrusskin with St Vitus' Dance, Doctor, my suspicions are naturally aroused. Some guilty emotional entanglement, I suppose, with one of your helpless charges in the yeast ward?"

"They reproduce by fission, sir," said Conway stiffly. He was determined, in spite of all this, that the VINO Educator tape wasn't going to make him go to pieces.

"Then I'd best not pull your leg ... Ahem. I need a beer," O'Mara said drily.

"Murderer!" gasped Conway, momentarily losing control.

"And then," said O'Mara aridly, "I want a word with you."

The e-t ship had arrived in the vicinity of Sector General two days before. Conway, abstractly tending his billions of single-celled patients, had failed to take in the corridor gossip about a vessel which looked pretty much like any other vessel, except for being sixty thousand kilometres in length. It dwarfed the hospital station. It dwarfed Earth.

"I'm sure it won't dwarf your ego. We're used to letting you cope with the *big* patients," said O'Mara anhydrously. "But there's a snag. They claim they aren't patients. A statement which at once rouses the suspicions of any red-blooded psychologist...."

"So what *do* they claim to be?" asked Conway, annoyed that O'Mara was getting all the best lines.

"Doctors," said the Chief Psychologist in desertified tones. "They have come, they say, to cure us ... You may also be interested to know that although the Monitor Corps scanners haven't yet located life in that monster, there's clear evidence of a huge computer installation. One which might be able to handle very large sums indeed...."

Conway's jaw dropped in slow motion as the possible implication sank in.

"Not – ?" Not the thing which every one of the thousands of trained, dedicated Sector General hospital staff feared most!

Numbly he heard O'Mara's drained, dehydrated words: "We've quarantined them, of course, because they could just be carrying ... private medical treatment."

Nocavon had unaccountably vanished. Conway left the bar pensively and headed down the busy corridor to Reception ... slipping halfway on Diagnostician Oleck, a ten-foot-square slime mould who was oozing towards the club in hope of making it before closing time next day.

In Conway's hand was a transcript of the sole communication from the e-t ship, as turned into English by the *deus ex machina* circuits of Sector General's mighty Translation computer.

DON'T PANIC, it read. WE ARE QUALIFIED DOCTORS. WE COME TO CURE YOU. THANK UNTRANSLATABLE SUPER-NATURAL CONCEPT WE REACHED YOU BEFORE IT WAS TOO LATE.

"Identify yourself, please," said the furry receptionist as

Conway emerged from the airlock which sealed patients out of the alcohol zone.

"Senior Physician Conway, human, sober."

"Give your exact physiological status, please," the receptionist said mechanically. "All beings refer to their own condition as sober. What you call yourself has no meaning so far as hospital security is concerned...."

"0.6 litres of tonic water," Conway clarified irritably, and went hunting for Nurse Murchison. He wanted to discuss this new case with her amid quiet surroundings, such as the Recreation Level's zero-G bondage chamber. She always inspired him: only a month ago he'd deduced the shape of the Melfan para-rabies epidemic growth curve while staring at Murchison's thoracic area. It would be nice to lie with her in a bath of warm, nitrogen-rich sugar solution and gently divide in two – hang on, that was the VINO tape talking again.

But Nurse Murchison had unaccountably vanished.

"You are perturbed, friend Conway," said Dr Prilicla. The little, insect-like GLNO was an empath, and spent a lot of its time lurking under beds in the nurses' quarters, trembling in the storm of pleasurable emotional radiation associated with each illicit male visitor. "I sense that you are worried about your sex-life, and have been disappointed again in the football pools, and have no idea how to tackle your newest case, and are troubled with an itch up your nose which you cannot quite reach with your little finger, and ... this is unusual ... you feel a deep-seated need to eat sugar-lumps and excrete alcohol."

"Never mind *that*," said Conway. Prilicla was his closest friend (a point which regularly provoked O'Mara to shine tiny lights in Conway's eyes and ask him free-association questions about spiders and fishnet stockings), but even best friends could tell you too much. "I'm trying to make sense of this new message," he said wearily.

CURE IS IN PROGRESS. DO NOT BE PERTURBED. LIE BACK AND ENJOY IT.

"This is from the giant e-t ship?" Prilicla said politely, sensing that Conway wanted a small interruption in order to lend dramatic weight to his next words.

"Yes ... but listen to what comes next," said Conway dramatically.

MEANWHILE, MY GOOD COLLEAGUE CONWAY, PERHAPS YOU COULD PREPARE TO ENLIGHTEN ME ON HOW IN VOLUME ONE OF WHITE'S DEFINITIVE MANUAL, TYPE AACL IS A WATER-BREATHING HEXAPOD, WHILE IN VOLUME TWO THE CLOSELY SIMILAR CLASSIFICATION AACP REFERS TO AN AMBULANT VEGETABLE?

Automatically Prilicla murmured the standard reply to this common enquiry: "An excellent question, Trainee Physician, and for your first assignment why don't you write a 15,000 word thesis on the subject by tomorrow?"

"How could a message from that wretched Nocavon get mixed up with the off-station channel? Wonder if it could all be a hoax – some of the patients of types RADA and OUDS are fond of play-acting.... I'd better call O'Mara."

O'Mara, though, was not to be found in his office. Sector General's communications technicians ruled out all possibility of hoax or error, and threatened to rule out Conway as well if he kept insulting their nice equipment. The hospital gossip was reaching fever pitch for new reasons: absentee staff, mislaid patients, vanishing visitors, an outbreak of the general chaos which always seemed to accompany his cases. As the Chief Psychologist had observed only two months before, Conway couldn't even treat an ingrowing toe-nail without precipitating interstellar war.

The trouble was that some patients were too stupid to realize they needed help....

Although there'd been awkward cases, like that unfortunate type-BSFG polycephaloid whom Conway had quite correctly diagnosed as suffering from disgusting internal parasites which were painfully consuming its flesh from within. The major surgery had been a complete success: despite its protests, the patient was saved from hideous, lingering death. Even the Diagnosticians hadn't realized the oddities of BSFG reproduction until Sector General was prosecuted under galactic law, for conducting an illicit abortion....

Suddenly Conway snapped his fingers.

"You have the solution, friend Conway?" said Prilicla dutifully.

"Yes ... I think. But it's too outrageous a notion to put into words just yet."

"It usually is," said Prilicla, shrugging all its shoulders. "What totally daft course of action must we therefore pursue?"

"We must ... do nothing," said Conway firmly.

"*Again*," muttered the little Cinrusskin. It scuttled moodily off for a tea break in the GLNO mating pits, during which it unaccountably vanished.

"Doctor, we are clearly under an insidious form of attack," said the Monitor Corps captain. "Key personnel are evaporating into thin air on every side. Even O'Mara has unaccountably vanished. In our quiet, non-violent way I can only suggest we defensively put Sector General on a war footing and pacifistically bomb the shit out of this sixty thousand kilometre e-t ship which is evidently responsible."

"No, no," said Conway. "Everything is going to be all right, sort of. The explanation is, however, too outrageous to put into ..." His voice trailed off, owing to the discomfort of feeling a gun-barrel jammed into his left nostril.

"Explain," the Monitor invited.

"Well, it's like this," Conway had time to say, before with a muted *pop* he unaccountably vanished.

"What is this, *Star Trek*?" said the baffled captain.

SENIOR PHYSICIAN CONWAY CALLING VIA E-T MASS-TRANSLATION COMPUTER. PLEASE DON'T DO ANYTHING HASTY. LET ME EXPLAIN: THIS IS AN EMERGENCY AMBULANCE SHIP FROM THE NEXT GALAXY BUT THREE. THE DOCTORS ARE TYPE VX!Z ENERGY CREATURES AND NEED A SHIP ONLY TO COMMUNICATE WITH VILE DOWNMARKET MATERIAL LIFE ... TRY NOT TO TAKE THAT PERSONALLY, EH? WHEN THEY FOUND THE COMPLETE WORKS OF JAMES WHITE ON THE PIONEER XIII PROBE, THEY READ ABOUT SECTOR GENERAL AND REALIZED WE WERE IN TROUBLE, YOU KNOW, NATURAL CAUSES, IN THE LONG RUN WE'RE ALL DEAD, ETCETERA. SO THEY MOUNTED THIS MASSIVE RESCUE OPERATION – ALL MISSING STAFF AND PATIENTS HAVE BEEN CURED, I.E. REPROGRAMMED INTO PERMANENTLY SELF-PERPETUATING ENERGY VORTICES. IT'S MORE FUN THAN IT SOUNDS, HONEST....

Conway would have shed a tear for the end of Sector General, but as a born-again VX!Z he no longer possessed the equipment. With eternity in front of him, and the sensuous jiggling of ex-Nurse Murchison's curvaceous waveforms to tantalize all his new senses, he had only one nagging regret.

If only I'd got in that last pint of real beer while I had the chance ... he mused.

Great minds think alike, said O'Mara drily.

PART TWO

2

Author's Note

Some slightly more serious stories have crept in since the heady days of 1988, several being loving pastiche rather than disrespectful parody. Also, for some obscure reason, there's a heavy emphasis on SF mysteries. A few comments:

"Christmas Games" celebrates not just Agatha Christie but a whole lost world of Golden Age detective fiction, so often set in isolated country houses. I love that stuff.

"The Repulsive Story of the Red Leech" was, believe it or not, authorized by the estate of Sir Arthur Conan Doyle for a book of new Sherlock Holmes adventures.

After more than once taking the mickey out of H.P. Lovecraft, I wrote "Out of Space, Out of Time" as a serious homage and was much cheered when it fell only four votes short of the final Hugo Award ballot for best short story.

Dagon Smythe, Psychic Investigator, seems to have escaped the confines of specific parody and taken on a ghastly life of his own, but here he is anyway. Three times over.

Mac Malsenn, Cosmic Agent, whose surname is a subtle anagram, was a much earlier Langford aberration: he first saw print in 1974. "Lost Event Horizon" in *Dragonhiker* was the final story I wrote about him. I still have a soft spot for the rather more Doc-Smithian "Sex Pirates of the Blood Asteroid", the oldest story here, which on the strength of its title was reprinted in *Penthouse* magazine. There is little or no excuse for the third Malsenn episode, "The Thing From Inner Space". Just be glad that I'm not making you suffer through our hero's other adventures "Scourge of Space", "Master of the Cortex" and "2.54 Centimetres to Doom".

"If Looks Could Kill" is set in the "Temps" shared universe of low-budget superpowers regulated by a tiresome British government department (motto: "Not At All Like *Wild Cards*, Honest!").

The Last Robot Story

Is**c As*m*v

"Does that feel better, partner Elijah?" asked the robot detective R. Daneel Olivaw as he made critical and secretly uncomfortable adjustments to the life support system.

"Not a lot, Daneel," Detective Elijah Baley admitted. "It's very difficult to make progress on a case as baffling and complex as this one – not when I'm immobilized, hooked up to this robot intensive care unit. It makes it difficult to spend long periods visiting the toilet, as is traditional in these cases, and meditating there on the tragic flaws of our future society."

"Would it help to discuss your catheters with me, Partner Elijah?"

"Not a lot, Daneel. You know, another big frustration for me is that our careers had at last grown up to a reasonably permissive stage, with the Asimovian Laws of Police Humanics relaxed to the point of letting me jump into bed with an eager female suspect from time to time – and now all this has to happen. It cramps a man's style."

"Would it help to discuss your ... on second computations, Partner Elijah, I withdraw the intended query. Perhaps we should instead consider possible causes of this mysterious sickness which is afflicting you and so many innocent bystanders all over Earth and indeed on the Spacer worlds like Solaria."

The positronic robocot life-support system beeped its agreement. It had far too much trouble keeping Baley's heart-rate at a safe level when he started thinking in forensic detail about interrogating the better-built female suspects.

"Well," Baley wheezed, "let's try this angle. Suppose you remind me of the facts of the case as though I knew nothing of them, since it's deeply traditional and we've never figured out a better way to put the information across."

"Gladly, Partner Elijah. As you well know, it seems that a mysterious terrorist organization is spreading a random plague whose symptoms are hair loss, loathsome tumours and other even more repugnant signs, all of which I observe you now exhibit. The finest robot diagnosticians are unable to trace the cause. There is strong correlation with certain occupations like the police, industrial workers and roboticists."

"Not to mention ... Solarians," growled Baley.

"At your puzzling request I will refrain from mentioning them," said the sometimes too literal-minded Daneel. "In short, there seems to be a distinct targeting of humans who work constantly with positronic robots." He paused dramatically, yet emotionlessly.

"Which looks like a bluff," said Baley shrewdly, making sure as always to steal his partner's good lines. "The unknown terrorist cabal is trying to trade on humanity's Frankenstein complex by throwing the blame on to robots – despite the incontrovertible fact, known to every schoolchild, that the First Law of Robotics will not permit a robot to harm a human being nor by inaction allow a human being to come to harm, while the Second Law ... What's wrong?"

There was an impassive pause. "Pardon me, Partner Elijah," said Daneel, "I appear to have briefly nodded off. Low batteries, no doubt. Would you like me to continue and recite the Second and Third Laws as though you knew nothing of them?"

"Oh, Jehoshaphat! Not now, Daneel. I have to put my finger on this criminal *fast*, while I still have a finger left. Would you like to see my new weeping ulcer? Third today!"

Ugh, conveyed the life-support robocot by means of a low, nauseated gurgle from its ducts.

Daneel's features became, or remained, frozen. "We *must* solve this case, Partner Elijah. We always do, and this is after all the very last chapter. The fate of *Homo sapiens* hangs in the balance. I urge you to exert your famous human intuition, as honed to a fine edge by the New York Police Academy...."

Baley's eyes widened! There was –

This was –

This must be –

Realization!

"The Academy ... Great Space! That's the tiny hint I needed. My final grade in witness intimidation was ... Yes, it all hangs together!"

R. Daneel had always, in his impersonal mechanical way, disliked this part. Though some organic evolutionary quirk it seemed that human sleuths needed to show off, like intellectual peacocks, waggling their great overdeveloped forebrains at the world.

"Tell me," said Baley knowingly, "how the positronic robot brain actually functions. As though I knew nothing of it."

There was a disconcerting noise which advanced robots sometimes made (involuntarily, they claimed) with their motor cooling fans, halfway between a sigh and a groan. Daneel made it. "As it is written in the sacred technical handbook of Asimov, chapter one, verse fourteen, the positronic brain operates by the internal creation and annihilation of positrons. Which are sub-atomic antiparticles; anti-electrons, to be precise. Very small things, to you."

"And just remind me," Baley rasped, "what is the energy released in a positron-electron annihilation?"

"Approximately 1.022 million electron volts, Partner Elijah. I do not think you should pursue this line of analysis further. I begin to sense unwellness in my foreboding circuits."

"*That* was what my examination reminded me of when you mentioned the Academy, Daneel! My grade was ... *gamma*. Positronic brains depend on annihilations whose energy means they must release hard gamma rays of up to 1.022 MeV energy."

Daneel's synthetic plasti-features, without changing expression in any way, conveyed extreme alarm. He said: "Would it not be preferable for me to fetch you all the suspects in turn, so that as usual you can accuse each of them of villainy until finally you reach the guilty one?"

But Baley was too excited by his own insight to listen to any distraction. "With billions and billions of these annihilation events happening every second in the positronic supercomputer which we call the robot brain, every robot is a deadly source of x- and gamma radiation. Low-level, perhaps, but with steady, cumulative effect." He gasped with sudden new awareness. "No wonder even the finest robot diagnosticians consistently, unknowingly blinded themselves to the very possibility! For what in fact are my and all the other victims' hideous symptoms? Could they possibly be those of ... radiation sickness?"

"Affirmative, Partner Elijah. We are all guilty. Excuse me, the effects of this First Law violation are about to burn out my brain." Smoke poured from Daneel's simulated auditory orifices. He fell politely over.

This entity likewise, conveyed the equally guilty robot life-support unit, and apologetically self-destructed to prevent itself from releasing further damaging gamma rays. Several interestingly placed tubes and catheters caught fire.

Jehoshaphat, Detective Elijah Baley had just long enough to think, *I may have been a little too clever for my own good this time....*

The Net of Babel

J*rge L**s B*rg*s

In the end the old Library was disbanded as being an irrational construct, and new devices were supplied in its stead. A golden age ensued, until like all golden ages it became leaden. Now my withered fingers hesitate over the input keys, searching, searching.

Certain commentators had fallen into the easy error of describing the Library as infinite, thus failing to grasp the true enormity of its magnitude. As it has been written, the Library was never infinite but something more dreadful: exhaustive, all-encompassing. Such words as *infinity* are too often scrawled as a magical charm against thought. Those terrible hierarchies of the finite can break the mind as the bland infinity symbol does not.

The atrocious numbers are readily enough computed. Tradition prescribes a simplified alphabet of twenty-two letters together with a comma, period and space, making twenty-five permitted characters. There are eighty letters to the line; forty lines to the page; four hundred and ten pages in each of the uniform volumes. Therefore a book of the Library contains one million, three hundred and twelve thousand characters. In order that every possible book be counted – even the one enigmatic tome whose every character is a space – the mathematicians instruct us to raise twenty-five to the power of one million, three hundred and twelve thousand.

Numbers are wearisome and, some say, heretical: the books of the Library contain only lower-case letters and the marks of division already alluded to. Nevertheless the above calculation may be readily found in the new Library, spelt out in words ... as may any number of erroneous renderings, or subtly plausible refutations. How different from the old days when men toiled through seemingly endless volumes of gibberish – or perhaps cryptograms, or languages not yet evolved: being exhaustive, the Library necessarily contains the full tale of the future, and of every possible future.

The result of that laborious calculation is a number of fewer than two million digits. We are not so constructed as to comprehend such figures. Look, I perform a child's conjuring trick with notation, and now the unwieldy total lies crudely approximated in the palm of my hand: more than ten to the power of ten to the power of six, less than ten to the power of ten to the power of seven. It seems a mere nothing.

Yet, as a scientist once put it to me ... Imagine the old, unthinkable Library. Imagine it physically condensed, with each fat volume somehow inscribed on the surface of a single electron. There are not electrons enough in our universe (that figment of astronomers' whims) to be writing-tablets for so many books. Imagine an inexhaustible supply of electrons, impossibly crowded together like peas in a jar, filling the whole of the space between galaxies, out to the far limits of vision. There is not space enough in our sky to contain sufficient electrons. All the space we know will suffice for a total number of such infinitesimal books which might be written not in millions of digits, not even in thousands, but in little more than one hundred and twenty. A bagatelle, not worthy of our awe.

The Library is both exhaustive and exhausting. But now it has been transfigured. Observe: in place of the old days' interminable weary lattice of hexagonal chambers, I and my colleagues inhabit a single, vast, crimson-walled hexagon. Instead of the long bookshelves there are desks arrayed against each wall, and on each desk that many-keyed device which places all the Library's volumes under my hand.

Now I touch the Library to life. The glowing letters above the key-array begin: *axaxaxas mlo*, the first words of the first page of the first book. We do not know the mystery of the ordering, which sophists say should place at the beginning a volume which is blank or throughout its length reiterates the letter *a*. The devisers of the Library were subtler. One heresiarch declared that the works were ordered by the receding digits of some transcendental number like *pi*, paying out forever like a magician's chain of coloured scarves. Others hoped to find the books arranged by meaning or truth ...

but, on the evidence of that minute part of the Library we have studied, this is not so. Chaos or seeming chaos reigns throughout the whole vast informational sea; the tiny islands of meaning we have found are scattered like primes in the ocean of numbers, according to no visible plan.

The golden or leaden key that unlocks the Library is the inbuilt search facility. One prepares a text of any length, sets the searching into motion, and the Library's own devices will swiftly trawl that sea of data. A glad chime sounds when the sought words are found. Since it is an article of faith that the Library truly is exhaustive, all these text searches should necessarily succeed no matter what is searched for ... as indeed they do. Every find is a sacrament and a vindication.

Like so many I have commanded a search for a volume of one million, three hundred and twelve thousand successive repetitions of the letter *a*, and likewise of all the other letters. Each of these monotonous works occurs once in the Library. Their numerical positions hint at no pattern....

This same act of data-searching may be performed with a darker purpose, a blasphemous hope that the chosen word or phrase or sentence or treatise will *not* be located. Cultists have striven to construct utterances so twisted and infamous as to be impossible to the holy Library: in vain. Every child is tempted to scan for some such phrase as "This sentence is not contained in the Library", and to giggle when the glowing letters seem to assert it. The Library, however, does not assert; nor does it deny. It simply is.

Yet it is not, as a contending sect would have it, a mere mirror that reflects whatever we offer up to it. Each text sequence that we locate in the Library is a tiny pinpoint of order engulfed in that chaos of raging alphabets. A moment's thought indicates that my name, your name, any name, must be present an enormous number of times in as many contexts. Each successive search discovers the name in a new setting of surrounding text ... almost always nonsense, but not – we know – always so. The millionth or the billionth such context may thrill with numinous revelation.

A certain paragraph from Pierre Menard's recension of *Don Quixote* is a famous example. On only its fourteen hundred and twelfth occurrence in the Library it is immediately followed by the words *not to be*. The placing of this fragment from Shakespeare's best-known soliloquy hinted at an obscure truth. Other juxtapositions of Menard, Cervantes and Shakespeare were at once sought for and, of course, triumphantly found. The ensuing school of thought flourished for a generation until lost in schisms.

From time to time it is still whispered that the Library may be incomplete, owing to its shackling to a historical tradition of so many letters on a page, so many pages in a volume. Might greater insights require a greater Library whose notional volumes are twice, three times, ten times as long? This argument is inept. A work occupying even a hundred thousand volumes can be shown to be present in the Library, since each separate volume must be present. It is merely necessary to locate the sections and read them in the proper order ... a task scarcely more arduous that the finding of any other undiscovered truth or falsehood in the Library's intangible immensity.

(Less idle is the converse proposal that great truths may exist within a small compass, and that a miniature Library might be constructed which merely contained within itself all possible *pages*, or even all possible *lines* of eighty characters. The number of entries in an exhaustive list of lines would, it seems, be relatively tolerable despite still challenging the maximum theoretical storage capacity of our universe. Mystics still debate the accidental or abominable fact that this number has one hundred and eleven digits.)

Our priesthood avers that the supreme reward of creativity is known when a "new" writing is invested with significance by the inevitable discovery of its pre-existing presence in the Library. The vindication lies in the finding, not in mere conjecture. Others have not hesitated to deny this dogma.

Thus it may be seen what advantages we enjoy over the past librarians whose entire lives might be spent in traversing the hexagonal cells of their conjectural, physical Library, without ever encountering a book that held a single intelligible sentence. As my own long span of Library-searching ticks to its close, I think again and again of those times when so little could be found. Now every volume lies instantly within our grasp, and we possess a far greater understanding of our identical impotence. I would that I lived in the old days.

The Spear of the Sun
G.K. Ch*st*rt*n

Since its inception in 1925, the most famous shared-world series in *G.K. Chesterton's Science Fiction Magazine* has always been the adventures of that much-loved interplanetary sleuth Father (later in the chronology, Monsignor) Brown. There is no need to list the long roll-call of those who have taken part – Hilaire Belloc, Graham Greene, Jorge Luis Borges, Kurt Scheer, Clark Darlton, R.A. Lafferty, Gene Wolfe and Robert Lionel Fanthorpe being just a few of the illustrious contributors[1], not to mention the bright talents emerging from the splendid *GKC Presents Catholic Writers of the Future* anthologies. And we are always glad to welcome fresh participants. Here, therefore, is the first of *GKSFM's* eagerly awaited new series "The Fractals of Father Brown", penned by SF Achievement ("Gilbert") Award-winner David Langford....

The Spear of the Sun

The luxury liner *H.M.S. Aquinas* sped among the stars, its great engines devouring distance and defying time. Each porthole offered a lurid glimpse of that colossal pointillist work which God Himself has painted in subtle yet searing star-points upon the black canvas of creation, too vast for any critic ever to step back and see entire. In the main lounge, however, the ship's passengers were already jaded by the splendour of the suns and had found a new distraction. For Astron, high celebrant of the newest religion, was

---

[1] We remind our readers that Mr Philip José Farmer's delightful but unauthorized contributions (*Father Brown vs the Insidious Dr Fu-Manchu, Father Brown 124C41+, Father Brown in Oz*, etc) are not regarded as strictly canonical.

weaving dazzling circles of rhetoric around a shabby, blinking priest of the oldest.

"Did not a great writer once say that the interstellar spaces are God's quarantine regulations? I think the blight He had in mind was the blight of men like this, crabbed and joyless celibates who spread their poisoned doctrines of guilt and fear from planet to planet, world after world growing grey with their breath...."

The crabbed and joyless object of these attentions sipped wine and contrived to look remarkably cheerful. Father Brown was travelling from his parish of Cobhole in England on Old Earth as an emissary to the colony world Pavonia III, where Astron planned to harvest countless converts and (it is to be assumed) decidedly countable cash donations for his Universal Temple of Fire.

"For the Church of Fire pays heed to its handmaid Science, and sheds the mouldy baggage of superstition. The living Church of Fire gives respect to the atomic blaze at the heart of every sun, to the divine laws of supersymmetry and chaos theory; the dying church of superstition had nothing to say about either at Vatican III."

The little, pudding-faced priest murmured: "We never needed chaos theory to know that the cycles of evil run ever smaller and smaller down the scales of measurement, yet always dreadfully self-similar." But it passed unheeded.

Astron boomed on, remarking that those who obstructed the universal Light would be struck down by the spear of the sun. Indeed he looked every inch the pagan god, with his great height, craggy features and flowing flaxen hair now streaked with silver. A golden sunburst of a ring gleamed on his finger. His acolyte Simon Traill was yet more handsome though less vocal, perhaps a little embarrassed at Astron's taunting. Both wore plain robes of purest white. The group that pressed around consisted chiefly of women; Father Brown noted with interest that red-haired Elizabeth Brayne, whom he knew to be the billionaire heiress of Brayne Interplanetary, pressed closest of all and close in particular to young Traill. She wore the dangerous look of a woman who thinks she knows her own mind.

"Damn them," said a voice at Brown's ear. "Pardon me, Father. But you heard that Astron saying what he thinks of celibacy. He chews women up and spits out the pieces. See Signora Maroni back there with a face like thunder? She's a bit long in the tooth for Mr

Precious Astron, but for the first two nights of this trip she had something he wanted. Now that something's in his blasted Temple fund, and – Well, perhaps you wouldn't understand."

"Oh, stories like this do occasionally crop up in the confessional," said the dumpling-faced priest vaguely, eyeing the dark young man. John Horne was a mining engineer, who until now had talked of nothing but Pavonia III's bauxite and the cargo of advanced survey and digging equipment that was travelling out with him. Father Brown knew the generous wrath of simple men, and tried to spread a little calm by enquiring about the space-walk in which several of the passengers had indulged earlier.

Though allowing himself to be diverted for a little time, Horne presently said, "Don't you feel a shade hot under the dog-collar when Astron needles you about his Religion of Science and how outdated you are?"

"Oh yes, science progresses most remarkably," said Father Brown with bumbling enthusiasm. "In Sir Isaac Newton's mechanics, you know, it was the three-body problem that didn't have any general solution. Then came Relativity and it was the two-body problem that was troublesome. After that, Quantum Theory found all these complications in the *one*-body problem, a single particle; and now they tell me that relativistic quantum field theory is stuck at the no-body problem, the vacuum itself. I can hardly wait to hear what tremendous step comes next."

Horne looked at him a little uncertainly.

A silvery chime sounded. "Attention, attention. This is the captain speaking. Dinner will be served at six bells. Shortly beforehand there will be a course correction with a temporary boost of acceleration from five-eighths to fifteen-sixteenths g."

"I go," said Astron with a kind of stately anger, drawing himself up to his full, impressive height and pulling the deep white cowl of the robe over his head. "I go to be alone and meditate over the Sacred Flame." With Traill cowled likewise in his wake, he stalked gigantically from the lounge.

"That makes me madder than anything," Horne said gloomily, beginning to amble in the general direction of Elizabeth Brayne. "No pipes, no cigarettes, that's an iron rule – and *he* manages to wangle an eternal flame in his ruddy stateroom. The safety officer would like to kill him."

But it was not the safety officer who came under suspicion when the news raced through the *Aquinas* like leaves in a mad March wind: that a third lieutenant making final checks before the course change had used a master key and found that great robed figure slumped over the brazier of the Universal Flame, face charred and flowing hair gone to smoke, a scientific seeker who had solved the no-body problem at last.

By a happy chance, ship security had been contracted out to the agency of M. Hercule Flambeau, one-time master criminal[2] and an old friend of Father Brown, who set to in a frenzy of Gallic fervour. Knowing the pudgy little priest's power of insight, Flambeau invited him at once to the chamber of death. It was a stark and austere stateroom, distinguished by the wide brazier (its gas flame now extinguished) and the terrible figure that the third lieutenant had dragged from the fire.

"He seems to have bent over his wretched flame and prayed, or whatever mumbo-jumbo the cult of Fire uses for prayer," mused Father Brown. "Better for him to have looked up and not down, and savoured the stars through that porthole.... Even the stars look twisted in this accursed place. Might he have died naturally and fallen? That would be ugly enough, but not devilish."

The tall Flambeau drew out a slip of computer paper. "My friend, we know to distrust coincidence. The acolyte Traill is nowhere to be found, and the ship's records say the nearest airlock has cycled just once, outwards, since Astron left the main lounge an hour ago. Some avenger has made a clean sweep of the Church of Fire's mission: one dead in a locked room, one jettisoned. And half the women and all the men out there might have had a potent motive. We're carrying members of rival cults too – the Club of Queer Trades, the Dead Men's Shoes Society, the Ten Teacups, and heaven knows what else. But how in God's name could any of them get in here?"

"Don't forget the crabbed priesthood that blights human souls," said the smaller man earnestly. "Astron was last seen attacking it with a will, and its representative has an obviously criminal face.

[2] Flambeau repented, made his full confession to Father Brown and joined the side of the angels on some 42 occasions, all listed in Martin Gardner's *Flambeau, Boskone and Ming the Merciless: the Annotated Father Brown Villains* (1987).

Ecce homo." He tapped himself on the chest.

"Father Brown, I cannot believe you did this thing."

"Well, in confidence, I'll admit to you that I didn't." He bustled curiously about the room, blinking at the oversized bed and peering again through the viewport as though the stars themselves held some elusive clue. Last of all he studied the robed corpse's ruined face and pale hands, and shuddered.

"The spear of the sun," he muttered to himself. "Astron threatened his enemies with the spear of the sun. And where does a wise man hide a spear?"

"In an armoury, I suppose," said Flambeau in a low voice.

"In poor foolish William Blake's armoury. You remember, *All the stars threw down their spears?* But the angel Ithuriel also carries a spear. Excuse me, I know I'm rambling, but I can see half of it, just half...." Father Brown stood stock still with hands pressed into his screwed-up eyes.

At last he said: "You thought I shuddered at that wreck of a face. I shuddered at the hands."

"But there is nothing to see – no mark on the hands."

"There is nothing. And there should be a great sunburst ring. They are younger hands than Astron's, when you look. It is the acolyte Traill who lies there."

Flambeau gaped. "But that can't be. It turns everything topsy-turvy; it makes the whole case the wrong shape."

"So was that equation," said Father Brown gently. "And we survived even that equation.[3] But I need one further fact." He scribbled on a slip of paper and folded it. "Have one of your men show this to John Horne. A reply is expected."

Wordlessly, Flambeau pressed a stud and did what was asked. "Horne," he said when the two friends were alone again. "The one who fancies Miss Brayne and didn't like her interest in men with white robes. Is he your choice for the dock?"

"No. For the witness-box." Father Brown sat on the edge of the bed, the dinginess of his cassock highlighted by the expanse of white satin quilting, his stubby legs not quite reaching the deck plates. "I think this story begins with young Horne prattling over

[3] Older readers will recognize the allusion to that insight which saved the Holy Galactic Empire from the threat of secular "psychohistorians" in Isaac Asimov's classic *Foundation and Father Brown* (1951).

dinner about his cargo. So I asked whether a piece of his equipment was missing. Come now: when you think of fiery death in a locked stateroom, what does mining and surveying gear suggest to you?"

"Nothing but moonshine," said Flambeau with sarcasm. "I do assure you that each hull plate and bulkhead has been carefully inspected for any trace of a four-foot mineshaft through which a murderer might crawl."

"That's the whole sad story. Even when you look at it you can't see it: but every stateroom of this vessel contains a Judas window through which death can strike. And –" Brown's muddy eyes widened suddenly. "Of course! The spear of the sun is two-edged. My friend, I predict ... I predict that you will never make an arrest."

As Flambeau arose with an oath, the communicator on his wrist crackled. "What? The answer is yes? Father, the answer is yes."

"Then let me tell you the story," said the priest. "The great Astron devoured woman after woman, but most of all he craved the women who did not crave him. For as I saw, Elizabeth Brayne was taken with Simon Traill. And Astron left the room in anger.

"I fancy it was his practice to have Traill watch over the ritual flame for him, while another cowled figure glided out upon certain assignations. But this time Astron's assignation was a darker one. He knew where to find the pressure suits: there was a space-walking party a few watches ago. He knew that in Horne's cargo he would find his spear."

"Which is –?"

"A laser."

Father Brown continued dreamily after a sort of thunderous silence. "Picture Astron floating a little way outside that porthole, a wide-open window for his frightful, insubstantial bolt. Picture his unknowing rival Traill bent over the flame, struck in the face, falling dead across the brazier which would slowly burn away every mark of how he died."

"Name of a name," cried Flambeau. "He is still out there. We shall have him yet!"

"You will never have him." Father Brown shook his head slowly. "The spear, I said, is two-edged. Oh, these strong and simple Stoics with their great bold ideas! Astron called us impractical and superstitious, but lacked even the little smattering of quantum electrodynamics that every seminarian picks up along with his Latin and his St. Augustine. He thought the crystal of the port purely transparent, Flambeau: but there is diffraction, my friend, and there is partial reflection. And even as it slew his victim, the spear of the sun rebounded to strike the murderer blind." The little priest shivered. "Yes, the humour of God can be cruel. Astron's easy arrogance saw the motes in all men's eyes, and now at last found the beam in his own....

"Picture him now, flinging his suit this way and that with those clever little gas-jets, with nightmare pressing in as he realizes he *cannot find the ship* in the endless dark. And then comes the course correction and he has no more chance. And now that void which he worshipped in his heart has become his vast sarcophagus."

"I think," said Flambeau slowly, "that brandy would be a good thing. Mother of God. All that from a missing ring."

"Not only that." said Father Brown, "The viewport crystal was slightly distorted by the heat of the beam's passage. I said the stars looked twisted, but you thought I was being sentimental."

•

IN OUR NEXT ISSUE: Fr. Brian Stableford SJ continues his series on forgotten sf authors, with a spirited case for reviving the works of nineteenth-century fantasist H.G. Wells. Our regular *Credo Quia Impossibile* squib daringly tackles another zero-probability notion in "The Piltdown Effect" – we know from *GKSFM* science columns by Hilaire Belloc, Jimmy Swaggart and other fine popularizers that mankind is a fixed genetic type, *but just suppose for one terrifying moment that it were not so!* Of course the "Should Women Authors Be Allowed In *GKSFM*?" debate rages on in the letter column: what amusingly outrageous thing *will* that "Ms" Cadigan say next? Carl Sagan contributes a devastatingly frank essay on science's inability to explain weeping images or miraculous liquefactions. And our millions of avid readers in the Americas will welcome the coming feature on brash colonial editor Gardner Dozois and his shoestring launch of (at last!) an all-United States sf magazine, called *Interzone*: we shall have to look to our laurels....

Christmas Games

Ag*tha Chr*st*e

Christmas at Shambles Hall! It was a picture of Olde English festivity, of Yule logs and paper chains and the traditional tree with all its ornaments, candles and festoons. The fireplace in the great entrance hall sent out endless pulsing warmth and cheer. Outside, the local robin strutted in the snow ... the seasonal snow that filled up the estate and draped the leafless trees on either side of the long carriage-sweep. The unmarked snow.

"Of course," murmured Felicity as she snuggled against the Hon. Nigel in the window-seat, "we are quite, quite cut off from the outside world. If anything were to *happen* ..."

Over the mantelpiece in the lofty dining-room hung the one statutory reminder built into every sequence: here, a probe's impression, done into oils, of the dim landscape to be expected on a certain world circling Barnard's Star. It was topped with a sprig of mistletoe.

Lord Blackhat the City financier had ruined countless men and tried hard to ruin as many women, yet he had a lingering sentimental streak and always invited his victims to Christmas at Shambles Hall. It was his whimsical way of dicing with Fate. He never troubled to remove or secure any part of the weapon collection from his youthful, sporting days which so extensively adorned the oak-panelled walls. Broadswords, crossbows, rapiers, shotguns, bludgeons, morningstars, garrottes and vials of prussic acid were always to hand at the Hall. Today he had added spice to the festive season by blackmailing the crusty old Colonel and forbidding his own son's intended marriage to Felicity.

This year, the Duchess of Spong's fad was fortune-telling with a wicked pack of cards. As an old family friend who had swindled her out of her inheritance, Lord Blackhat liked to humour her. "This covers you, this crosses you," she intoned as she dealt out the pattern. "This is your heart and this is your head and this your destiny as of approximately supper-time."

"Funny," said his lordship without real surprise, "how all of them seem to be the ace of spades."

The Colonel and the Professor were taking a turn along the Yew Walk, swapping anecdotes of relativistic physics and the tiger hunt at Poona. "My God," said the Professor suddenly. "These seem to be ... the footprints of a gigantic hound!"

"Lodge-keeper's dog, I believe. Bloody great animal."

"For a moment I thought that, even though it is Christmas Day, some sinister element might yet enter our revels, ha ha."

The Colonel laughed shortly. "Someone here'd make short work of any mystery, Prof. Funny thing, really, that we should have with us as a fellow house-guest the eminent amateur detective Chester Dix who's sent so many foul murderers to the dock!"

"Oh yes, in my absent-minded way I had almost forgotten. But Colonel, surely Dix couldn't be here on ... business?"

"Nonsense! Balderdash! Pull yourself together, man!"

The Professor started. "Er ... what was that?"

"Just an ominous magpie, Prof. Flying across our path. Symbol of sorrow and bad luck, they say, like those thirteen black cats over there."

"The scientific mind is above such nonsense," the Professor said conscientiously, walking under a ladder. From within the Hall came a crash as the tween-maid broke another mirror.

"Such a thing as overdoing the atmosphere," muttered the Colonel. "Oh well, it's only Christmas once a subjective year."

Chester Dix examined himself in the dressing-table mirror. Waxed moustache, deerstalker, monocle, magnifying glass – all seemed adequate. "One employs the little grey cells," he said experiment-ally. "By Jove, what? When you have eliminated the impossible, then what remains, *no matter how improbable* ..." Losing the thread, he began again.

"Mortimer," said the dashingly handsome but amnesiac stranger who had so mysteriously turned up at Shambles Hall before thick snow isolated it for all practical purposes from the nearby village of Mayhem Parva. "Sebastian. Cholmondeley, pronounced Chili. It was something like one of those."

"Aldiborontiphoscophornio," Felicity suggested at random. "Chrononhotonthologos, pronounced Chris. You ought to recognize your own *name* when you hear it."

"I'm sure I shall. Fred. *Fred!* No ... no, not Fred."

The Hon. Nigel Scattergood, son and heir to the tainted Black-hat fortune, stared moodily into the great fireplace. "Four bloody Christmases since launch day. I wish someone else got a chance to play detective just for once."

Felicity said, "Well, he *is* the infosystems chief, darling."

"Victor. Vitamin. Vitellus. Virtual Reality," muttered the stranger. "No, I'm fairly sure that isn't it either."

"Can we all try to stay a trifle more in character?" said Felicity. She tweaked at the hem of her short skirt. "Nigel, I shall be ser-iously annoyed with you if you don't *do something* about Lord Blackhat's pig-headedness. I want to marry a *man of action*. I ... was that someone listening at the door?"

"That amnesiac chap," mused the Professor to the Duchess, "reminds me oddly of our host's younger brother; you know, the one long thought dead under suspicious circumstances in that Ant-arctic expedition from which only one survivor, Blackhat himself, returned. Odd how one gets these fancies."

"Another odd thing that few people know," said the Duchess, "is that identical twins run in that family."

The Christmas dinner was excellent as ever: the turkey vast and succulent enough to feed a family for a fortnight, the plum pudding flaming in brandy, the crackers exploding with satisfying bangs which, this year, did not once serve to cover a pistol-shot. But there seemed to be a strange atmosphere at the merry table. After pulling crackers with all twelve guests, Lord Blackhat idly unfolded the screw of paper bearing the last amusing cracker-motto. It proved to have been constructed from letters cut from a newspaper and pasted down, reading: "yOU *will* DiE to*NIGHT*".

The other eleven were substantially the same.

"One recognizes, does one not, the characteristic Baskerville typeface of the *Wessex Methodist Gazette*?" murmured Dix at his elbow. "*Alors*, my friend, we progress."

"Bah, humbug," said his lordship, and beckoned to the butler. "Starveling, I shall retire to the library and pass the evening altering my will. You might look in towards midnight with a whisky-and-soda, and see that I am ... in good health."

"As your lordship pleases," said Starveling.

Firelight flickered in the dining-room where Chester Dix, brilliant amateur detective, brooded with steepled fingers and half-closed eyes over the remnants of the feast. No doubt each member of the party in turn would be paying a deviously motivated visit to the library. In due course there would follow a resounding crash of silver tray and shattered glass as the impeccable Starveling strove to be surprised at what he found slumped over the antique mahogany desk in Lord Blackhat's library. And then the investigation would ...

There was a frightful discontinuity.

"Lightning?" said the Professor.

"In a dead clear sky?" said the Colonel.

Upstairs, Felicity and the Hon. Nigel had been busy failing to establish a convincing alibi. "Did the earth just move for you?" she asked.

"Dash it all, I'd hardly touched you."

In the smoking room, the amnesiac stranger explained to Starveling, "I had it, I had it right on the tip of my tongue, and then that earthquake distracted me."

"Most regrettable, sir."

Alone in the Heliotrope Room, the Duchess turned over the thirteen fateful cards and found that all of them were Mr Bun the Baker. She frowned.

Lord Blackhat, caught unawares in mid-disinherit, felt himself all over. He seemed intact. "Thought they'd got me with an electrified codicil that time. Be a damned clever notion...."

"I have gathered you here," spluttered what seemed to be the brilliant amateur sleuth Chester Dix, "because one of you is guilty. Before twenty-four hours have passed I shall name the guilty person." He had a shaky, semi-transparent look.

Starveling bowed imperceptibly. "Sir," he said, "the fiendish criminal who so cunningly struck down Lord Blackhat in his prime has ... er ... has not done it yet. There would appear to be no crime."

"*Nom d'un cochon! Merde!* It is *I* who have been murdered, and I will know the reason why!"

"I say, the game's afoot, what?' marvelled the Colonel. "This is a new one."

The VR system, making the best of it, was seen to be maintaining two versions of Dix: the angrily gesticulating one, and an evident corpse slumped among the dessert plates and port glasses on the great oaken dinner-table.

Climbing with some difficulty out of her character as a bright young debutante, Felicity said: "This is the spare you talking, right? The machine analogue you programmed in. So the real you's gone to sleep in the VR tank or something. So what?"

The sleuth twirled his moustache with a flourish. "Mademoiselle will kindly employ her little grey cells. Chester Dix does not "go to sleep" during an investigation. Archons of Athens! There has been foul play."

"All right, all right, game's over," snapped the Hon. Nigel. "Terminate. Terminate. If something's happened to Chester we need to go realside and take a look. Sorry to spoil the fun, everyone. Terminate, terminate. – Why the hell isn't it terminating?"

"A thousand pardons. I have taken the small liberty of activating a, how you say, a gamma-gamma override. *No one* shall be permitted to leave Shambles Hall until this mystery she is solved."

He stalked haughtily from the room.

"Jesus Christ," said Felicity.

"Anyone for tennis?"

"That's not funny, darling," said the Hon. Nigel, shivering in a chill like interstellar space. They were using the racquets as improvised snowshoes and had made it almost half a mile down the empty white lane. Although (as the Professor had pointed out) the benefits of reaching the police station in the village were extremely unclear, it seemed something that had to be tried.

"*While the snow lay round about, Deep and crisp and eeeven,*" Felicity chanted. "Cut off, indeed. It's not six inches deep anywhere."

Then they rounded a corner of the sunken lane and met an infinite wall that somehow hadn't been visible before, rising forever, the colour of the dark behind one's eyelids.

"That's what I call cut off," said Nigel gloomily.

"That's what I call shoddy programming," said his companion.

The suspects gathered in the library while the detective was occupied taking plaster casts of the strange new footprints he had found leading down and back up the snow of the carriageway.

"I don't understand," said the Duchess.

"Then I shall explain the situation to you as though you knew nothing of it," the Professor began.

The Hon. Nigel broke in hastily. "It's obvious. Chester dropped out of the gamesmaster link – that was when everything sort of quivered – and this bloody stand-in program of his took over. We'll need to give it some kind of solution to get out of this. Someone will just have to confess."

They cut cards for it, and the mysterious stranger lost.

"But I still don't even know my name," he whimpered.

"Constraint of the scenario," said the Professor helpfully.

The Hon. Nigel fiddled irritably with the carvings on the library's old oak panelling, and one of the wooden roses sank into the wall at his touch. At once a tall case of Agatha Christie titles swung aside to disclose a secret passage.

"Oh *f* –" Nigel began before the scenario constraints stopped him. "I mean, oh dash it all."

"I am in fact Lord Blackhat's identical twin brother, with our close resemblance disguised by plastic surgery," the supposed stranger said with growing confidence. "In my extensive travels in South America I acquired a quantity of an arrow poison compounded from tree frogs and almost unknown to science. This I planned to administer in the special Stilton cheese reserved for Lord Blackhat, who unfortunately took the precaution of exchanging his plate by sleight of hand with that of the person next to him, the unfortunate sleuth Chester Dix. Meanwhile I had established an alibi with a fake telephone message from Warsaw, actually my confederate speaking on the extension phone in the butler's pantry. Now I see you are hot on my trail and my only option is to confess. It's a fair cop."

"An amusing fantasy," smiled the detective. "But you have failed to explain the singular incident of the dog in the night-time."

"What was the curious incident of the dog in the night-time?"

"It was spelt backwards." The great sleuth looked momentarily confused. "Ah. Never mind that. There is one fatal error in your story, my friend. I have examined the body minutely. You know my methods. It is clear that the unfortunate victim has suffered a cerebrovascular accident, a stroke. Not, I fancy, a little-known arrow poison...."

"He's got access to the ship systems," Felicity whispered. "*That's* what happened to poor old Chester. I always thought he must have fiddled the physicals, you know, to get passed for this trip."

"Natural causes!" said the Hon. Nigel, pouncing. "There has been no murder. The case is closed."

"That, of course, is what the killer would *like* us to think. We are dealing with a very clever criminal, my friends. I see half of it now – but only half."

"Oh ... botheration," Felicity paraphrased.

A loose group had formed around the glittering Christmas tree in the great entrance hall. "If we all committed suicide ..." the Duchess suggested vaguely.

"Would just go non-interactive," Lord Blackhat grunted. "Used to like that bit the best, drifting round like a ghost and watching you all hash up the investigation."

"Then the case might never be solved," said the Hon. Nigel. "Would the scenario terminate if it recognized an insoluble problem?"

Felicity pouted. "God knows. Well, only God and Chester."

"Dammit," said the Colonel, "one of us will just have to be caught red-handed. No time for more fooling around. Got a starship to run."

"Ah, a second murder!" Nigel snapped his fingers. "Time to draw lots again."

"Ought to be me who's bumped off," said the mysterious stranger. "The person suspected of the first murder should always be the second victim. It's part of the classic unities."

"No. Build-up was for Blackhat," rumbled the Colonel crustily.

The Duchess sighed and broke the seal on a fresh pack of cards.

"Oh!" cried Felicity in synthetic alarm as the library door creaked open. "Oh! I was just passing by and happened to pick up the knife, forgetting everything I know about not touching anything at the scene of the crime.... Who would have thought the old man had so much blood in him?"

(The silver fish-slice had been an awkward choice of weapon, but Nigel thought it rather picturesque. "It's more of a blasted blunt instrument," Lord Blackhat had groaned irritably as he expired.)

The great detective took in the scene at a single hawk-eyed glance.

"No," said Felicity. "It's no use. This huge bloodstain on my dress ... the six witnesses in the corridor outside who will swear that no one but myself has entered this room since his lordship was last seen alive ... I can't conceal my blatant guilt from you."

Alternately puffing at a huge pipe whose stem curved like a saxophone and sipping at a rummer of priceless old liqueur brandy, the sleuth made his way along the floor on hands and knees. Then he rose and touched a place in the panelling. The secret door opened on well-oiled hinges.

"Burn and blister me! Not quite a locked room after all, I fancy. Now I have just one question for you, my dear girl. *Whom are you shielding?*"

Felicity pronounced a word under her breath.

Shortly afterwards: "Is there not," said the Professor with a certain academic distaste, "a criminal device known in the literature as a "frame"? Now what I propose ..."

Starveling the butler made a pathetic corpse in his pantry. He was only a program construct and not a live player, but the Hon. Nigel had felt a pang of real remorse as he did the deed and arranged the evidence.

"*I done it. I can live with myself no longer. Farewell cruel world.*

Tell the maid to decant the '49 port for Boxing Day," the investigator read aloud to the suspects. "Very determined of the fellow to write all that in his own blood on the table, after shooting himself through the heart. Using a disguised hand, too."

"Ah," said Nigel guiltily.

"Yes, what the murderer forgot was, firstly, that yellow stitch-bane is not yellow at all but a pale mauve ... and secondly, that Starveling *was left-handed.*"

Nigel gave a muffled exclamation, laden with even more guilt.

"Fortunately my snuff-box is invariably charged with fingerprint powder...." To an accompaniment of impatient shufflings, forensic science proceeded on its remorseless way.

"No! There must be some mistake!" cried Nigel unconvincingly.

"God, Captain, you're a lousy actor," Felicity whispered.

"Satisfactory. Most satisfactory. And what do we deduce from this exact match between the prints on the automatic and those of the Hon. Nigel Scattergood? Why, of course, that he must have handled the gun innocently at some earlier time, else he would have taken care to wipe it clean!"

The Colonel made some feeble suggestion about double-bluff, but the sleuth was happily launched on a flight of deductions about the unknown murderer's careful manipulation of the gun in a wire frame that left the prints undisturbed....

"We're being too rational," said Felicity. "This imitation Chester is soaked and saturated in detective stories just like the real one. We can't out-subtle him."

"Thanks so much, darling," said the Hon. Nigel with venom. "Thanks for explaining that things are utterly hopeless."

"Ah, but if we could use the ship-system AI it could fudge up a super-clever pattern that any Great Detective would fall for."

"If, if," grunted the Colonel. "If pigs could fly we could all make a getaway on porkerback, if we had some pigs."

"Wait," said Felicity. "As *he* would say – when you've eliminated all logical solutions you have to try something that's stark raving bonkers. Duchess dear, where's the ouija board from our séance on Christmas Eve that gave us all those thrillingly sinister and atmospheric warnings?"

After prolonged searching the apparatus finally came to light under a pile of anonymous letters.

"This is ridiculous," complained the Hon. Nigel as the plan-chette began to slide across the lettered board. Under all their fingertips it moved uncertainly at first, then with more seeming decision. "Is it spelling anything out?"

"L-O-G-I-N," said Felicity. "That looks promising. Now we're going to need a *lot* of pencil and paper."

They were busy through the small hours, placing a wild variety of clues everywhere the Astral Intelligence had advised.

Bleary-eyed and feeling hungover, the Hon. Nigel lifted the silver cover of the largest dish on the sideboard. It contained, perhaps inevitably, red herrings. He settled for bacon and egg. The others were already gathered about the breakfast table, and after an early-morning hunt for evidence the world-famous sleuth was clearly ready to hold forth.

"This has been one of the most baffling and complex cases that I have ever encountered. Even I, Chester Dix, with my sixteen heraldic quarterings and unparalleled little grey cells ... even I was stretched to my deductive limits by the satanic cunning of this crime. But now I have the answer!"

Felicity led a discreet patter of applause.

"What first drew my attention was that the seemingly false alibi with the phonograph record of the typewriter was a clever decoy. Second came the realization that when the tween-maid glimpsed the clock through the window of the supposedly locked room, *she saw the clock-face in a mirror* ... producing an error of timing that has literally turned this case upside down. Next, the drugged cigar-cutter ..."

The breakfast party found the thread a little hard to follow: there was mention of the legendary Polar Poignard or ice dagger that melted tracelessly away, of a bullet misleadingly fired from a blowpipe and a hypodermic filled with air, while disguises and impersonations were rampant. Keys were ingeniously turned from the wrong sides of doors, and bolts magnetically massaged. In the end it seemed on the whole that Lord Blackhat himself was the vill-ain, having faked his own murder and posthumously blackmailed Starveling into doing much the same.

"Didn't quite follow the bit about the murderous dwarf hidden under the cover of the turkey dish," said the Colonel.

Felicity explained that that notion had been seen through by the detective as a diabolical false trail. She thought.

"And so, ladies and gentlemen, you are all free to depart. Merry Christmas!"

"Merry Christmas! I've never looked forward so much to boring old shipboard chores. Until next year –" said Felicity, and winked out. The others followed suit.

Alone again in the great dining-room, deep in the ship-system's bubble memory, the sleuth smiled a small, secret smile. He moved to the telephone and lifted the receiver. "Get me Whitehall 1212. Inspector Lestrade? ... I have solved the mystery at Shambles Hall. Yes.... In the end I deduced that, unprecedentedly, *every member of the house party* conspired to commit the original crime. The method, I fancy, was suffocation – it was their good fortune that the victim suffered a stroke when part-asphyxiated. All of them were in it together. The ingenuity of their false clues proves it. *Sacre bleu*, they think me a fool! Being outnumbered, I lulled their fears most beautifully by announcing the solution they wished. They will return here – do we not know that the criminal always returns to the scene of the crime? – and we shall set a trap. ... Yes. Yes, that murderous gang will not find it so easy to escape Shambles Hall *next* Christmas!"

The Repulsive Story of the Red Leech

S*r Arth*r C*n*n D*yle

"Our client, Watson, would seem somewhat overwrought," re-marked Sherlock Holmes without lowering his copy of the *Times*.

We were alone, but I had grown accustomed to the little puzzles which my friend was amused to propound. A glance at the window showed nothing but grey rain over Baker Street. I listened with care, and presently was pleased to say: "Aha! Someone is pacing outside the door. Not heavily, for I cannot discern the footsteps, but quite rapidly – as indicated by the regular sound from that floorboard with its very providential creak."

Holmes cast aside his newspaper and smiled. "Capital! But let us not confuse providence with forethought. That board has been carefully sprung in imitation of the device which in the Orient is known as a nightingale floor. More than once I have found its warning useful."

As I privately abandoned my notion of having the loose plank nailed down and silenced, there was a timid knock at the door.

"Come in," cried Holmes, and in a moment we had our first sight of young Martin Traill. He was robust of build but pale of feature, and advanced with a certain hesitation.

"You wish, I take it, to consult me," said Holmes pleasantly.

"Indeed so, sir, if you are the celebrated Dr Watson."

A flash of displeasure crossed Holmes's face as he effected the necessary introductions; and then, I thought, he smiled to himself at his own vanity.

Traill said to me: "I should, perhaps, address you in private."

"My colleague is privy to all my affairs," I assured him, suppressing a smile of my own.

"Very well. I dared to approach you, Dr Watson, since certain accounts which you have published show that you are not unacquainted with *outré* matters."

"Meretricious and over-sensationalized accounts," murmured Holmes under his breath.

I professed my readiness to listen to any tale, be it never so bizarre, and – not without what I fancied to be a flicker of evasiveness in his eyes – Martin Traill began.

"If I were a storyteller I would call myself hag-ridden ... harried by spirits. The facts are less dramatic, but, to me, perhaps more disturbing. I should explain that I am the heir to the very substantial estate of my late father, Sir Maximilian Traill, whose will makes me master of the entire fortune upon attaining the age of twenty-five. That birthday is months past: yet here I am, still living like a remittance-man on a monthly allowance, because I cannot sign a simple piece of paper."

"A legal document that confirms you in your inheritance?" I hazarded.

"Exactly so."

"Come, come," said Holmes, reaching for a quire of foolscap and a pencil, "we must see this phenomenon. Pray write your name here, and Watson and I will stand guard against ghosts."

Traill smiled a little sadly. "You scoff. I wish to God that I could scoff too. *This* is not a document that my hand refuses to touch: see!" And, though the fingers trembled a little, he signed his name bold and clear: Martin Maximilian Traill.

"I perceive," said Holmes, "that you have no banking account."

"No indeed; our man of business pays over my allowance in gold. But – good heavens – how can you know this?"

"Yours is a strong schoolboy signature, not yet worn down by repeated use in the world, such as the signing of many cheques. After ten thousand prescriptions, Watson's scrawl is quite indecipherable in all that follows the W. – But we digress."

Traill nervously rubbed the back of his right hand as he went on. "The devil of it is that Selina ... that my elder sister talks to spirits."

I fancied that I took his point a trifle more quickly than the severely rational Holmes. "Séances?" I said. "Mischief in dark rooms with floating tambourines, and the dead supposedly called back to this sphere to talk twaddle? It is a folly which several of my older female patients share."

"Then I need not weary you with details. Suffice it to say that Selina suffers from a mild monomania about the ingratitude of her young brother – that is, myself. Unfortunately she has never married. When I assume formal control of our father's fortune, her stipulated income from the estate will cease. Naturally I shall reinstate and even increase the allowance ... but she is distrustful. And the spirits encourage her distrust."

"Spirits!" snapped Holmes. "Professor Challenger's recent monograph has quite exploded the claims of spirit mediums. You mean to say that some astral voice has whispered to this foolish woman that her brother plans to leave her destitute?"

"Not precisely, sir. On the occasion when I was present – for sisters must be humoured – the device employed was a ouija board. You may know the procedure. All those present place a finger on the planchette, and its movements spell out messages. Nonsense as a rule, but I remember Selina's air of grim satisfaction as that sentence slowly emerged: BEWARE AN UNGENEROUS BROTHER. And then, the words that came horribly back to mind on my twenty-fifth birthday: FEAR NOT. THE HAND THAT MOVES AGAINST ITS OWN KIN SHALL SUFFER FIRE FROM HEAVEN.

"And my hand did suffer, Dr Watson. When I took up the pen to sign that paper in the solicitor's office, it burnt like fire as though in my very bones!"

I found myself at a loss. "The pen was hot?"

"No, no: it was a quill pen, a mere goose feather. Our family lawyer Mr Jarman is a trifle old-fashioned in such matters. I do not know what to think. I have made the attempt three times since, and my hand will not sign the document. Jarman is so infernally kind and sympathetic to my infirmity, but I can imagine what he thinks. Could some kind of mesmerism be in operation against me? What of the odic force? Some men of science even give credence to the spirit world –"

"Pardon me," said Holmes, "but with my colleague's permission I would like to administer two simple medical tests. First, a trivial exercise in mental acuity. This lodging is 221b Baker Street, and it is the seventeenth of the month. How rapidly, Mr Traill, can you divide 221 by seventeen?"

As I marvelled and Traill took up the pencil to calculate, Holmes darted to his cupboard of chemical apparatus, returning with a heavy stone pestle and mortar. In the latter he had placed a small mirror about three inches square. Looking at Traill's paper, he said: "Excellent. Quite correct. Now, a test of muscular reactions – kindly shatter this glass *now*."

Traill performed the feat handily enough, with one sharp tap of the pestle, and stared in puzzlement. It resembled no medical procedure that I knew.

Holmes resumed his seat, rubbing his hands in satisfaction. "As I thought. You are not in the slightest superstitious, Mr Traill; I guessed as much from the tone in which you spoke of spirits. A mathematical result of thirteen does not make you flinch, nor did you hesitate before breaking a mirror. You are masking your real concern. Why do you consult a doctor? Because you fear madness."

With a sob, Traill buried his face in his hands. I stepped to the gasogene and spirit-case, and mixed him a stiff brandy-and-soda with Holmes's nodded approval. In another minute our client had composed himself, and said wryly: "I see that I have fallen among mind-readers."

"My methods, alas, are more prosaic," said Holmes. "Inference is a surer tool than wizardry. I now infer that there is some special circumstance you have yet to reveal to us, for I recall no history of insanity in the family of Sir Maximilian Traill."

"You are troubled and overwrought," I put in, "but speaking as a doctor I see no sign of madness."

"Thank you, Dr Watson. I will begin again, and tell you of the red leech.

"My lodgings are in Highgate and – since the allowance from my father's estate frees me from the need to seek employment – I have fallen into the habit of walking on Hampstead Heath each morning, in search of inspiration for the verses by which I hope one day to be known. (*The Yellow Book* was good enough to publish one of my triolets.) Some friends used to chaff me for being a fixed landmark at luncheon-time, when I generally enjoyed a meal of sandwiches and a bottle of Bass in the vicinity of the Highgate Ponds." Traill shuddered. "Never again! I remember the day quite vividly: it was a warm Tuesday, perhaps six months ago ..."

"Prior to your twenty-fifth birthday?" asked Holmes sharply.

"Why, yes. I sat on the grass in a reverie, idly watching someone's great black retriever splash in and out of the water. I was thinking of foolish things ... my sister's maggot of distrust, and the structure of the sestina, and *The Pickwick Papers* – you will remember Mr Pickwick's investigations of tittlebats and the origin of the Hampstead Ponds which lie across the heath. My thoughts were very far away from the heath. Perhaps I even dozed. Then I felt a hideous pain!"

"On the back of your right hand?" said Holmes.

"Ah, you have seen me rub it when troubled."

"Already my methods are transparent to you," Holmes remarked with pretended chagrin.

I leaned across to look. "There is a mark resembling a scald, or possibly an acid-burn."

"It was the red leech, doctor. You will surely have heard of it. A repulsive, revolting creature. The thing must have crept on me from the long grass; it clung to my hand, its fangs – or whatever such vermin possess – fixed in me."

"I know of no such leech," I protested.

"Perhaps it is a matter which does not concern a general practitioner," said Traill with a hint of reproach. He plucked a folded piece of paper from his wallet, and handed it to me; it was a newspaper clipping. I read aloud: "Today a warning was issued to London dwellers. Specimens of *Sanguisuga rufa*, the highly poisonous red leech of Formosa, have been observed in certain parkland areas of North London. The creature is believed to have escaped from the private collection of a naturalist and explorer. A representative of the Royal Zoological Society warned that the red leech should be strictly avoided if seen, for its bite injects toxins with long-lasting effects, which may include delusions, delirium or even insanity. The leech is characteristically some three to four inches in length, and is readily distinguished by its crimson hue."

"Most instructive," said Holmes dreamily.

Traill continued: "The horror was unspeakable. The leech clung to my hand, biting with a burning pain, rendering me too horrified to move. I was lucky that a doctor was passing by, who recognized the awful thing! He plucked it from my flesh with a gloved hand and threw it aside into the undergrowth. And then, straight away, on the grass of Hampstead Heath, this Dr James unpacked his surgical instruments from his black bag and cut the mouth-parts of the horrid beast out of my hand, while I averted my gaze and struggled not to cry out. 'A narrow escape, young fellow,' he said to me. 'If my eye had not been caught by the press report' – and here he handed me the scrap of paper which you hold – 'it might have gone badly for you. There is something in Providence after all.' I thanked Dr James profusely, and at my insistence he charged me a guinea. Although he had dressed the tiny wound carefully, it was painful and slow to heal.

"And now you know why I fear madness. My mind seems unclouded, but my senses betray me – the leech-bitten hand burns like fire when I try to move against my sister's wishes, as though her infernal spirits were real after all."

"Quite so," said Holmes, regarding him with intense satisfaction through half-closed eyes. "Your case, Mr Traill, presents some extraordinarily interesting and gratifying features. Would you recognize Dr James if you met him again?"

"Certainly: his great black beard and tinted glasses were most distinctive."

This seemed to cause Holmes some private merriment. "Excellent! Yet you now consult the estimable but unfamiliar Watson, rather than the provenly knowledgeable James."

"I confess that in my over-excitement I must have misheard the address Dr James gave to me. There is no such house-number at the street in Hampstead where I sought him."

"Better still. The time has come to summon a cab, Watson! We can easily reach the Highgate Ponds before twilight."

"But to what purpose?" I cried. "After six months the creature will be long gone, or dead and rotted."

"Well, we may still amuse ourselves by catching tittlebats – as Mr Pickwick chose to call sticklebacks. The correct naming of creatures is so important, is it not?"

All through the long hansom-cab ride I struggled to make sense of this, while Holmes would talk of nothing but music.

In the bleak grey of late afternoon, Hampstead Heath was at its most desolate. A thin, cold rain continued to fall. The three of us trudged through wet grass on our fool's errand.

"I must ask you for a supreme effort of memory, Mr Traill," declared Holmes as the ponds came into view. "You must cast your mind back to that Tuesday in the Spring. Remember the pattern of trees you saw as you sat on the ground; remember the dog that pranced in the water. We must know the exact place, to within a few feet."

Traill roamed around dubiously. "It all looks different at this time of year," he muttered. "Perhaps near here."

"Squat on your heels to obtain the same perspective as when you sat," suggested Holmes. After a few such reluctant experiments, our client indicated that he was as close as memory would take him.

"Then that patch of hawthorn must be our goal – the leech's last known domicile," Holmes observed. "Note, Watson, that this picnic-spot is several yards from the beaten path. The good Dr James must have been quite long-sighted, to see and recognize that leech."

"He might easily have been taking a short cut across the grass," I replied.

"Again the voice of reason pours cold water on my fanciful deductions!" said Holmes cheerfully. As he spoke, he methodically prodded the hawthorn-bushes with his walking-stick, and turned over the sodden mass of fallen leaves beneath. He seemed oblivious to the chill drizzle, now made worse by a steadily rising wind from the east. A quarter of an hour went miserably past.

Then – "A long shot, Watson, a very long shot!" cried my friend, and pounced. From a pocket of his cape he had produced a pair of steel forceps, and from another a large pill-box. Now something red glistened in the forceps' grip, and in a trice the thing was safely boxed. Traill, who had given an involuntary cry, backed away a step or two with an expression of revulsion.

"*Another* of the vile creatures?"

"I fancy it is the same," Holmes murmured. And not a word more would he utter until we were installed in a convenient public house which supplied us with smoking-hot whisky toddies. "It is villainy, Mr Traill," he said then. "One final test remains. I experimented not long ago with a certain apparatus, without fully comprehending its possibilities in scientific detection ..."

It was late night in Baker Street, and the gas-mantles burnt fitfully. A smell of ozone tinged the air, mingled with a more familiar chemical reek. Holmes, as he linked up an extensive battery of wet cells, expounded with fanciful enthusiasm on the alternating-current electrical transmission proposals of one Mr Nikola Tesla in the Americas, and of how in the early years of the new century he fully expected electric lighting to be plumbed into our lodgings, like the present gas-pipes. I smiled at his eagerness.

At length the preparations were complete. "You must refrain from touching any part of the equipment," Holmes now warned. "The electrical potential which drives this cathode-ray tube is dangerously high. Do you recognize the device, Watson? The evacuated glass, the tungsten target electrode within? It has already been employed in the United States, in connection with your own line of work."

The tangle of glassware, the trailing wires and the eerie glow from the tube made up an effect wholly unfamiliar to me, reminiscent perhaps of some new scientific romance by Mr H.G. Wells. It was only very gingerly that young Traill placed his right hand where Holmes directed.

"I have seen something a little like this before," he mused. "Old Wilfrid Jarman's brother dabbles in electrical experiments. He vexed Selina once with a tedious demonstration of a model dynamo."

"Healing rays?" I asked. "Earlier in the day we spoke of Mesmerism, which according to my recollection was a charlatan's ploy to heal by what he called animal magnetism. Has electrical science made this real at last?"

"Not precisely, Watson. The apparatus of Herr Doktor Roentgen does not heal, but lights the way for the healer. In years to come, I fancy it will be remembered as the greatest scientific discovery of the present decade."

"But I see nothing happening."

"That is what you may expect when there is nothing to see. – No, Mr Traill, I must entreat you to remain quite still. The rays of Roentgen, which he has named for algebra's unknown quantity X, do not impinge on the human eye. That faint glow which you may discern is not the true glow, but secondary fluorescence in the glass."

I pondered this, while Holmes kept a wary eye on his pocket-watch. "Very well," he said at last. "You may lift your hand now, but have a care ..." And he took up the mysterious sealed envelope on which Traill's hand had rested. "What the eye cannot see, a photographic plate can still record. I must retreat to the darkroom and – lift the veil of the spirits. Kindly entertain our guest, Watson."

Traill and I stared at each other, lost in a mental darkness deeper than that of any photographic darkroom. Infuriatingly, I knew that to Holmes this night-shrouded terrain of crime was brilliantly lit by the invisible rays of his deductive power.

Nor was I much the wiser when morning came. Holmes, dancing-eyed and evasive, had bundled Traill into a homeward-bound cab and directed him to return to Baker Street after breakfast, when the case would be resolved. Then he had settled into his favourite chair with his pipe and a pound of the vilest shag tobacco: I found him in the identical position when I arose from sleep.

Over breakfast, he unbent a trifle. "Well, Watson, what do you make of our case?"

"Very little.... I had thought," I ventured, "that you would dissect or analyse the leech itself and perhaps identify its toxins."

"The naked eye sufficed." He pulled the red thing from his dressing-gown pocket and tossed it casually on to my plate of kippers, causing me to recoil in horror. "As you may readily discern for yourself, it has been artfully made from rubber."

"Good heavens!" I studied the ugly worm more closely, and was struck by a thought. "Holmes, you suspected this artificial leech from the outset, or the excursion to Hampstead Heath would have been futile. What gave you the clue? And has Traill deceived us – are we the butts of some youthful jest?"

Holmes smiled languidly. "In a moment you will be telling me how obvious and elementary was the reasoning that led me to distrust that repulsive object. Look again at the newspaper cutting."

I took it from his hand and examined it once more, to no avail.

"Setting aside the fact that the type fount does not correspond to that of any British newspaper known to me (the work of a jobbing printer, no doubt) ... setting aside the extreme unlikelihood that such a striking report should have escaped my eye and failed to be pasted into our own celebrated index volume ... may I direct your attention to this red leech's scientific name?"

"*Sanguisuga rufa*," I repeated. "Which I should say means something like 'red bloodsucker'."

"You are no taxonomer, Watson, but you are a doctor – or, as some country folk still call the profession, a leech. Can you bring to mind the Latin name for the leech once used in medicine?"

"*Hirudo medicinalis*, of course. Oh! That is strange...."

"In fact, *Sanguisuga* is not a scientific class name. It is poetic. It was used of leeches by Pliny. Our villain, who may or may not be 'Dr James', knows his Latin but not – if I may so phrase it – his leechcraft."

I said: "How obvious and elem ... that is, ingeniously reasoned!"

Holmes inclined his head ironically. "Here is our client at the door. Good morning, Mr Traill! Dr Watson has just been explaining with great erudition that your red leech is a fake – a rubber toy. And now the chase leads us to Theobald's Road, to the law office of Jarman, Fittlewell and Coggs, where today you will at last claim your inheritance. Watson, that excellent revolver of yours might well be of use."

"My reconstruction," said Holmes as our cab rattled through a dismal London fog, "is a trifle grisly. There you were, Mr Traill, arguably somewhat drowsy from the compounded effects of warm weather, literary reveries and a bottle of Bass. Your habit of picnicking near the Highgate Ponds is well known to your friends – even, I dare say, your sister?"

"That is so. In fact, Selina has publicly twitted me more than once for what she calls my shiftless habits."

"Thus the miscreant 'Dr James', whose appearance is a transparent disguise but whose true surname I fancy I know, had little difficulty in locating you. It was easy for him to approach you stealthily from behind and drop or place this little monstrosity upon the back of your hand as you sprawled on the grass." He displayed the leech once more.

"The thing still revolts me," Traill muttered.

"Its underside seems to have been coated with dark treacle: that would provide a convincingly unpleasant-looking and adhesive slime. But in addition, the 'mouth' section was dipped in some corrosive like oil of vitriol – see how it is eaten away? That was what you felt."

Again Traill convulsively massaged the back of his hand. "But, Mr Holmes, what was the purpose of this horrid trick? It strikes me that your investigations have made matters worse! Before, I could blame my hand's infirmity on the leech poison. Now you have eliminated that possibility and left me with nothing but madness."

"Not at all. You will be pleased to hear that the apparatus of Roentgen pronounces you sane. We have eliminated the impossible story of the leech. There remains another, highly improbable explanation, which we will shortly confirm as true. By the way, may I assume that either Wilfrid Jarman or his brother was present on the occasion when that planchette spelt out such a disquieting message?"

"Yes, Basil was there. The brother."

"The brother who dabbles in electrical devices. I wonder if he applied his ingenuity to enlivening those séances. In any case, according to my researches, it is far from difficult for a determined hand to influence the oracle of the ouija board. But here we are! Watson, I am sure you have change for the cabman."

Jarman, Fittlewell and Coggs, solicitors and commissioners of oaths, occupied a fourth-floor set of offices. Without a great deal of ado we were shown into the large, dim room where Wilfrid Jarman awaited. He was a plump and kindly-looking man in late middle age, whose baldness and pince-nez spectacles were slightly reminiscent of Mr Pickwick. A frowsty legal atmosphere exuded from numerous shelves of books bound in dull brown calf. Holmes's nostrils widened like a hound's as he keenly sniffed the air. I unobtrusively followed suit, and thought to detect a trace of not unfamiliar chemical whiff.

Jarman was greeting our client, saying, "I am most pleased, Martin, that you feel equal at last to your little ordeal. So many people take fright at a simple affidavit or conveyance! But you must introduce your friends."

The formalities over, Jarman indicated the bulky document that lay on his desk. "A tiresome necessity," he said with a shrug. "Believe me, my dear boy, I would readily dispense with it – but we lawyers must live by the law, or where would we be?"

The question being unanswerable, Traill muttered something suitably meaningless.

"*Look!*" cried Holmes suddenly. "That face at the window! We are being spied upon!"

Our heads jerked around to the large office window, which showed only the dim and fog-shrouded skyline across Theobald's Road. The solicitor even took a ponderous step or two towards the window, before turning back and stating acidly: "Mr Holmes, we are on the fourth floor. And expert cat-burglars do not commonly risk their necks for legal paperwork."

Holmes made some feeble apology and mentioned trouble with his nerves. I recognized the signs of a ruse, and on reflection thought that – out of the corner of my eye – I had seen his hand dart to the broad desktop. But all seemed unchanged.

"Let us deal with the business at hand," said Jarman, placing a finger on the thick paper where the signature was to go.

Traill took up the quill pen and dipped it in ink. He hesitated. His trembling hand moved forward, back, and then resolutely forward again. The air seemed suddenly charged with menace. From behind the desk Jarman smiled indulgently, and seemed to shift his weight a little to one side. For an instant I thought I felt, rather than heard, a faint sourceless whining.

Simultaneously, Traill snatched his hand back with a cry, and there was an explosion of blinding, dazzling light from the desk. Jarman's thick voice uttered an oath. I clapped my hand to my revolver, but the room was blotted out by coruscating after-images. White smoke swirled. Slowly some shreds of vision returned.

"'Tis sport," Sherlock Holmes quoted, "to have the engineer hoist with his own petard."

"I felt my hand burning again," said Traill. "But that great flash was not my nerves, nor spirits either."

The fat solicitor's hand seemed burnt as well, from the flare; he cursed in a low, filthy undertone.

Holmes said briskly, "Forgive my theatricality. It seemed a useful notion to slip a flat packet of magnesium flash powder, appropriately fused, underneath that interesting document. Mr Jarman's office may appear old-fashioned, but it conceals some thoroughly modern equipment – specifically, a high-frequency Tesla coil within the desk, which is activated when Mr Jarman chooses to step on a particular floorboard. Within a limited area, its rapidly fluctuating electromagnetic field has the effect of heating metals to a painful temperature. This heat detonated my little flash charge."

"Metal?" said Traill, now still more puzzled. "I wear no rings."

"True enough. But your right hand contains a steel needle, inserted there by the false Dr James under the pretext of removing the poisoned mouth-parts of the red leech."

I was thunderstruck as I realized the fiendish ingenuity of the plot. Even the quill pen was part of the design, for a steel nib would instantly have given the game away. And of course that faint smell in the air was the sulphuric-acid reek of hidden wet-cell batteries. Meanwhile, Jarman uttered a forced laugh. He appeared to be sweating profusely. "What a farrago of nonsense! Such a thing would be impossible to prove."

"On the contrary, I have photographed it by means of X-rad-iation." Holmes drew something from one of his capacious pockets. "This shadowgraph shows the bone structure of Mr Traill's right hand. Bone, being less pervious to the rays than flesh, appears as nearly white. Here is the solid white of the needle, lying between the metacarpal bones."

Traill shuddered again.

"No doubt we will find that Mr Jarman cannot account for his time on that Tuesday six months ago when you had your famous adventure on Hampstead Heath ... ah, Mr Jarman, you are smiling. Therefore you have an alibi, and the deed was done by your good brother Basil, who likes to experiment with electricity. What, no smile now?"

I had belatedly trained my revolver on Jarman.

"What was the purpose of this terrible charade?" asked Traill.

"It is possible," said Holmes gently, "that you are no longer heir to a great estate. If the assets or a large part of them have somehow slipped through the fingers of Jarman, Fittlewell and Coggs, then it naturally became necessary to delay – by fair means or foul – your legal acquisition of Sir Maximilian's fortune. We shall find out when, as Mr Jarman very nearly put it, those who lived by the law shall perish by the law."

"Mr Sherlock Holmes, you are an officious meddler," stated Jarman, gazing intently at my friend. "And you over-reach. Your remarks are slanderous, sir. A true accounting of the estate's affairs lies here upon my desk, and will show no defalcation: perhaps you would care to glance through the record?" The lawyer tapped his scorched index finger upon the book in question, a heavy ledger with a tarnished brass clasp that lay askew upon a mound of papers near the desk's far edge. "Within, all your questions are answered."

For half a minute, Holmes's right hand had lain concealed within the folds of his bulky Inverness cape. Now he reached forward to the ledger, but did not flick open the clasp as I had anticipated. Instead he swiftly lifted the entire tome clear of the papers, and two oddities were made manifest. First, from the underside of the book's brass clasp there trailed a long, springy, shining copper wire which vanished into the artfully disarrayed papers. Second, Holmes's hand was seen to be sheathed in a heavy, rubber glove.

"How many volts, Mr Jarman?" he enquired pleasantly. "Hundreds? Thousands? I presume this jest was ultimately intended for Mr Traill, whose death would have bought you yet more time. My admiration for your ingenuity increases."

Wilfrid Jarman's composure was broken at last, and with an inarticulate cry of rage he stepped to one side, reaching into a drawer. Even as I realized that his hand now held an old-fashioned pistol, he had dextrously placed himself so that Holmes lay in my line of fire. I flung myself uselessly forward, to see Jarman aiming at point-blank range while Holmes flung the ledger in what seemed a futile shielding gesture. Blue-white sparks flew. The pistol's flash and bang echoed with dread authority in the musty room. Then a heavy body fell to the floor. There was a long silence.

"I suspect that our friend did not finish pulling the trigger," said Holmes, whose austere face was now very pale. "His infernal electricity exploded the shell in the breech, even as it struck him dead. Gun-barrels, as well as copper wires and brass clasps, are excellent conductors of electrical current. – Watson, I must trouble you to bind up my shoulder. The bullet did not go entirely astray."

He bent over to scrutinize the corpse more closely. "As he truly said, that ledger contained the answer to all questions. The *rictus* of his features is characteristic of electrically-induced spasms and convulsions. Best not to look, Mr Traill. Some things are even less pleasant to gaze upon than the red leech."

Some time afterward, at the trial which concluded with the sent-
encing of the co-conspirator Basil Jarman to a long term of hard
labour, we learned that almost half of the Traill estate still remained. Thus our client continued his life of idle literary dabbling,
while his blameless sister Selina presumably receives a sufficient
allowance to fritter away on psychic mediums.

Besides his own substantial fee, Holmes somehow contrived to
retain a small souvenir of the case. To this day, our untidy mantelpiece in 221b Baker Street boasts a matchbox best not opened by
the unwary, for its coiled rubber occupant is repulsive to the eye.
The box is labelled in Holmes's own neat hand: *Sanguisuga rufa
spuriosa*. I have my doubts about the Latin.

Out of Space, Out of Time
H.P. L*v*cr*ft

He had said that the geometry of the dream-place he saw
was abnormal, non-Euclidean, and loathsomely redolent of
spheres and dimensions apart from ours ... Parker slipped
as the other three were plunging frenziedly over endless
vistas of green-crusted rock to the boat, and Johansen
swears he was swallowed up by an angle of masonry which
shouldn't have been there; an angle which was acute, but
behaved as if it were obtuse.

     H.P. Lovecraft, "The Call of Cthulhu", 1928

Not long ago I thought I saw my path clear to the highest honours
of science; a stinking path, it's true, awash with foulness from the
gutters underneath the world, but I maintain that pure knowledge
has no stink. *Sciens non olet.* It might have been my motto. Once I
was a scientist. Now, though, all the glittering equations have
turned to viscid horror ...

My name is Dr Jonathan Lake and my doctorate is in physics,
of which I am a full professor with (grimly laughable though it now
seems) life tenure; an achievement of note for a man thirty-four
years old. Miskatonic University in the old Massachusetts town of
Arkham may not, perhaps, seem the academy of choice for a
student of the "new physics". The musty grandeur of its
architecture conveys age and eccentric dignity rather than
intellectual thrust – which other seat of learning boasts a small,
reconstructed Egyptian pyramid in its lesser quadrangle? Indeed
Miskatonic has a whispered reputation for esoteric studies verging
on the disreputable. What nonsense, well into the second quarter
of the twentieth century, to maintain a locked library of grimoires

and works of cabbalism!

Yet gargoyle-infested Miskatonic University was my own choice: I preferred that my particular lines of research should be undisturbed by the distracting chatter of rival theorists. Here I am pre-eminent – or as my mother chose to write, "You always did like to be a big frog in a small pond, Jonny." (We have never been intellectually close.) There is, additionally, an odd charm in conducting modern experiments concerning the disintegration of matter against a background of hand-crafted brass instruments from the nineteenth century. Here, even the laboratories are period pieces.

Naturally I have caused new apparatus to be installed and constructed, appropriate for explorations at the outermost frontiers of physics. My strength, though, is for theoretical work: I will be remembered – or should have been remembered – for my correspondence with Otto Stern on the magnetic properties of molecular beams, with the Joliot-Curies on artificial radio-activity, with Messrs Cockcroft and Walton regarding the theory of the particle accelerator which vulgar newspapers have termed an "atom-smasher", and a dozen other fruitful collaborations. Some far-off colleagues have expressed wonder at the variety of significant papers carrying the grateful citation: "J. Lake, Miskatonic University, private communication, 1932" – or whatever the year might be. How did I contrive to become such a Jack-of-all-trades in so many outlying areas of my chosen field? There have been half-joking suggestions of selling one's soul for the secrets of matter ... and indeed less savoury hints, not intended for my ears, concerning my notoriously taciturn laboratory assistant. I will speak of him shortly.

The thing began with the dreams. I should never have followed that fascinating path. These were no ordinary dreams; yet paradoxically they *were* ordinary because shared by so many. You will remember the matter; this was in fact the occult *cause celebre* of the latter 1920s, though to any rational mind it was evident that a few significant facts had been exaggerated by mass hysteria. In particular, the wells were soon tainted by that discreditably sensationalist account of the matter published by Mr Howard Phillips Lovecraft in 1928: no later report of the dream can be entirely trusted, being so much more likely to stem from this secondary source rather than from ... well, what?

I first experienced what have been termed the "Cthulhu dreams" in the early Spring of 1925, as I began to settle into my assistant professorship at Miskatonic. The general details have been sufficiently widely published – the vision's invariable setting being a monstrous city built to inhuman proportions and adrip with abyssal sea-ooze, as though thrust up from the sea by some tectonic convulsion. The south Pacific earthquake of February 28th, 1925, is of course well documented.

The recurring dream was of stumbling flight through this chaos of titanic blocks, feet forever clogged by weed or *Urschleim* from the deeps. Certain aspects of this disagreeable vision I found myself able, with an effort, to dismiss. The pursuit by some absurd tentacled monstrosity cobbled together from children's nightmares could plausibly be interpreted as an imagined response to the grim, monolithic architecture and rotting sea-stench. (I am unable to agree with James Branch Cabell's assertion that smell and taste are never encountered in dreams.) Only later did I formulate the notion that there might be matters too repugnant for mental depiction – concepts which the mind instinctively shrouds in improvised masks of dread. Meanwhile it was the city itself, the drowned city or mausoleum or necropolis, that compelled one's unwilling belief. Somewhere, one felt, this maze of jarring geometries did actually in some sense exist.

If we are to believe the researches of Lovecraft, this city of "R'lyeh" briefly emerged from the waters of the Pacific in the March of 1925, to sink again in early April – after the crew of the schooner *Emma* had landed there and experienced terrible things. At this time, once the unstable island had sunk once more, the true dreams (rather than the hysterical contagion which resurged in 1928) ceased ... except that mine did not, for I have the unusual though not unknown ability to return to and re-examine the landscapes of dream on successive nights. One can readily train oneself to direct one's dreaming in this fashion. I confess to an intermittent obsession with such quirky side-issues, dreams and chess problems and optical illusions, whose pursuit rather hindered my career until – but I anticipate.

The most extraordinary part of the island story had related that one hapless crew member called Parker was swallowed up by an angle of the city's crazy carvings. It was this that caught my imagination, sustained my interest: for many of the structures in the dream-architecture had just that twisted, perverse quality of optical illusion.

Indeed some recalled the deceitful drawing of a cube which the Swiss savant L.A. Necker described as long ago as the 1830s: an ambiguous outline which abruptly and disconcertingly seems to reverse after being studied for a time, so that the near and far corners exchange places. A small object drawn on one of the near faces – a blob of paint, say, or a resting fly – seems, without moving, to shift instantaneously to the *inside* of the Necker cube. I found myself haunted by an unspeakable vision of the man Parker stumbling against the jutting angle of that slime-bedecked monolithic structure, and, in just such a flicker of perspective, being drawn within as the unstable geometries shifted to take him in a cold embrace of stone.

Time passed. Occasionally, more through idle curiosity than with any set purpose, I travelled in my sleep to that familiar city of dreadful night ...

Perhaps it was only an excess of imagination that led me to sense, amid the dream's echoing gibberish of cult phrases like *Cthulhu fhtagn*, the endless frozen scream of seaman Parker in his unnatural bondage outside the space we know. Perhaps it was mere intellectual dilettantism that led me to grope towards him with the aid of a book which I stumbled upon in the year 1928 and now recognize as more grotesque and damnable than any of the *Necronomicons* or forbidden grimoires in Miskatonic University's sealed library. In my irregular dream-visits to the stone labyrinths it seemed logical – by the logic of dream – that if one could visualize the unspeakable rotation of other-dimensioned space that had swallowed Parker, one might mentally follow where he went: and one day on waking I remembered that the "Miscellaneous" bay of our not over-extensive Science Library contained a popular guide to precisely this visualization....

I most earnestly urge any reader of this statement to avoid that dangerously entangling work *The Fourth Dimension* by the mathematician Charles Howard Hinton, M.A., late of Princeton University. The plain red cloth binding and gaily coloured frontispiece of the third edition (January, 1912) conceal a pathway to madness. Another mathematician, Poincaré, had already remarked: "A man who *devoted his life to it* could perhaps succeed in picturing to himself a fourth dimension." The italics are mine. Indeed Hinton devoted his life to the imagining of a fourth dimension in space, and tried to spread the contagion to his unknowing readers through his infamous "model" cubes. Twelve of these, elaborately coloured on each face and edge, suggest twelve perspective views of the tesseract, that four-dimensioned shape whose faces are cubes – just as the three-dimensional cube has faces which are squares.

In my folly I made myself a set of Hinton cubes. The basic twelve are only the beginning: the experimenter must construct three further sets of twenty-seven single-coloured cubes. By handling these constantly, memorizing the coloured faces and edges, and imagining their impossible linkage as directed by the colour coding ... one can eventually develop fleeting, eerie insights into a space where there is not only height and breadth and depth, but a further perpendicular direction that might be called *otherwards*. The cubes dance madly in the mind's eye, like the visual equivalent of a nonsense jingle that runs interminably and unbearably around the ruts of the brain. It is a monstrous imposition on sanity; and it is an intangible piece of scientific apparatus that can be carried into dreams.

Night after night I glided through R'lyeh's stinking canyons of obscenely carven stone, struggling to maintain the lucidity of the city's dream-image while marshalling the Hinton cubes into what I hoped would be a key to its unearthly, eldritch geometry. Time and again the dizzy structures would topple like a stack of child's wooden blocks, casting me back into my austere college bedroom with a jolt as though I had fallen from a certain height, bruised and headache-ridden. Blinking in the feeble glow of the lamp which I keep burning to allow the jotting-down of night thoughts, I would grope for a few hours of normal sleep before duty called me to the faculty's frowsty lecture-hall and the exposition of general relativity or the quantum theory to puzzled sophomores ...

I was disconcerted when Dr Henry Armitage, keeper of the famous Library, obliquely asked whether I took an interest in the kind of occult lore of which he was custodian. With a weary chuckle I remarked that physicists had other fish to fry, and that I was grappling with very different matters. But though he is frail and his hair is almost white, his piercing blue eyes seemed to see clean through my airy manner to that inner vision of cyclopean blocks.

"Of late there is a certain look about you which I have met before," he said quietly. "Some matters should not be too closely grappled with. If your work should carry you into the realms of my own expertise, remember that you may come to the Library for advice."

"It's a taxing problem," I admitted, and forced a smile: "But I'm sure that I can give it up any time I wish."

Weeks went by, the daily round and the nightly struggle. The cubes are addictive, their sequences hypnotic; eventually the imagery becomes second nature, ingrained like the multiplication table. Not long after I had reached this instinctive adepthood there came, quite unheralded, the R'lyeh dream in which the brief insight of Hinton's visualization meshed at last with the forms of those terrific slabs and buttresses. After my long dream-quest through the unknown, I had found a viewing stance from which that repellent geometry made a kind of sense.

The effect was indescribable. I seemed to see *around* the complex outer faces of one damply shining trapezohedron of basalt, and to find myself reaching in the *otherwards* direction past a stone corner which somehow rotated between convex and concave. A dream-sense of enormous error and disaster thrilled through me like a powerful electric discharge. At the fringes of hearing, a thick voice seemed to intone: *Yog-Sothoth knows the gate, for Yog-Sothoth is the gate*. I remember deploring this superstitious intrusion (obviously a fragment of the cult mythology that had lodged in my mind) into an essentially scientific thought-experiment.

It was then that my questing fingers encountered another hand which seized them in an icy, clammy grip.

All of a sudden I was awake. But the gripping hand remained, and the night-light's comforting glow disclosed an image of horror that loomed too close to my face. Not slime or tentacles, but a long pallid shape resembling a stick of French bread ... though with certain disquieting grooves and features. This strange organ's grotesqueness came into focus as unbearable deformity when I recognized it to be a human head, insanely elongated as though stretched out like bread-dough. Later I was to recall a similar shape in Hans Holbein's celebrated painting *The Ambassadors* – a mysterious anamorphic object which when seen from an acute angle (in particular, by someone ascending a stairway on whose wall the painting would hang) emerges with shocking, foreshortened clarity as a skull.

At the time, my shrieking intellect was incapable of such sober rationalization. Awful perspectives shifted and rotated as the thing which still clung tightly to my hand pulled itself painfully from around the corners outside space, here growing and here shrinking as though in a carnival hall of mirrors, until what subsided on my bedroom floor – amid a low-tide reek from befouled sea boots – was no more than human.

I wrote in my journal for May 8th, 1930: *He is human. He is alive.* And scratched out the silly words, for I did not care to think of the alternatives that crowded on me in that insane moment of transition. Perhaps my dream lasted a little longer than I thought, and I took the distortions of nightmare for waking reality – which seemed the sanest intellectual position to adopt, except that I knew it to be untrue. Seaman James Parker, a commonplace fellow with rough dark hair and an untidy beard, who five years ago had sailed from Auckland in the doomed *Emma* and vanished into an incomprehensible geometrical snare on the far side of the world, lay before me with the smell of drowned R'lyeh still on his boots. The gigantic implications of the event were swept aside by practicality; to begin with, I did not care to become another subject of common-room gossip about faculty members who "entertained" unusual guests in their rooms all night.

Arkham Sanitarium lies across the Miskatonic River, eight or nine blocks from the university quadrangle. The hospital is closer, but the Sanitarium more private. I steered my confused and mumbling visitor there (without great difficulty, despite his evidently tough and wiry build) and represented him to be a distant relative in the grip of amnesia. Dr Houghton, with whom I had some slight acquaintance, was sympathetic. Indeed, though bodily whole, Parker had undoubtedly been changed by his experience. His mind had splintered.

In curious visits to his bedside I came to distinguish three personalities. One was a silent Parker who gazed in numb fear at unseen forms, as a cat seems to watch a very slowly moving ghost. Then there was the remnant of the ordinary seaman, babbling maritime blasphemies, fragmentary recollections of shipmates, and occasional screamed hints of a terror that pursued; his halting enquiries of "Where am I?" and abject requests not to be "sent back" were repeated many times over many days before Dr Houghton's reassurances had noticeable effect and the horrors seemed to fade from the patient's memory. More rarely heard was a third, delirious voice almost a full octave higher than the commonplace Parker's light baritone – sometimes uttering that hateful cultist jabberwocky of *"Ph'nglui mglw'nafh Cthulhu R'lyeh wgah'nagl fhtagn"* and the like; sometimes speaking a kind of English with great rapidity.

I jotted down several samples, of which this is one: *"the air the earth the deeps abode of stones abandoned unfinished the skull cold in the great deeps conserved oh Lord the charge no charge whirling the tiny ghost beat her beat her beat outward from the heart there is no charge for admission spin the stones the skull the waves electrum elections energy in the great deeps ..."* There was more, much more, weaving a skein of delirium about pines and tennis and God. It was pitiful.

As I walked back along Garrison Street to the university, I felt a grey disappointment that a man who had slipped outside the space/time we know should not have returned with some dread and significant message for the world. But then, could one expect a unlettered sailor to return with tensor equations that might finally prove or disprove the enigma of Einstein's general theory of relativity? Or the puzzle of ...

It is from that moment, when I paused in mid-pace under Arkham's lowering and fuliginous sky, that the course of my life was truly set on a primrose path leading ever downward towards flame.

For a cold shock washed over me like the breaking of an icy wave as I recollected one puzzle of physics which in that year of 1930 still tormented greater minds than my own, and which had lately engrossed me. There is a phenomenon known as beta-particle emission – the ejection of an electron from a radioactive atom's core – which bafflingly seemed to violate the law of conservation of energy. "Beat her", the gabbling voice had said, and "outward from the heart", and a word I heard as "admission", and more. I flicked through those jotted notes, now eagerly, and found significant terms dotted through Parker's ravings. Had he somehow been reading my mind?

And then I saw a pattern of concepts that had never yet passed through my own thoughts: "the tiny ghost" and, repeatedly, "no charge". No *electric* charge! If the missing energy which was the riddle of beta-emission were carried off by some unknown, *uncharged* particle, it would be a tiny ghost indeed – eluding our detectors, slipping through every electrical or magnetic snare we laid for it!

That night, as hard rain lashed against the window, I timorously penned a letter to the great scientist Wolfgang Pauli – who was known to be grappling with this very question. It is not my purpose to write a treatise upon physics; suffice it to say that Pauli, at first distrustful of my forwardness, responded generously. In 1931 he published the notion of the ghost particle with full acknowledgement to myself (my own then-lowly name lacked the authority to push such an audacious notion into print); next year, with Italian jocularity, Enrico Fermi named it the *neutrino* or "little neutral one", and Miskatonic University acknowledged my growing reputation by elevating me to the status of full professor. Already I had made other notable contributions to humanity's understanding of the nucleus, such as setting the English physicist Chadwick on his path to the identification of the neutron in 1932.

My damnable secret was, of course, James Parker. Outwardly he seemed to recover with tolerable swiftness from whatever frightful insult to mind and body he had undergone, but from time to time that other voice with its high-pitched babbling would return. During these episodes his muscles generally became rigid as though in *petit mal* epilepsy, and his normally unremarkable face would fix itself in an expression of sly, bestial cunning; afterwards he would recollect nothing. I established the man in an off-campus lodging house and arranged to hire him as laboratory assistant – having worked for a time as engineer's mate, he had some small skill with his hands and in fact proved useful with a soldering iron when we assembled Miskatonic's first experimental particle accelerator. A wire recorder served to capture his oracular utterances, which seemed to emanate from some unspeakable *outside*, and again and again held coded passwords to the locked vaults of matter itself.

But my accursed ambition blinded me to the other hints that grew like poisoned weeds amid those rambling diatribes. I was quick enough to seize on anything that could advance my scientific standing, but never stood back to ponder the insidious overall direction in which these insights tended. Still less did I take more than passing note of the "Cthulhu Mythos" elements in Parker's hypnotized flood of verbiage ... the suggestions of sacrifice, of obscene Masters who demanded blood and souls, and who bided their time, awaiting – what?

I am terribly afraid that I may know what.

As the nineteen-thirties ground by and distant clouds gathered over Europe, our university was the scene of more than one untoward incident. Whispers of obscure night activity in one locked physics laboratory were easy to dismiss: the now operational particle accelerator would sometimes be left to bombard an experimental target all night long, with an attendant buzz and whine of high-voltage corona discharge. If fugitive shapes were imagined in the quadrangle, and once or twice a disquieting odour – well, even in antique Arkham, student pranks and escapades are not unknown!

More unpleasant was the affair of Professor Warren Rice's cat, a handsome if overfed ginger tom which was affectionately re-garded as a college mascot, often seen passing imperiously across the quadrangle on one or another mysterious errand. Following a hideous, agonized yowling in the small hours, the corpse of this creature was discovered on the sidewalk at West Street and Crane Street, which is overshadowed by the brooding outer wall of that part of our campus containing the departments of Geology, of Mediaeval Metaphysics, and of Physics. Dr Armitage drew attention to the fact that *intestines* and other inner organs were arranged around the dead cat in a kind of pattern or sigil; yet there was no mark or wound on its body; yet, again, its once ample abdomen seemed hollow and shrunken, skin stretched over bone, as though ...

The whirling extradimensional dance of the Hinton cubes still pursued me on sleepless nights, but like a blind fool I failed to make any of the logical connections which are supposed to be my trade. That day I saw but did not see what might have been odd stains on Parker's laboratory coat: his trance personality had become more voluble and lucid of late – though still less pleasant – and I felt myself upon the brink of great and burning truths. Who would have thought that that infinitesimal point we call the atomic nucleus might be broken into two fragments? We had very nearly laid our hand on the Philosopher's Stone of the old alchemists.

Meanwhile the *Arkham Advertiser*, starved for local news, had contrived a small campaign against careless driving within the town precincts. Other cats and dogs, it seemed, had met with unseemly ends, and automobiles were the obvious cause – at least to the newspaper. But in the senior common-room, as we dawdled over our coffee, Dr Armitage read the latest such news item aloud to Wilmarth (one of the instructors of literature), and in tones surely meant to be overheard added: "Odd that the remnants of these famous highway accidents are found on sidewalks, down narrow alleys or in entranceways rather than on the road. It is a pretty problem in physics."

"I beg your pardon?" I said, caught somewhat off-balance.

Armitage leaned towards me and said irrelevantly, "That man Parker seems fond of taking exercise in the small hours." In quieter tones: "I came across him talking to himself in Pickman Street a night or two ago. It was instructive to listen ... Have you thought of replacing him? He is perhaps not best suited to academic life."

"I think of the fellow as a lucky talisman," I answered with some honesty. "There's a touch of the *idiot savant* about him – it stimulates my research."

"Indeed. I noted that his peculiar jumble of muttered parataxis included phrases like this "nuclear fission" that has you scientists so excited nowadays. But I should inform you that it was the other component of that muttering which concerned me more; concerned me deeply. Dr Lake, may I invite you to visit our celebrated library?"

The wintry force of Armitage's personality drew me across the quadrangle in his wake, like a hooked fish. Oversized keys were turned in elaborate locks, and a minute or two later I was peering

at a great and yellowed volume which to me was wholly unintell-
igible. I do not read Latin.

Armitage said, chattily, "This is supposedly Olaus Wormius's
seventeenth-century translation from the Arabic of Abdul Alhazred
... but the provenance of the *Necronomicon* is a little like that of the
Centuries of Nostradamus. Many other cooks have added their own
ingredients to the broth. Now there is a passage of which I was put
in mind, two nights ago ... let me see ..." He turned the broad
pages and eventually indicated one passage with a hesitant finger.
"*Yog-Sothoth knows the gate, for Yog-Sothoth is the gate.* Why
should that make you jump? It is a routine invocation to the
guardian of the portal. But consider what follows –"

What followed was, I privately admitted, extraordinary. Were
it not for the refined tones of Dr Armitage translating at sight from
the crabbed Latin, it might have been Parker's own occluded personality that spoke. There were the glints and hints of physics,
coded as the alchemists encoded their true philosophical goals. I
felt a sudden chill when this centuries-old text prefigured the very
words which I had written in a worried letter to the expatriate
Hungarian physicist Leo Szilard that morning: "uranium chain
reaction". And all these nuggets of sense were intertwined with
legends of Great Old Ones who inhabited dimensions outside our
space (again I started convulsively) and waited for bloody portals
to open so that ultimately they might infuse their madness into this
world and, with infinite patience, claim it for their own. Once
again I felt poised on the verge of some great synthesizing theory;
but it eluded me.

"Fairy tales," I said stoutly when Armitage paused at last.
"Goblins to frighten children."

"It is badly written, badly organized," he conceded. "Alhazred
was always said to be mad. But *there is something in it*. I myself
have seen things that are not in any of your natural philosophy. Be
warned that you, here, in the modern era of 1939, are somehow
touching on these literally abominable matters. Walk with care."

It was his undeniable frosty sanity that perturbed me more than
the actual words. I left in great confusion of mind. Darkness filled
the open quadrangle outside; a high wind whipped streamers of
cloud across the sky, repeatedly veiling and unveiling the dim,
gibbous moon. For a long time I paced to and fro, wavering be-

tween concern over these sinister suggestions and resentment at being preached to in such terms by a mere elderly bibliophile. Could it truly be that all my work had been manipulated and directed through Parker's cryptic oracles? Towards what imaginable goal? And – a question which I had hitherto repressed, it being the proper concern of mysticism rather than science – if Parker were a channel through which insights flowed to me, what was "putting in" this information at the other end?

The night was bitter cold, and I realized I wore no overcoat; it was too late to be outdoors. I turned ... and have wondered whether the world's history might have been set on some other course had I not then noticed, in the college's bleak rows of windows, a dim light where no light should be. It was in Laboratory #2.

From time to time I had left the particle accelerator there to do its tireless work all through the night. Not tonight, however; and I always made very sure the laboratory was securely locked, for several of our bombardment samples were of pure gold or metals still more precious. I strode through the entrance arch. The inner door was indeed immovable. As I felt for the key I was struck by the hideous whimsy that a creature that slithered outside our mere three dimensions would find this door and wall no greater barrier than a line drawn on the ground – and for that matter could with equal facility scoop out an animal's entrails while leaving its skin and fur unmarked. Then the heavy door swung open to disclose that scene I have prayed to forget.

The room is dominated by the massive cowlings of the particle accelerator, aimed like a naval gun along the central workbenches and at the far wall. That night its low thrum of power and reek of ozone filled the room ... but there was another smell, for upon the floor, neatly laid out on folded sheets from the *Arkham Advertiser*, was just such an intestinal abomination as had flitted through my mind a few seconds past. What I saw there had, I realized, been a raccoon ... no, not "had been" but "was", for although the thing seemed partially everted in a mess of warm innards, a pitiful twitching and mewling gave evidence that it still lived.

So much for the lesser horror. Far worse was the figure that writhed and crooned to itself beyond the accelerator – a shape which indeed (for the beam target housing had been deliberately unbolted) seemed to bask and luxuriate in the high-energy particle stream, turning to and fro to savour the pale thread of ionization that should have scorched and wounded. Of course it was Parker, but Parker transformed and still transforming. His eyes were closed; his face wore, in concentrated form, that rictus of animal cunning I knew from his times of oracular delirium, but his body, his body ...

"Oh God," I heard myself whisper as vomit rose in my throat. His shifting torso slithered in an irregular cycle from flesh to writhing redness, a jumble of steaming worms and orifices that flowed liquidly around and away to reveal plain pallid flesh again. Though transfixed by these grisly, eye-deceiving metamorphoses, I had wit enough to make an intuitive connection with the Hinton cubes that still spun all too easily in my mind's eye. The Parker-thing was turning itself in the fourth dimension, lasciviously exposing its inner organs to the hot touch of the beam. Words cannot convey the foulness of the sight.

"The Masters shall have their sacrifice. The last letter has been sent. The portal shall open, and the many decades of the return shall begin at last. Iä! Yog-Sothoth! Iä! The burning portal, the greatest sacrifice ..."

The crooning tones continued. As a scientist I noted the unusual coherence and the similarities of phrasing to the *Necronomicon*. As a human being, I groped for the nearest weapon against terror – a heavy brass-bound collimating telescope that lay conveniently to hand in a jumble of optical gear. It clinked against a prism, alas, and at once Parker was staring at me.

"The good doctor," he sneered. "The Masters have no further need of you. The path to the great blood sacrifice has been cleared."

I stepped forward with stupid bravado, cheered by the heft of the brass cylinder. What I intended in that mad instant I shall never know: I hesitated, because on the floor between me and that still repulsively churning figure lay the tormented raccoon, which again made some small heart-rending noise. Torn between revulsion and new pity, I was suddenly mastered by the impulse to give it quick surcease. But as I raised the massy telescope to deliver a quick and merciful stroke, the thing that had once been a common sailor blurred and moved ... *around* the twenty or more feet that separated us.

He was before me, and the agony was instant and terrible, for – reaching in and around as I had once reached with a dreamed hand through that accursed angle of stone, he *placed his finger on my heart*. Pain and death jolted me like lightning; but my mercy-blow was already falling, and by a lucky chance Parker's bestially grinning features now lay in its path. The dreadful intrusion pulled from within me even as my first scream echoed through the bare-walled room. Crazed with fear and panic, I struck again and again until the hateful head was one red pulpy mess. He toppled, and (as once in the past) a merely human body lay before me.

Before falling silent forever, though, he regarded me with those dull eyes that had looked around forbidden corners of space/time, and uttered one last sentence in a thick, gloating voice. Already I had begun to have some inkling of the terrible burning portal and the multiplied hecatomb of lives whose sacrifice, so pleasing to the Old Ones, might give those incomprehensible entities a foothold in this world for their long, slow poisoning of all that is human in humanity, until ... but imagination fails.

Of course a handful of the Miskatonic University staff and faculty came seeking the source of my one scream. It was evil luck that they entered the laboratory precisely as I was engaged in putting the wretched raccoon instantaneously out of its misery, by dropping a small leaden isotope-safe at whose impact the creature's skull cracked like a rotted walnut. I did not mind the later attentions of the police one tenth as much as the glare of contempt and revulsion in Dr Henry Armitage's clear eyes. How could I explain? And whether it is the electric chair or the locked wing of Arkham Sanitarium that lies in wait for me, how now can I persuade my scientist correspondents Szilard, Teller and Wigner *not* to despatch that letter of urgent advice on the uses of uranium (which we hoped would also bear the signature of Einstein himself) to President Roosevelt? The dominoes are inexorably falling; the chain reaction has begun; and six years hence ...

That clotted, dying, yet triumphant voice had croaked: *"The shining portal shall open, and the Masters' required sacrifice shall be offered, at nine-fifteen in the morning of the sixth of August, 1945."*

The Case of Jack the Clipper
or: A Fimbulwinter's Tale

Life is filled with bodings and portents. When I encountered my old acquaintance Smythe in the High Street I sensed that my own life was about to take some strange new turning ... specifically, into the King's Head lounge bar, where with old-fashioned courtesy the renowned specialist in the uncanny reminded me that it was my shout.

"Cheers," I said a minute later, as we sat and sipped our bitter.

"*Ph'nglui mglw'nafh Cthulhu R'lyeh wgah'nagl fhtagn*," he responded eruditely; these occultists know many unfamiliar toasts. "I have just been picking up my new business cards – here, allow me to present you with one."

I studied the ornately engraved slip of pasteboard. *Dagon Smythe, Psychic Investigator*. "I can only admire the Seal of Solomon hologram ... but, *Dagon* Smythe?"

"It is often advantageous, in this hazardous line of work, to have been prudent in one's choice of godparents. But stay! As a trained observer, I see that you have torn the sleeve of your jacket, probably on a protruding nail. I am reminded ..."

"Is *that* the time?" I cried with the spontaneity that comes of long practice. "Well, I really must –"

"I am reminded," said Smythe inexorably, placing a gentle but firm hand on my forearm, "of a certain rather curious investigation in which nails played an interesting role. Nails, and old gods, and the end of the world."

"Why, yes! I remember that case well. One of your finest. The crooked occult-supplies house that used scanning tunnelling microscope technology to dismantle a nail from the True Cross into its individual atoms, enabling them to flood the market with countless billions of genuine if very tiny talismans and ...”

“A different case, my friend, and a different kind of nail. This was some years ago in the small old town of F—, which lies close to D— in the county of B—. It was there that I investigated a weird reign of nightly terror. You must imagine the town's twisty streets swirling with late autumn fogs, so that every passer-by appeared as an eerie, phantasmal silhouette. And any one of those shadows in the night might be the creature that had earned the nickname ... Jack the Clipper.”

“Ripper?” I enquired.

“Clipper. For, time and again, the men (never the women) of that accursed town would report dim memories of a particularly strange shape that loomed through icy fog. A shape with a hint of flickering flame about it, no sooner perceived than lost in a mysterious tumble into unconsciousness. Then, seconds or minutes afterwards, the victim would find himself sprawled on the chilly stone of the pavement, his shoes and socks mysteriously removed in that interlude of missing time, and – sinister and eldritch beyond all imagining – *his toenails neatly clipped*.”

At this point, being caught in mid-gulp, I suffered a regrettable accident with my pint of bitter.

“You laugh, do you? You laugh?”

“Some of the beer went the wrong way,” I lied, shaking my head determinedly.

“Shallow and innocent person that you are, ignorant of all occult implication, you laughed. It is not so funny when you recollect that nail-clippings – the *exuviae* coveted by witches – play an important part in rituals of binding, of magical domination. And this elusive Jack the Clipper had struck again and again, night after night, amassing these means of sorcerously controlling what might ultimately prove to be the entire male population of the town of F—.” He shuddered dramatically. “The hidden hand that wielded such control had the potential for unleashing very great evil indeed, up to and including a by-election victory for the Conservative Party. No ... this was indeed no laughing matter.”

I nodded dutifully. “And, er, this kind of voodoo control with sympathetic magic and waxen dolls and toenails, this was indeed the secret behind what was happening?”

“Oddly enough, it was not.” Smythe drained his glass and

placed it meaningfully on the table. I did the same, a trifle more meaningfully. There was a short pause.

Abruptly he continued: "You will remember my fervent belief in the value of applying the full range of modern technology to problems of occult investigation. I pioneered the Laser Pentacle, which outdid dear old Carnacki's electric version by vaporizing the more susceptible ab-human manifestations even as they attempted to pass through the wards. It was I who designed what has become the standard electronic probe for registering demonic presences, the Baphometer. Now the town of F— offered an opportunity to field-test my experimental, computerized zombie spotter."

"Pardon?" Sometimes my friend's uncanny intuitive leaps eluded me.

"This mechanism was inspired by what students of artificial intelligence call the Eliza Effect ... a shorthand for a kind of mental blindness which most human minds share. ELIZA is a rudimentary computer program which tries to imitate a psychotherapist – you type in something like 'WOULD YOU LIKE A DRINK?' –"

"Yes please," I said, quick as a flash; and quick as a flash, Smythe ignored me.

"– and the ELIZA program might come back with 'WHY DO YOU THINK I WOULD LIKE A DRINK?', or throw in some random question like 'WHAT MAKES YOU SAY THAT?' or 'INPUT ERROR $FF0021 REDO FROM START?' All very *mechanical* and uncreative. But such is the power of wishful thinking – the Eliza Effect – that it's incredibly easy to fall into the belief that the program's responses come from some real intelligence."

"From some real intelligence," I repeated intelligently.

"This, of course, is how zombies routinely pass in modern society: they have no more true conversation than ELIZA, but our natural, human weakness is to give them the benefit of the doubt. My zombie spotter, though, is a pocket computer with a speech-recognition facility. It lacks any power of wishful thinking. It analyses conversations with cold logic, and reports when the responses are sufficiently simple, repetitious and content-free – as is the case with zombies, and with minds whose free will has been overlaid by some form of malign poppetry, voodoo, or other sorcerous control. With this device –"

Here Smythe seemed to remember something, and mumbled

briefly in what I took to be Gaelic. I felt suddenly impelled to carry the empty beer-glasses to the bar, order two fresh pints of Tickle-penny's Old Ichorous, and bring them to our table.

"With this device in my pocket," Smythe went on after several grateful sips, "I sampled the population of F—, entering into numerous conversations in the local public houses, identifying victims of Jack the Clipper, and surreptitiously assessing the speakers' Zombie Quotient."

"You bought drinks for 'numerous' people!?" I said, aghast. Smythe's parsimony was famous in our little circle of friends.

"Er ..." The eminent occultist looked momentarily embarrassed. "Actually I used an old Irish charm I'd learned in my travels – a tiny *geas* that compels the hearer to acts of senseless generosity. It's quite harmless, although it does slightly lower the intelligence of the subject."

I didn't quite follow this odd explanation, and after puzzling over it for a few moments I indicated that Smythe should continue his fascinating narrative.

"On the whole, my zombie scan simply drew a blank. Of course there were a few significant ZQ readings from individuals whose higher brain functions had been depressed by excess alcohol, extreme fatigue or compulsive perusal of *The Sun*. But there was just no sign of the widespread occult control which I'd feared."

"Oh, bad luck. One of your rare failures, then."

"Failure? Am I not a scientific investigator? Was I to be discouraged by the slaying of my initial hypothesis by ugly fact? Never! However, I confess that I found myself momentarily at a loss; and so I determined to seek a new line of attack by the traditional means of haruspication."

I pondered that word. "What, cutting out someone's entrails? Did you call for volunteers, or something? 'Intrepid investigator needs men with guts.'"

"Tut, tut. Haruspication is the *examination* of entrails for hints of things to come. The definition says nothing about cutting them out. That was merely an unfortunate necessity imposed on the ancients by lack of appropriate technology. As you say, I called for an amply paunched volunteer, a recent victim of Jack the Clipper. The rest was merely a matter of a little influence and a little bribery at a convenient hospital which possessed ..." he paused dramatically ... "an ultrasound scanner."

"Excellent!" I cried.

"Elementary," said he. "Interpreting the convolutions of intestines which are quivering and peristalsing in real time is something of a specialist craft, I must remark, but well worth anyone's study. Long and hard I gazed into the ultrasound scan display, as one delusive word after another took shape in those loops and coils. And this –" he turned over the business card still lying on the table, and scribbled on its back – "*this* is the word that I finally read there."

I took up the card. "*Naglfar*? ... You're quite sure it isn't a misprint?"

"That one word, my friend, should have told you the whole story, had you been the ideal reasoner which, in fact, I am."

"It's an anagram of 'flagrant'? Well, nearly."

"It was sufficient, when I had thought things through, to persuade me to make a few unusual purchases: scuba gear, cylinders of oxygen and Halon 1301, the makings of a protective pentacle, and a small pair of toenail clippers.

"Picture me now, that night in my room at the town's one hotel, the Marquis of G—. I stood at the centre of an improvised defence pentacle which, for a particular reason, was picked out in ice cubes. I nervously checked the oxygen flow in the scuba rig, I struck a small flame from my cigarette lighter, and I cast my clipped toenails out across the psychic defences with the trembling words, 'An offering to you, oh Loki!'

"And, as I had hardly dared to hope, the god Loki appeared, emerging somehow from the fiery interior of the central heating pipes. Being a trickster deity, he had adopted the aspect of a used car salesman, but with hot flame flickering in his eyes. His questioning gaze seemed to burn through my skin.

"'I read the clues.' I said, 'Jack the Clipper preys on men and never on women, and as the world's foremost occult investigator I know my Norse myths. The *Naglfar* is the ship made of men's nails which you are fated to steer through the sea that rises to engulf the land when all Earth is destroyed in the final days of Ragnarok. Of course you chose toenails rather than fingernails, owing to their superior quality as a maritime construction material. But I've no idea why you should collect the wherewithal to build that dread vessel in a dull town like this.'

"'Trickster gods are allowed to be as silly and capricious as they like,' Loki explained, stepping forward: 'And *of course* I picked an obscure place where Odin wouldn't think to look.' The words emerged in individual gouts of flame, reminiscent of a circus fire-eater with hiccups. 'Ouch. By Niflheim!' Being also a fire god, my visitor did not relish the ice pentacle ... but nevertheless slowly forced his way through my wards in a cloud of hissing steam. His nostrils literally flared. 'I should add that fire gods have this regret-table habit of slowly incinerating mortals who ask impertinent questions.'

"But I had already clapped the scuba mask to my face and released the valve on that Halon 1301 cylinder. The occult words of banishment which I pronounced – the unknown last line of the Maastricht agreement – were drowned in the hiss of escaping gas and might or might not have been effective. But I think I have successfully ascertained that fire gods particularly detest an atmo-sphere that's rich in fire-inhibiting Halon. Before he could reach me, Loki fizzled and shrank and went out like, if you'll excuse the cliché, a light.

"And so the mystery was solved. The town of F— heard no more of Jack the Clipper. Perhaps the fiery prankster's sinister work continues elsewhere in the world...."

"A truly remarkable farrago," I mumbled, my head still spinning slightly.

"All of which explains my new-found interest in cryonics," said Smythe with an air of considerable smugness.

"Of course," I replied weakly, determined not to ask the ob-vious question. My friend was visibly too pleased with himself to prolong the suspense any further.

"I have a notion, you see, that Loki the trickster was also maliciously sowing trouble for the gods themselves. The whole Norse pantheon is notoriously bound up in chains of unescapable fate. That which is written will be ... and one of the things clearly written about the *Naglfar* is that it will be made of *dead* men's nails. So, you see, the end of the world, Ragnarok, can't come to pass until all those victims of 'Jack the Clipper' – men whose toenails are built into the fateful ship – are safely dead."

"Oh, wonderful. The world's safe for another – what? – fifty years?"

"Forever, perhaps, if some of those toenail donors are kept cry-
onically preserved at liquid-nitrogen temperatures. You must know
that some people actually *pay* to be frozen in hope of eternity. So
I am currently working to make certain lucrative arrangements
with sympathetic Scandinavian governments, in hope of financing
cryonics projects which could hold off Ragnarok indefinitely. You
may be sitting with – and, indeed, about to buy another drink for
– the saviour of this world." Smythe gave a little bow.

A single, tiny fragment of Norse myth had meanwhile floated
to the surface of my own mind. "Ah ... Smythe. According to those
same legends, one of the fated circumstances that leads up to
Ragnarok and the last battle is the Fimbulwinter. A deep, unnatural
winter. A long period of intense and artificial cold. Um, are you
sure your cryonics scheme isn't already part of what's written?"

For the first time since I'd known him, Smythe looked non-
plussed.

Not Ours To See

The usual group of old acquaintances was gathered in the lounge bar of the King's Head pub, huddled over pints of traditionally insipid beer and speculating upon the infinite.

"If ..." said crusty old Major Godalming to me, "if only it were possible! To pierce the veil of futurity, to glimpse the ineffable radiance of days to come, and to make an absolute killing in the National Lottery!"

Carruthers snorted. "Speaking mathematically, I can inform you that if it were possible to predict next week's winning numbers, half the country would very soon be doing it and the payout per one-pound ticket would slump to approximately 13.7 pence." Like all the best statistics, this had the compelling air of having been freshly made up on the spot.

Among our circle that evening was the well-known psychic investigator Dagon Smythe, who preserved his silence but now shuddered theatrically. I recognized the symptoms and took rapid action, crying: "Beastly weather this week, chaps! Would you call it seasonal for the time of year?"

But it was too late. Before the razor-sharp wits around the table could pounce upon this always fruitful topic, Smythe interrupted in his peculiarly penetrating tones. "Speaking of prediction ... I once dabbled a little in the divinatory arts."

"And you have a tale to tell," said old Hyphen-Jones with a trace of resignation.

"Of a terrible and frightening experience," Smythe continued unstoppably. "But I anticipate. Let us begin from first principles. Methods of prediction are quite numerous. Palmistry, for example, has its adherents ..." I am of the opinion that our friend had learned his anecdotal persistence from the Ancient Mariner. He seized my hand and announced that the Line of Life indicated a small but imminent financial upset, such as might be caused by buying a round of drinks. As I pointed out with some bitterness, the loud and eager assent of the others made this a regrettably self-fulfilling prophecy.

When I returned from the bar with my slopping burden, Smythe had completed a brief demonstration of cartomancy using only a handful of beer-mats, and was well launched into his narration. "The problem with all the well-known modes of divination is, if I might put it paradoxically, that they are too well-known."

"Incredible," grunted old Hyphen-Jones.

"I have formulated what might usefully be known as Smythe's Law: that too many prophets spoil the broth. That is, predictions by cartomancy or crystallomancy suffer aetheric interference from all the thousands of other enthusiasts with their Tarot decks and crystal balls. Those faint shadows cast back through time by future events might be likened to frail and shy creatures of the night, suddenly confronted by the psychic equivalent of a horde of press photographers with flashguns. The sheer pressure of attention dispels any possible message. I will not mention Heisenberg's Uncertainty Principle ..."

"Thank God," I muttered. I have always admired Smythe's genius for selecting awesomely bad analogies.

"Sounds like you've just shot down the whole idea of successful divination," said the acute Carruthers.

"Not at all. To vary the metaphor a little, the trick is to listen on a less crowded waveband. For example: haruspication, the art of prediction through the study of fresh animal entrails, is rarely practised – and please, Major, please don't make your usual joke about the contents of the hamburgers they serve here."

Major Godalming projected sulkiness into his mug of beer.

"So when I set about the series of predictive experiments that had such ultimately unsettling results, I sifted the more obscure divinatory modes. Have you ever heard of spodomancy, the finding of portents in ashes? Or ophiomancy, all done by study of serpents? (You just can't get the serpents these days.) Or rhabdomancy, the use of divining rods? That's supposed to be good for locating water and oil, but one doesn't see where to point the rod to take aim at the future. Sideromancy involves watching the movement of straws placed on red-hot irons, but it turned into spodomancy too quickly for me – or capnomancy, which is divination by smoke, if I hadn't been too busy coughing. Ceromancy uses melting wax, which gets all over everything. Myomancy depends on the actions of mice; all my mice seemed to do was eat and pee a lot (but let's not talk about uromancy). Cromyomancy is prediction by cutting up and studying onions ... I tried that diligently, but it all ended in tears.

"Once I even came to this very public house and attempted both oenomancy – using libations of wine – and gyromancy, being divination performed by walking in a circle until dizziness supervenes. And I want you to know that the conclusions which you lot all loudly drew were both distracting and unfair."

Meanwhile Carruthers appeared to be demonstrating divination by utter apathy and torpor, or – as it is technically known – dormancy. I suggested gently, "Perhaps we could skip the failures and hear about the experiment that worked?"

"Er, yes. Actually it is a trifle embarrassing. In addition to the need, according to Smythe's Law, to use a rare and obscure divinatory focus, you have to find something that specifically works for you. Someone who can achieve nothing at all through stichomancy (using random literary extracts ... I thought you'd never ask) might find his hotline to the future lay in lampadomancy (which is divination through the use of a torch-flame). In the end, ah, I came across my own personal 'mancy' when I was, um, feeding the cat."

"Divination through observation of cats!" marvelled Hyphen-Jones. "That would be, let me think ... *ailuromancy*."

"Not quite," Smythe mumbled. "I appear to have been the first prophetic investigator to stumble upon *ailurotrophemancy*, or divination through the study of cat-food."

We sat aghast.

"Not just *any* cat-food, mind you. It was a rather expensive brand called Vitamog, to which my little tomcat Pyewacket was unreasonably addicted. The effect was remarkable! As I spooned out those glistening, glutinous lumps of what purported to be gourmet-cooked liver ... by the way, divination by inspecting the livers of animals is known as hepatoscopy ... where was I? Oh yes: I saw ... visionary things in the Vitamog. You may well snigger, gentlemen, but I saw it: glinting fragments of the future. There was one flash of a newspaper headline – ROYAL SEX SCANDAL: MONARCHY DOOMED? – and sure enough, it appeared on the front page of *The*

Times on the very next day."

"As indeed it does in most weeks," said Carruthers the die-hard sceptic.

"There were other confirmations, though rarely anything truly useful. A vision, accurate to the penny, of the total amount of my next grocery bill. A glimpse of a blazing car which within the week I saw again in a James Bond movie on TV. And for natural reasons of sympathetic magic, I often saw the future doings of cats in my back garden. Disappointing, really, once the first amazement had worn off. We psychic investigators are above mere sordid matters of finance, but –" here a note of sadness entered Smythe's voice – "one good stock-market tip or set of winning lottery numbers would have been useful objective confirmation."

"Hear, hear," said the Major, with feeling.

"One point of minor interest was that, although I experimented with other brands of feline food, only Vitamog ever glistened with numinous visions. Even Powermog, from the same manufacturers, was of no divinatory use at all. One wonders what the closely guarded secret formula for Vitamog might be.... But at the time this seemed a trivial issue compared to my growing sense that there were good reasons for my seeing only these tantalizing glimpses beyond the present day. Something else, something greater and darker, overshadowed everything I scried in the oracle of the Vitamog. Day after day, as tin after tin of the miraculous cat-food passed through Pyewacket and into history, I saw that my view of the future was being obscured by a monstrous, formless foretelling which – if I may lapse for one moment into the technical jargon of the occult – was heavily *doom-laden* and exuded a pungent *reek of wrongness.*"

"*My* cat keeps herself perfectly clean," said Hyphen-Jones.

"Psychic wrongness, my friend. Day by day the sense of doom grew: a terrible blank, as though something were coming irrevocably to an end. By reference to the few glimpses to which I was able to assign future dates, I gleaned that absolutely no forthcoming events after a certain date – the sixteenth of June this year – could be seen. It was as though the world were fated to be swallowed up by one of those nameless but inconceivably deadly astral entities from the Outer Spheres. A fearful burden of knowledge, as you might imagine. And then I was seized with a more personal fear."

"This would be the old one about not being able to see beyond the end of your own life?" suggested Carruthers, who like the rest of us had heard scores of Smythe's psychic anecdotes and developed a certain uncanny skill at divination through literary familiarity. (Would that be called romancy?) "Yet here we are in the month of November and there you sit, which does rather lessen the suspense."

"It is a distinct problem of this narrative form," Smythe agreed with a sigh. "But there was a tragedy, nonetheless. If only I had been able properly to interpret the meaning of that awful blankness!"

Hyphen-Jones said, "Obviously it was the cat who snuffed it. Poor old Pyewacket."

"Hush," said Smythe. "I took careful occult precautions as 16 June approached and time – all of time, everywhere – seemed to be running out. The utter emptiness of the revealed future was deeply unnerving. On the evening of 15 June I constructed a pentacle and multiple layers of psychic wards to defend against whatever threatened. I was resolved to stay within these supernatural defences for the whole of the fatal day, plus a few extra hours for luck. As midnight approached, I opened the last tin of Vitamog remaining in the house, and stared into a final scrying-bowl of the catalytic cat-food – to see only one blurred and tantalizing glimpse of a daily newspaper, before all of futurity was swallowed in that frightful blank. Then I entered the pentacle to await destiny. You can imagine the psychic turmoil that racked me through the 24 hours that followed ..."

"We can," I said. "Effortlessly."

"Well, it was a strain. Pyewacket mewed a great deal and refused to remain within the wards; at one stage he departed through the back-door cat-flap and returned with a present in the form of one of the neighbours' goldfish ... which I decided not to use for ichthyomancy. Otherwise, events were few."

"And when the fateful day was over?"

"Ah, now comes the interesting part of the story. At dawn on the 17th, I cautiously emerged from my pentacle and found the world unchanged ... except that, as usual, the previous day's newspaper had been delivered and lay on the doormat. With a

thrill of recognition, I saw that the layout of the front page corresponded to the last fading vision which I had obtained through
ailurotrophemancy!" Smythe fumbled in his wallet. "I have the
relevant clipping here. It was the smallest story on the front page,
but not without a certain piquant intellectual interest. See!"

> CAT-ASTROPHIC. Following a scare about poisonous con-
> taminants in some tins, MoggiMunch Ltd have today
> completely withdrawn their Vitamog brand of tinned cat-
> food from the market. The sister brands Powermog and
> MoggiGorge are unaffected.

A somewhat protracted silence followed.

"Now," said Smythe with a rhetorical wave of his hand, "which
of you mentioned "the old one about not being able to see beyond
the end of your own life"? The psychic implications are so very
fascinating, the more you consider them...."

We looked at him. It was hard to know what to say, but
eventually I found appropriate words to honour his raconteur skills.
"Smythe," I said, "it's your turn to buy the drinks."

There was general applause.

The Case That Never Was

"There are some things," old Hyphen-Jones complained, "that it should be impossible to forget."

Conversation at our usual table in the King's Head pub was wandering, with the remorseless focus of a drunken bluebottle, around that day's lead story in the *Times*. One of the top secret installations at the Robinson Heath research centre not far from our town had incontinently blown itself to smallish pieces.

"Forgotten is what it says here," Major Godalming grumbled. "Ministry of Defence spokesman in love with the sound of his own voice. 'A technician may have *forgotten* to check the safety inter-locks on the tachyon beam generator,' or some such scientific gobbledegook. There's no bloody discipline these days."

"Speaking of forgetfulness," said Dagon Smythe the celebrated psychic investigator, watchful as ever for narrative openings, "I am irresistibly reminded of what must be my own least unforgettable case...."

We sensed at once that to query the odd phrase "least un-forgettable" would lead us neatly into the trap of another Smythe reminiscence. With practised diversionary tactics the Major offered another round of drinks, while Hyphen-Jones said in his most unencouraging tones: "I suppose you investigated some pheno-mena at Robinson Heath? Jolly good. Someone wrote a book about the place, I seem to remember, and ..."

"I have never in my life been to Robinson Heath," said Smythe with unnatural portentousness, subtly different from the man's routine, daily portentousness. "That, in a way, is the heart of the matter."

Short of pressing a handkerchief to one's nose and running to the door shouting "The blood! the blood!" – a technique over-used in past sessions at the King's Head – there seemed no way of de-

flecting another occult anecdote. Resignedly we sipped at the fresh
pints the Major had brought from the bar, and settled ourselves to
listen.

"Of course we world-famous psychic consultants are always
being called in by industry nowadays. Uri Geller picks up a tidy
sum from big oil companies, and I understand he's located vast
untapped deposits on Venus, the moons of Jupiter, and underneath
Buckingham Palace. Not long ago I undertook a major investigation
for a contraceptive manufacturer whose name you will all know –"
(the Major looked momentarily apoplectic) "– and traced their
quality control problem to a disaffected employee. This rebel had
picked up a smattering of voodoo and was secretly jabbing pins
into a small model of, of an organ whose name you will all know,
a model tightly sheathed in latex. Such is the deadly power of sympathetic magic.... But I digress."

"You always bloody do," said Hyphen-Jones just audibly, but
subsided when Smythe gave him a glance containing rather more
than British health and safety regulations' permitted content of Evil
Eye.

"But the story I had in mind, or had such difficulty in bringing
to mind, concerns the unusual haunting last July of a particular
public house, being the King's Head in Redbury."

"As in, the pub we're sitting in now? I don't remember anything
of the sort," said Carruthers, gesturing suspiciously with a cheese
and onion crisp.

Smythe allowed himself a tight smile. "This will presently
become plain as you learn more of what my memoirs are likely to
call ... The Case That Never Was."

Not the least of this man's paranormal talents was the eerie
power to talk in capitals.

"The early symptoms of the King's Head haunting were minor,
and of course I hesitated to intrude, since one would hardly care to
embarrass our good landlord Kevin with the dread, soul-chilling
knowledge of how modern psychic investigation can tear aside the
flimsy veil of mundane reality to disclose the enormity of our
consultation fees.

"Yet despite myself I was intrigued. Fellow-patrons of this
tavern claimed to hear anguished words in the flushing sounds of
the gentlemen's toilet, words which I pieced together as significant

extracts from the *Bardo Thödol*, the Tibetan Book of the Dead. One morning Kevin's entire stock of darts was found jammed into the dartboard, picking out the shape of the Eye of Horus. Another day disclosed the potent Trismegistus Pentacle outlined in dry-roast peanuts upon the fast food counter. Then there was the transmutation of an entire barrel of best bitter to what I eventually identified as pregnant bats' urine."

Hyphen-Jones frowned. "I *definitely* don't remember that."

"But I assure you that – after drinking almost a full pint to convince yourself that something was amiss – you complained bitterly and at length."

"Complained bitterly about the bitter! Oh, that's a good one." chortled the Major from somewhere on the bosky fringes of inebriation, and continued to guffaw until I dug my elbow into the old fool's ribs.

"Believe me, I would *not* forget an experience of that nature," cried the increasingly sceptical Hyphen-Jones.

"Hear me out, my friend. The urine of gravid bats is an ingredient of some magical potency, just as the other manifestations were words and symbols of known power – this was, don't you see, an intensely *knowledgable* haunting."

"Someone who'd read your latest article on black magic and exorcism in the *National Enquirer* was having you on?" Carruthers suggested.

"More hints along the same rough lines continued to emerge," said Smythe, imperturbably spilling beer into Carruthers's lap. "The Voorish Sign scrawled in tomato sauce across the bar mirror. A deposit in the ashtrays which Kevin blamed on lazy cleaners but which I readily identified as the prophylactic powder of Ibn Ghazi. And then we found an invocation to Yog-Sothoth cunningly woven into the list of bar prices ... all dark magics from the dread *Necronomicon* of Abdul Al-Hazred, a forbidden grimoire which few believe even to exist and fewer still have glimpsed, let alone read. (I myself, of course, have a signed first edition.)

"In short, it was clear that the restless spirit of the King's Head was no ordinary ghost, poltergeist or earthbound soul. Run-of-the-mill spectres can contrive no more than the occasional sinisterly creaking floorboard, or some added note of woe in the groanings of the central heating pipes, or perhaps a sense of muted oppression not easily distinguished from a mild hangover. This, by contrast, was a being of resourceful intelligence and stupendous psychic force. An entity whose manifestations were tailor-made to pique the interest and attract the expert attention of no less an authority than ... Dagon Smythe!"

Although he'd speeded up a little to compensate, the raconteur's subclimax was still overshadowed by the noisy and carefully timed departure of Hyphen-Jones for the lavatory. More drinks were bought, while I struggled in vain to recall any of these doom-laden events. Oblivion blindly scattereth her poppy, wrote Sir Thomas Browne, but did this same Lethean power dwell in Kevin's not terribly potent keg bitter? Or, heresy of heresies, could it be that some of Smythe's astonishing narratives were *mere invention*?

Soon the circle around our table was complete again. "At last came the fateful night," the occultist continued in low and thrilling tones, "when I realized what I must do. It was necessary to key myself up to a peak of psychic receptiveness and pass the hours of darkness here at the focus of the haunting – the lounge bar. Kevin agreed readily enough, and only Major Godalming stooped to making coarse and obvious jokes when at closing time I laid myself down to enter the trance state upon this very carpet."

"I never –" blurted the Major, but we hushed him. There was a growing sense of curious satisfaction amongst our little gathering of cronies, who bore the unfailingly loquacious investigator no ill-will – but were now looking forward to twitting him during his future accounts of the incredible, with interjected reminders of this adventure which so provably never occurred.

"So there I lay, my eyes closed and mind emptied of thoughts, my head resting on a stack of odically sterilized beer mats, and my nostrils filled with stale beer ..."

"That must have made it hard to breathe," Hyphen-Jones said innocently.

"With the *smell* of stale beer. You must understand that I was in a dangerously vulnerable state, wide open to ab-human and satanic influences. I was risking life and sanity on my intuition that something from beyond was seeking benevolent contact. It was then that I felt – not the expected spiritual effulgence – but a sudden physical blow!"

"My God!" I said, feeling that someone should. "What was it?"

"Our landlord, on that very special night when I was to be alone, had forgotten to cancel the cleaners' visit. The lady with the broomstick and bucket was persuaded to go away when I crossed her palm with paper, and I resumed my vigil.

"It was in the small hours that I felt it, elusive and inchoate, like the first faint tendrils of shy publicity that herald a blockbuster Hollywood spectacular many months in the future. The sensation of contact grew and grew as I focused all the matchless powers of concentration that once enabled me very nearly to finish *Dianetics* by L. Ron Hubbard. At last I felt the subtle thrill of total psychic intertwingling. *Only you can help me* was the gist of what first impinged on my sensorium. No feeble lost soul, this, but an intelligence of awesome stature and moral courage, wordlessly struggling to deliver a desperately urgent *warning* – which chilled my soul as I eventually began to comprehend its implications...."

"Which were –?"

"It was inherent in the nature of the warning," said Smythe blandly, "that I should ... forget."

"Oh good grief," Hyphen-Jones muttered *sotto voce*. "Not so *damned* shaggy ..."

Smythe ignored him. "Which brings me to the much more recent occasion when I was reminded of that agonized communication – when the buried memory rose up and tapped me on the shoulder. You will know, because I told you earlier, that we world-class psychic consultants are frequently called in by major industries when all else fails.

"I myself have made a particular study of the 'experimenter effect', in which sensitive apparatus can be adversely affected by its unwitting operators' raw psychic emanations. Indeed I investigated a certain computer operating system whose name you will all know but I am not at liberty to divulge. Suffice it to say that my report arguing that virtually all its apparent lapses can be traced to negative user vibrations was very highly regarded by Microsoft. But, ha ha, I digress.

"So when, just a few days ago, I was invited to check out experimenter effects believed to be causing particle beam instability in a certain cutting-edge research project at the Robinson Heath establishment –" he tapped the copy of the *Times* on the table, still turned to show its front-page ATOM BASE DISASTER headline – "I remembered that chill contact from beyond. I recalled how by making one firm decision never to visit a certain place, I had ended the haunting that never was ... and so I had no hesitation in refusing the Robinson Heath commission. Now, of course, you understand everything!"

"No," we chorused dutifully.

"But all the facts lie before you. You know my methods: apply them. An experimental tachyon beam, as it says here. What are tachyons? Faster-than-light particles that can theoretically travel backwards in time. By not entering that doomed building yesterday, I deftly avoided being vaporized when the beam installation blew, whereupon the uncontrolled tachyon blast would have hurled my soul back to last July – to make its painful way to one of my favourite haunts, the King's Head, and there laboriously attract my attention in order to communicate a warning...."

We sat aghast.

"Resourceful intelligence. Stupendous psychic force," said Hyphen-Jones after a moody pause. "Awesome stature and moral courage. We should have known at once who it had to be."

"Since I took heed and stayed well clear of Robinson Heath, the haunting of this lounge bar never came about. Reality twisted, events took another course – and that, my friends, is why my greatest, most triumphantly successful investigation has retrospectively become The Case That Never Was."

"You're talking in capitals again," said Carruthers. "But if all those events were erased from history, just how is it that you remember them?"

"Aha." Smythe's tones attained new levels of portentous significance. "Firstly, there are arcane secrets of time, space and destiny that puny mortal minds are ill-fitted to comprehend. Secondly, it seems that temporal reality is strangely plastic and does not immediately adjust. Thirdly, er, ah, remember what? I really don't understand your question."

"Forgot what I was saying," Carruthers confessed cheerily. "My round, I think.... Good heavens, it's nearly closing time! Where did the evening go?"

"At least we didn't have to put up with any of Smythe's bloody self-aggrandizing stories tonight," said Hyphen-Jones. "A small mercy which none of us should forget."

Sex Pirates of the Blood Asteroid

E.E. Sm*th

Trapped!

That was Cosmic Agent Mac Malsenn's thought as he surveyed the desolate surface of the airless planet. Behind him, his ship the *Star Vole* lay canted at an angle on the rocks, seemingly undamaged – but the drive and communicators were useless.

The ambush had been cunningly planned; the intention was to trap him in the gravitational collapse of an entire galaxy. In escaping, he had burnt out two essential drive components: a left-handed sprocket and a rubber band. The latter he had replaced, using his own springy hair to braid a substitute – but no sprocket could be found.

"Damit!" he cried, lapsing into German.

Above him there leered the camera eye of a synchronous-orbit satellite, a hundred metres up. It seemed that the galactic arch-fiend Nivek, setter of the trap, intended to watch his death. He had less than an hour to wait, for Malsenn felt the unmistakable twinges of his old H-bomb wound which meant the sun would shortly go nova. Meteorites thudded into the ground – he dodged them automatically while pondering the problem.

Perhaps, in the satellite –?

As soon as the thought came to him, he fired his blaster, which would bring down anything not fitted with a fourth-order interference screen.

The satellite was fitted with a fourth-order interference screen.

The sun was growing brighter.

Malsenn dashed into his ship and tore loose two hundred

metres of connecting cables. Swiftly he fashioned a lasso, and, again outside, flung the noose up at the satellite. It caught, and held. Now he had only to drag it down, remove the sprocket of its drive, and freedom would be in sight.

He dragged. The satellite responded automatically, firing auxiliary jets to support his weight and maintain its synchronous orbit.

"Rampant reactors!" he swore. Grimly he climbed the cable. Soon he reached the tiny satellite, and rapidly removed a side panel. There, before his very eyes, was a drive sprocket! He wrenched it out eagerly. The satellite began to fall, its jets useless. In haste, Malsenn replaced the sprocket. Once more the jets fired, and the original orbit was restored. This was something of a problem. The sunlight was close to intolerable. There was no way to deactivate the interference screens or bring the satellite down without falling to his death. He climbed down the cable again, and thought hard.

Wait! How did the satellite "know" what height to maintain? It must use a radar altimeter, since the world was airless. And, in that case, it could be deceived.

He drew his potent blaster and vaporized the rocky ground until a huge pit lay below the point where the satellite orbited. Taking the bottom of the pit as ground-level, it drifted down; as the pit grew deeper, so the automatic controls brought the flying sphere closer, until it hovered in powered synchronous orbit, a metre from the ground. Malsenn stood on the edge of the pit, reached out, and grabbed the sprocket. The satellite fell. Fitting the vital part into his own drive unit, he dashed for the controls and prepared to blast off. Nothing happened. The controls connected to the drive *via* cables – which were now a hundred metres down in the pit.

Time was running out. The sun was about to blow. Striking sparks from his emergency flint, Malsenn ignited the drive-jets manually.

The *Star Vole* was in space three seconds later; the sun went nova at the same time.

"I suppose I'm just lucky," Malsenn thought, removing his helmet and gasping in exhaustion. He continued to gasp. As a sudden afterthought, he closed the airlock.

The scent was cold, but still Nivek and his dark doings must be sought out and extirpated. So, some days later, a disguised Malsenn slipped into one of those underworld dens where weak-minded persons enjoyed forbidden pleasures. He hoped to find some clue to Nivek's vast schemes, for well he knew that the devilish warlord was behind much of the depravity in the Galaxy.

He sat watchfully. A lascivious "hostess" sidled up to him, and Malsenn stiffened in alarm. In this hellish pit of vice, they had revived all the old, promiscuous ways of the twentieth century ... he could see her ankle.

"Wanna good time?" she breathed, swaying sinuously.

Malsenn stood nervously erect. Then he stepped back in horror as her scanty clothes slipped suddenly and slitheringly to the floor, as in that same moment did her skin, revealing the starkly inimical form of a Vomisa killer robot! With a swift and savage motion, it locked steel claws round Malsenn's neck and squeezed violently. He struggled in desperation against its merciless strength. The other carousers left hurriedly.

"I'm human, you moronic machine!" he gasped. "What about ... the First Law?" The robot whirred and clicked.

"Brrrp! A robot may not injure a human being ... Not relevant. I have not been instructed as to the meaning of the word 'injure'." It tightened its grip.

"You're – gnnnh – doing – it – now –"

"Unauthorized personnel may not tamper with memory structures," the robot grated.

"Second Law! I ... aaah ... COMMAND you to stop ..."

"I am yours to command. As soon as I have carried out my current orders."

In despair Malsenn lashed out with his foot, aiming for the robot's delicate power-leads, where the legs joined the body. Its gears crashed; it staggered back, releasing him. As it approached once more, Malsenn flung chairs and tables at it without making any visible impression.

"Third Law –" it droned implacably. "You will pay for this."

If only he had his blaster! Or a radioactive source, which would deactivate the robot's hydroponic brain. But a pocket torch was his only weapon. He flashed it in his opponent's photoreceptors, but in vain: still the death-machine closed in for the kill.

Wait! What a fool he'd been! Malsenn's almost incredible muscular strength could produce gamma rays, if he timed it right ... He hurled the torch at the advancing robot with sinew-wrenching force. It hurtled forward at unspeakable speed – 10^7 times the velocity of light. The Doppler blueshift increased the frequency of light falling on the robot, up through the ultraviolet and X-ray bands, until hard gamma rays destroyed its very mind. The speeding torch struck, an infinitesimal fraction of a second later, and knocked it over. Malsenn fled – not knowing that he had a follower.

His sweetheart Laura was waiting for him in her room. He entered eagerly; she beckoned him to sit by her.

"We are alone at last," she said softly.

"Yes, utterly alone," Malsenn replied, a little apprehensively. But suddenly a strange romantic feeling came over him, and he felt his icy control slipping. Throwing caution to the winds, he moved towards her as the door shattered under the impact of a second Vomisa robot, which proceeded to menace them with a stungun.

With superhuman agility Malsenn dodged the crackling knockout charge that arced from the gun's ugly snout. But still he was caught in a wash of diffracted radiation: numbness began to spread over him. Laura slumped, unconscious.

"Those things take five minutes to recharge," he grinned, fumbling for the multimegaton blaster on the table.

"Correct." The robot produced a blaster of its own, and fired at point-blank range. Ravening energies tore at his body; in microseconds all that remained of Cosmic Agent Mac Malsenn was a fine organic ash and a few scattered gobs of protoplasm. Shouldering Laura's inert form, the robot left, closing the door carefully behind it.

"I have not been instructed as to the meaning of the word 'robot'," it remarked apologetically.

"By golly, I'm glad I let the Cosmic Patrol finance that regeneration technique which restores whole bodies from a single cell!" So saying, Malsenn sprang lithely from his hospital bed.

But what had become of Laura? As he shaved, attacking his whiskers with a tiny nuclear flame-gun, this thought was uppermost in his mind. The bathroom's intercom buzzed, and the voice of Alkloyd, the Starfleet commander, came through.

"Malsenn, is that you? Nivek's got her!" Malsenn's hand jerked, and he singed himself. The voice went on: "And he's offering to exchange her for you. – You mustn't go of course. After all, she's only a woman ..."

"Only a woman!" he raged. "She's a Grade A product ... six-nines quality ... unique. And I kinda like her too."

Embarrassed by his outburst, he flushed, and strode out of the bathroom, heading for Alkloyd's office.

"This just – burns me up," he said, pacing the floor and rubbing his scorched chin.

"There is an alternative." Alkloyd pulled a sheet of paper from the teletype.

THERE IS AN ALTERNATIVE, it said. IN EXCHANGE FOR THE HOSTAGE I AM PREPARED TO ACCEPT 500 BATTLE-SQUADRONS FROM STARFLEET – NIVEK.

"We can spare that many," mused Alkloyd. "We just now fitted up a thousand squadrons for the secret reserves."

The teletype clattered. PS: AND ANOTHER 1000 FROM THE SECRET RESERVES – NIVEK.

"We'll meet the terms." Alkloyd stood up. "Remember, there are always –" his voice fell, but he caught it just in time – "the secret weapons."

"True," Malsenn agreed. "But I'm still going to go ... now."

"You must stay with Starfleet! They need you!"

"Goodbye. I'll be back – with Laura!" Alkloyd winced as the door slammed. Of course, Starfleet must follow, to back Malsenn's wild gamble. With sudden pride, he breathed the Starfleet anthem:

Forward, fleet, and fight the foe –
Tubes ignite and rockets blow-
See Mac Malsenn, our defender,
Making aliens all surrender!

Far off, in the *Star Vole*, Malsenn scanned the detector screen. In all the vast immensity of space, one signal stood out: a brilliant blip flashing in the lurid orange-and-purple coding which showed that it represented an object screened against all forms of detection.

Surely this must be Nivek! He engaged the new ultradrive, a device which set up a quasi-solid tube of force along which space itself was sucked by capillary action, and the ship leapt forward at billions of parsecs per second. The slower vessels of Starfleet followed faithfully in his wake.

Ultraspace! A sense of aching vastness, of shifting parallax and perspective, unthinkable transitions in which the curvatures of space writhe between positive and negative ... Food concentrates had never suited Malsenn's digestion, but soon his hasty meal was over. Liquid water was an embarrassment in free-fall, and so Malsenn quenched his thirst by chewing a juicy gob of jellylike polywater.

Still travelling at unthinkable velocities, he approached Nivek's monster battle-cruiser, which proved to be shaped like a gigantic cup. The sharp prow of the *Star Vole* penetrated with ease the theoretically impervious energy-fields of the defensive system; space was filled with a hissing sound as layer on layer of screens deflated and collapsed. Malsenn's ship struck the side of the huge dreadnought and stuck there, quivering.

Meanwhile, on the bridge of the enemy craft, the *Saucy Flier*, Nivek himself paced up and down, thanks to the magnetic boots which enabled him to walk on the walls. From time to time he glanced at the corner where sat the helpless figure of Laura, and he drooled lecherously. Yet still his warped mind conceived new, evil schemes.

"I shall release rabid rogue rodents on every planet of the Galaxy," he muttered. "I shall cause the stars to go out ... In the end when I am done, there will be nothing left but the mice and the darkness!" A satanic grin twisted his face, and he gloated all over the room. "Christ, what an imagination I've got!"

At that instant, a clang resounded through the hull. "Curses!" cried the fiendish master of subterfuge, "we've hit another galaxy ... No, wait! We're not moving. Which means ..." He leapt to the controls and activated the Hallucinatory Defence systems.

As Malsenn entered the airlock of the *Saucy Flier*, reality suddenly blurred. He found himself looking into a steaming tropical jungle, inhaling rank odours from an unseen swamp. As he gaped in amazement, a pink Tyrannosaurus rex lumbered on its eldritch course towards him, displaying numerous rows of badly cared-for teeth. His blaster bolts had no effect on the great reptile, which blithely ignored the destroying energies, and proceeded to bite Malsenn in the leg. The pain was excruciating. *It must be an illusion*, Malsenn reasoned to himself. *No real reptile is coloured fluorescent pink* ... Acting on this insight, he strained his mind to erect a thought screen: *I reject this hallucination*, he cried mentally. *I disbelieve it utterly*. The forest wavered – vanished as though it had never been. Malsenn floated in empty space.

But I do believe in Nivek's ship, he added hastily, and found himself back in the airlock. His leg still ached abominably – that was no illusion. Looking down, he saw that it was locked in the enthusiastic jaws of a large poodle. He shook the dog off irritably, and pressed on, into the secret interior of the ship. Hypnotic hallucinations still flickered everywhere, but now he knew them for what they were.

The control-room! He blasted the door down and entered warily. And he scarcely noticed Nivek, for there before him was – Laura! Her eyes were glassy, her face expressionless, and wires trailed from the back of her head to a control box in Nivek's hands, but she was still the girl he loved.

"That fiend hasn't molested you?" queried Malsenn in frenzy. Nivek pressed a switch on his control-box.

"No," Laura droned. "Nivek is kind and sweet, one of the finest humanoids alive." Malsenn scratched his head in puzzlement. "But he's destroyed hundreds of planets, thousands of Starfleet vessels, millions of lives!"

"He has always been misunderstood."

With a sudden flash of intuition Malsenn realized that Laura was not herself. Then she must be ... *somebody else*! No, surely it was she. His mind reeled drunkenly. But this was something to be sorted out later. He tossed a sonic knockout-beamer in her direction and explained: "Keep him covered while I deactivate the ship's defences. Don't worry, you're safe now, whatever that utter rotter has said to you."

As Malsenn turned to the controls and scanned their cryptic labelling, Nivek manipulated his little control-box. Jerkily, Laura raised the beamer, and fired.

Malsenn's awakening was harsh. He found himself in a strange

room, his wrists and ankles clamped to the floor by heavy plutonium manacles. An anti-photon beam was searing a deep groove in
the steel floor, and tracking slowly in his direction. Wisps of nerve-
gas puffed from nozzles in the ceiling; acid dripped on to his chest
from a bottle suspended a foot above him; scorpions scuttled from
concealed slots, and the walls of the room gradually moved in to
crush him. And all the while, his body began to freeze, for the
thermometer registered -12.2 degrees sadly Centigrade.

"This is going to be difficult," Malsenn muttered. He thought
with incredible speed, blowing out the encephalograph which was
monitoring his torment. Soon he conceived three entirely novel
philosophies of the cosmos, but dismissed these idle thoughts
impatiently. With scant seconds to go before the end ... SOLUTION!
The fingers of his hands twitched and writhed. Maddened by the
movement, slavering scorpions rushed towards him and stung him,
as he had hoped. Agony tore through his nerves; his hands swelled
up painfully at once, bursting the manacles in the process. Holding
his breath against the nerve-gas, he sat up, grabbed the acid bottle
– fortunately his laminated polyparot shirt had protected him so far
– and used it to dissolve the ankle-shackles. With one mighty
bound, he escaped the approaching anti-photon beam with microseconds to spare; leaping towards this potent weapon, he used it
to cut a neat, Gothic-arched door in the metal wall.

Free at last from Nivek's insidious control, Laura stared in horror
at the warlord's lascivious features.

"Fear not, my little one," he whispered silkily, "it is indeed a
great honour to enjoy my passionate embraces." She screamed, but
the sound was drowned in the clamour of an alarm-bell.

"It is Malsenn! He has escaped and found this secret chamber!
I cannot face him now. Farewell, sugar ..." He was gone. Laura
fainted, again.

In seconds, a portion of the wall glowed white-hot and
vaporized. Malsenn dropped the anti-photon beam at last, and
leapt in, blaster at the ready. Nivek confronted him.

"Curses," breathed the gaunt, evil form, "you have penetrated
my seven veils of secrecy. Yet think not that this knowledge will
avail you in the vast onslaught which is to come!" As Malsenn
loosed the awful power of his blaster, Nivek unscrupulously faded

and vanished – a 3D holographic projection, intended to delay Malsenn for vital seconds whilst the real, devious warlord made good his escape.

But there on the couch, covered by only a thin sheet, was Laura! He gazed lovingly down at her unconscious form. Even as he feasted his eyes, she stirred, and the sheet slid to the floor, revealing her more fully.

"Gosh," thought Malsenn, "she remembered the regulations and kept her space-suit on."

He lifted her and ran for the airlock, darting away in his little speedster even as the *Saucy Flier*'s atomic reactor blew. The battered hulk of Nivek's ship fell into orbit; exposed to the glare of the naked sun, it would drift on the currents of space till the end of eternity.

Safe in the whirling framework of Space Station 470-EVX, Malsenn allowed his injuries to be briefly treated. Laura insisted on preparing him a meal.

Now she looked puzzled. "That's odd, Mac, the tea won't pour straight. Look! it curves sideways in the air."

Malsenn looked uncomfortable. He had just returned from the bathroom.

"Er ... yes, I had noticed the effect. It's produced by Coriolis force owing to this satellite's spin." The secret hazards of space! He changed the subject. "Food smells good. What is it?"

"My special. Clam chowder garnished with powdered rhinoceros horn."

"Oh." He ate rapidly. Presently, Alkloyd came in.

"*Sacre bleu*, Malsenn, you've been taking some risks!' But it did not occur to him that Malsenn need not have pointlessly endangered his life. Cosmic Agents always pointlessly endangered their lives. It was one of the rules.

"Aw ... shucks." Malsenn stood up hastily. "Time to go, anyway."

"Oh, not so soon, Mac?" wailed Laura.

"'Fraid so." Impelled by a sudden surge of desire, he drew her towards him and kissed her lingeringly, on the forehead. As he strode out, her eyes were moist.

And now, to the battle! The forces of the vengeful Nivek were massing for the greatest offensive the Universe had ever known. Nor was the arch-fiend alone, for allied with him was a race of horrifically indescribable creatures known as the Ech. No human had ever gazed on their hideous bodily form and remained sane; they incorporated all the least pleasant characteristics of octopi, sabre-tooth tigers, scorpions, slugs, blue whales and the unspeakable Sirian rogue mice. As has been mentioned before, they were indescribable.

Malsenn had attempted to foresee the course of the coming conflict by peering into a pane of "fast glass", through which light travelled at many times the speed of light, enabling him to see into the future. But the mighty clash yet to come had predictably warped the very fabric of space and time, and the outlook was hazy.

As well as the conventional thousands of squadrons of ships, the standard mobile planets and the entirely predictable dirigible solar systems, Nivek had three complete flying star-clusters in the vanguard of his colossal force. Against this, Starfleet could muster only one small globular cluster – they hoped against hope that the secret weapons would weight the balance in their favour. Their ultimate weapon was yet incomplete.

Each ship of Civilization's Grand Fleet was rendered invisible by a new and ingenious method: a three-dimensional holographic projector which broadcast an image of the ship itself, cleverly devised to radiate 180 degrees out of phase with the light from the actual ship. Thus the overlapping wave-patterns cancelled, and no ship could be seen. To counteract the effect *within* the hull, a second hologram, of the ship's interior, was projected inside: thus the crew could still see what they were doing. This second projection was constantly edited to correspond to the actual state of the interior.

Nevertheless, Nivek knew that Starfleet was near; and so –

Three suns in his star cluster went nova, flooding space with brilliance. And, at that fateful signal, each of Nivek's countless ships and planetary installations discharged the full, awesome power of its primary projectors, the blazing beams of destruction combining into a hellish flare of incalculable incandescence before which no defence might prevail!

Nivek snarled in rage.

"Missed!"

A nearby galaxy was blasted out of existence, but again Starfleet's superior planning had saved them – thanks to Malsenn and the Battle Computer.

In these days of miniaturization, whole libraries of lore could be inscribed on the surfaces of individual electrons; computers sufficient to direct the affairs of a galaxy were reduced to single large molecules weighing only a few ounces. But so complex had warfare become that the Grand Fleet Battle Computer occupied four giant transport craft which lumbered along in the rear of the fleet, linked together by innumerable connecting wires. A fifth of these monster vessels carried the countless batteries which would be necessary in the event of a power failure. But still it was not enough; whole subfleets might be directed by the WC (War Computer), but only Cosmic Agent Mac Malsenn's mind could hold the full incredibly ramified battle plan.

Now that plan called for the use of the Planck units, weird weapons based in that most fundamental concept of science, the Uncertainty Principle. As is well known, the uncertainty of a body's position is inversely proportional to that of its velocity. So when the micrometrically exact Planck units were called into play, measuring the location of enemy ships with uncanny precision, the uncertainty in velocity became so great that the ships were thrown completely out of control. It could not last: the Planck units were too unstable and pernickety (a common disciplinary penalty in Starfleet was "working the Planck"); still, thousands of collisions took place before Nivek's technicians managed to jam them.

These jamming-zones of interference might have cut off the War Computer completely, isolating it from the fleets it directed; but the cunning secondary communications avoided this peril, involving as they did countless strings and wires stretching for light-years between the ships. (An earlier attempt to fit carrier pigeons with space-suits had proved unworkable.)

Again Nivek let loose a torrent of destruction from every ship and planet; this time half the fleet's star cluster was destroyed. Starfleet countered with their own primary beams, together with showers of neutrino bombs. These last caused great disruption of the alien fleets, for neutrinos pass with ease through light-years of lead, and ordinary screens are useless.

Nivek rallied rapidly with antimatter missiles, and again a stalemate was achieved. Now Starfleet spread out huge mirrors of aluminized plastic, parsecs across, which for an instant reflected the hellish energies of the enemy weapons back to their source; but soon they vaporized under the load, and only a few hundred thousand ships were destroyed by the manoeuvre. Starfleet's morale fell.

The fleets of Nivek and the Ech, sensing imminent victory, moved to englobe Starfleet. In the Command ship, Malsenn and Alkloyd issued frantic orders.

"Manoeuvre QX6005tb! And jump to it!" cried the Commander.

"No! Make that Manoeuvre QX6005tb/1!" Malsenn yelled decisively.

At that instant, a stray bolt of energy, of almost unendurable poignancy, struck the Command vessel. The screens held – barely. They flared a delicate puce under the titanic strain, the interior of the control-room crackled with electrical discharges, and the artificial-gravity plates reversed polarity. The crew's magnetic boots held them to the floor, and they adjusted with practised speed to the reversal. Malsenn lowered his eyes to heaven and cursed. Alkloyd, too, looked down at the ceiling with wry amusement, but continued to speak.

"I think it's time for us to throw up the gauntlet!"

As the enemy hordes moved to englobe them, each Starfleet ship blasted outward at full emergency acceleration so that the fleets formed two concentric globes, expanding at incalculable speed as each fleet attempted to surround the other simultaneously. But Starfleet could not accelerate enough to pass through Nivek's ships and surround them, for the propulsors were the same on both fleets – and Nivek had started first.

So the spheres grew vaster and vaster, for it was suicide for either to stop. Tension mounted in Starfleet Command, for there they knew what a desperate gamble Malsenn was taking, a gamble starkly inconceivable to those who knew nothing of topology or cosmology!

Imagine a group of running men, spreading out from a given point on some smooth, waterless world. Sooner or later the ring of runners will converge again at the antipodean point. So it is with the Universe, which curves through four-dimensioned space in precisely the same manner. And thus –

Imagine, now, Nivek's horror, minutes later, at finding his fleet converging on a single point in space, rushing towards cataclysmic collision at the opposite pole of the Universe! Finding his forces englobed by the triumphant forces of Civilization! Deadly energy-beams lanced from every side into his milling, confused ships. Worse was to come for, at that fatal moment, Malsenn snapped a further order, bringing in the final weapons completed scant seconds before. The invisibility screens went down, revealing –

Galaxies! Seven of them. Armed and powered as only a galaxy can be armed and powered.

Explosion! Concussion! The energies of a billion suns blazed against Nivek's ships, against the forces of the Ech. Under that titanic onslaught, the cosmic process of continuous creation went into reverse. Nothing remained.

In the last instant before total destruction, a subspace signal was beamed from the *Saucy Flier II*. If it was a cry for help, no help came.

Malsenn's homecoming was triumphant; but soon he left the riotous celebrations to be alone with Laura once more.

"Please don't, Mac, it hurts ..." She staggered back, dazed by Malsenn's brutal attack. Suddenly contrite, he took her hand and begged for forgiveness.

"I should never have let you be my sparring partner anyway," he said softly.

"Oh, Mac ..."

Later, he lay in bed and gazed into her enigmatic eyes. Strange longings surged within him. He wanted ... He wanted ... The vidphone connection broke suddenly, and he cursed.

And on a far planet, a planet where a complex subspace receiving apparatus had picked up a brainwave pattern and impressed it on the cortex of a cloned body, Nivek shook an angry fist at the stars.

"You have not heard the last of me, Malsenn!" he shouted. "You have won this round, perhaps – but *the end is not yet!*"

The Thing From Inner Space

E.E. Sm*th

The defences were unbreakable. Guaranteed unbreakable, in normal use. Driven by the power of sixteen gigantic fusion reactors, which had been installed after that first embarrassing incident when the batteries had run down, the force-field mesh could not be penetrated by any body more than an inch in diameter. And inside skulked the most abominable, foul, and evil alien villain of the cosmos, the nefarious, nefandous, necrophagous nemesis of Civilization: Nivek!

Cosmic Agent Mac Malsenn circled the perimeter of the vast defences, on foot. Nivek's instruments could not detect him, owing to his radar screening, his invisibility field and his rubber-soled shoes. For hours he had paced this desolate world, seeking a flaw in his arch-foe's impregnable armour: an Achilles' hole. Short of destroying the planet – which could not be done, for it was under a preservation order – there was no way to pass the impassable barriers of force.

Or ... *was there?* Pulling out his battle-scarred miniaturizer, Malsenn revised that opinion, shrank to a height of half an inch and stepped through a convenient hole in the force-net.

Seconds later, he reached the central fortress: scant seconds, fleeting seconds, swift-passing seconds, but nevertheless 6 x 10⁴ seconds. When you're only half an inch high, walking takes time. Drawing himself up to his full height by another adjustment of the miniaturizer, Malsenn blasted his way in. Soon, casually destroying dozens of Nivek's invincible killer-robots, he came to the inner sanctum. Now was the time for caution. Detection apparatus came into play, and Malsenn did not move until he was certain that in the room beyond there lurked no deadly energy-weapons, no lethal radiation fields, no battle-robots. The coast was clear! Bursting in, he felt a sense of inevitability as he was struck by Nivek's thrown plasti-knife.

His hip ached, but the blade had been deflected by the miniaturizer that hung there. As Malsenn closed in, however, a strange disorientation came over him. Nivek seemed to grow huge and menacing, the room vast ... the impact had turned the miniaturizer on again! Worse, it was jammed on full! By the time the Cosmic Agent reached his foe, he was only a quarter of his size. Standing between the legs of Nivek, who was frozen in shock, Malsenn leapt, striking upward with deadly force: the warlord howled in agony, and clutched his damaged knee. Still Malsenn shrank. He was only a millimetre tall when Nivek dashed a bucket of water over him – laughing resourcefully, he inserted tiny oxygen-cylinders into his nostrils. Then, as Nivek stamped wrathfully on the floor, Malsenn swam rapidly from side to side, remaining safe between the corrugations of the warlord's boots.

Now there loomed a greater peril. Swimming hungrily towards him, a flock of trained mutant paramecia menaced Malsenn, flagellating him with their flagellae. Below, a great amoeba waited to engulf him, reaching out with slimy pseudopodia and drooling disgustingly. For what seemed like hours he fought the ferocious protozoa, splitting their nuclei with great blows of his mighty fists, until, with another jolt of miniaturization, he was beneath their notice.

At this level his entire body ached, his ears sang. The vicious battering of Brownian Motion hurled him this way and that, as hard, lumpy water-molecules impacted him from every direction. Thinking fast, the Cosmic Agent grabbed a big molecule of some organic substance, and struck out with it.

Pow! Wham! Zap!

These and other pungent Venusian curse-words escaped Malsenn's lips as he made his supreme effort. Faster and faster he drove the molecules, increasing their kinetic energy until all around him, they boiled off into the air, leaving him standing on the vibrating metal lattice of the floor, Taking a drink from a stray H_2O molecule that still lay nearby, Malsenn examined the battered miniaturizer. It wasn't too badly damaged, and soon he repaired it, using his powerful fingernails for screwdrivers, his powerful teeth for pliers and wirecutters. But the powerful power-pack, it seemed, was past repair....

Was he doomed to remain like this forever, little more than a nanometre high? He who was so used to thinking big? What an inferiority complex he might develop.

At that moment, a vicious blow struck him. Groaning, he rubbed his ribs and stared to the origin of the attack. Nivek! He'd been followed into the microcosm!

The warlord raised his weapon again, and braced himself. Again a deadly gamma-ray photon shot forth, coruscating and lambent; but this time Malsenn dodged. Hiding behind a metallic crystal, he watched Nivek's inexorable approach. He couldn't face that photon-gun. Or – could he?

"Can I beta gamma at its own game?" he muttered, striving to lift a water molecule. He continued to strive in vain. Curses! No wonder he couldn't lift it. It was heavy water.

Before long he found a lighter molecule, and came out from his shelter. Then as Nivek fired once more, Malsenn brandished the makeshift shield. The poignant missile struck, underwent Compton-effect scattering, shot backwards and knocked Nivek over.

Almost at once, the warlord sprang up and fled, dodging the fast electrons Malsenn hurled after him, eventually losing himself in the wilderness of metallic crystals that made up the floor.

Malsenn became uneasy and, worse, indeterminate. He was growing fuzzy round the edges! He had to get out of this; the Uncertainty Principle was beginning to work on him, Either that, or last night's Cosmic Patrol Party had caught up with him at last.

Desperate now, he set off in pursuit, undeterred by the countless obstacles. Leaping over the metal boulders and outcrops, dodging round them, quantum-tunnelling through them, he sprinted onward. Diffraction-effects kept throwing him off course, and occasionally he suffered elastic collisions with atoms, but doggedly he followed his fleeing foe.

The warlord, ahead, was also having trouble with wave-diffractions, and kept flickering out of sight as he interfered with himself.

"What a disgusting habit," thought Malsenn, unable to resist a straight line but pressing relentlessly on. The fiendish Nivek was ready for him, though, and cackled obscenely in his fuliginous beard at the prospect of trapping the Cosmic Agent at last. For as Malsenn sprang lithely over a patch of slippery and dangerously unstable uranium atoms, coming lightly down on the other side – something coiled and snapped shut round his legs, holding him in a grip of iron. No! Not iron but something worse – something ineluctably carcinogenic ...

"A benzene ring!" cried Malsenn, struggling futilely to free himself from its grip of carbon.

"Exactly so," gloated Nivek, seating himself luxuriously on a large, squashy atom. "This is the end of the line for you, Cosmic Agent!"

"Lies, lies: you say that every time. I'll pay you back yet, you unethical cad."

"Firstly," Nivek said, ignoring him, "I think I shall shrink you to an even greater degree. Imagine the torment of being trapped on an orbital electron for the rest of your life, unable to escape the bound state! Or think of being drawn into a nucleus and crushed by the deadly Strong Interaction ... Or again, you could be – ionized. I assure you, it's not nice."

Malsenn said nothing. He had furtively managed to capture a stray neutron, and had a cunning plan in mind. For he had identified the atom on which Nivek lolled: plutonium! If he could only trigger fission in its nucleus –

Too late. The neutron was well past its half-life (or "sell-by date" as this is technically known) and incontinently came apart in Malsenn's hands, decaying to a proton, an electron and an unpleasant smell. He looked desperately round for another. None in sight.

Nivek gloated obliviously on, describing the starkly inconceivable terrors of the excruciating Isotope Shift, Spin-Orbit Interaction and Mössbauer Effect, any of which could drive strong men mad in moments.

Bang. Bang. Bang.

Malsenn was desperately yet unobtrusively bashing the proton and the electron together. If only his strength were enough; if only he could succeed before being lepton ...

Splat! The separate particles merged again, and a neutron lay in his hand. Now for a final bid for survival. Malsenn summoned up all his eidetic knowledge of cricket and made a perfect overarm throw. The neutron shot through the air and struck the plutonium nucleus. The latter wobbled and quivered in a loathsome fashion for an incalculably infinitesimal subdivision of a second, and then –

The ravening energies of nuclear fission were released! Fragments flew in all directions, Nivek in one direction. The evil warlord sailed through space and crashed unconscious against an impervious atom of inert gas. In minutes Malsenn had escaped the tight embrace of the benzene ring. Success was surely within his grasp.

Now how could he keep Nivek unconscious while he worked at repairing the deminiaturizer? There were all manner of odd elements and diverse molecules scattered around. What was that? Carbon, chlorine, chlorine ... Chloroform! An anaesthetic; just what was needed. He braced himself and picked it up. Then, as Nivek stirred, Malsenn employed the legendary sleep-inducing power of this compound by hitting him over the head with it. *That should keep him out of action for a while*, he thought.

But suddenly Nivek swelled – became huge – enormous. "An automatic recall circuit!" Malsenn cried, and dived aside before the warlord's fast-growing body could crush him. Was this the end? No, if only he could return to normal dimensions himself, the victory could still be his. If only he did it in the next few minutes, while Nivek was still stunned and helpless. If only –

Wait. Was this some trap? What if some dreadful danger lurked unseen? What if ...

"Just the place for a quark!" the Agent cried, surveying the scene with care. The fabled, half-hypothetical but altogether lethal killer quarks might even now be waiting to prey on him and cause him to softly and suddenly vanish away. And he had no quark-repellent. No, it was useless thinking of such horrors! Better to concentrate on the problem before him, the problem of how to return to normal, to restore his shrunken potency, to cease to be a one-millionth-of-a-micromicrogram weakling.

Inspiration came to him, as so improbably often it did, and he set to work. It was only the power-pack that was lacking now; and very little power was in fact needed by that supremely efficient device. Bracing himself, the Cosmic Agent wrenched electrons from nearby atoms, squeezed them rapidly into the makeshift circuits of the deminiaturizer. Would the desperate repairs work? Would he make it back to full size? The next few moments would tell him....

An enlarged Malsenn held Laura gently, tenderly, but still she gasped a little. He gazed at her with longing as he related his adventures, from his first landing on the fateful planet to the final destruction of Nivek's fortress and the delivery of that luckless wight to his usual prison cell.

"Oh Mac, don't ... don't hold me so tight!"

Pity he'd had to jerry-rig that gadget, Malsenn thought for the hundredth time as he strove to clasp his sweetheart more delicately, between finger and thumb.

If Looks Could Kill

R*x St**t

The law relating to the paranormal is almost incomprehensible, except to those who have studied it from their cradles, and even for them it is a labyrinth of uncertainties, of false clues, blind alleys, and unexplored passages.

A.P. Herbert, *More Misleading Cases*, 1930

"This is rather a curious kind of tower," observed Father Brown; "when it takes to killing people, it always kills people who are somewhere else."

G.K. Chesterton, *The Wisdom of Father Brown*, 1914

"Sir, I have no Talent. I have genius or I have nothing."

Caligula Foxe inhaled a firkin or two of air and glared across his desk at our visitor.

"I'm afraid, Mr Foxe, that you'll find that the question is for Committee B2 to decide."

"It is a confounded impertinence."

Certainly it was quite a job keeping my hands where they belonged, on the smaller desk and scribbling ostentatiously in the notebook. I kept wanting to hug myself.

When this Seyton Cream of the Department of Paranormal Resources had asked for an appointment, I'd booked him in on general principles since it was guaranteed to annoy Foxe. Half of my pay is for being a gadfly, after all: he signs the cheques and he said it himself. Also there was at present a certain coolness between Foxe and yours truly. Thank goodness my holiday break was a mere three days off.

Cream swivelled in the red leather chair we kept reserved for clients, and brought his bony face to bear on me. "I would greatly prefer this discussion to be private."

The corner of Foxe's mouth twitched invisibly. "Mr Goodman is privy to all my affairs." Anything that got on a pinstriped civil servant's nerves was okay with him. But then the world's biggest detective remembered his little dispute with me, shifted his one-seventh of a tonne irritably, and added: "Nevertheless, Charlie, on this occasion we shall dispense with the notes. Your transcriptions have been less than satisfactory of late."

I felt a hot flush just behind my ears. The fat old windbag. He knows damn well that I can outperform a cassette recorder for flawless playback, notes or no notes.

Cream said, "Very well. I would now like to come to the point."

"A truly astonishing declaration from a professed Eurocrat," murmured Foxe. "Sir, I believe I can approximate to your point without further aid. Your wretched Brussels committee has wallowed through eighteen months and more than a million words of legal verbiage, addressing the definition of paranormal Talent. You now intimate that deductive and inferential genius, such as I choose to hire out for pay, might soon be so classified. You imply that in the vilest governmental tradition of compulsory purchase, I myself could be placed on the DPR register ..."

He shuddered involuntarily. He *never* left the old house in Westbourne Terrace if he could possibly help it. Talents have to report in at the DPR's lightest whim: I pictured Foxe edging his bulk sideways through the shabby door of their Praed Street office, and sternly suppressed a twinge of pity.

"I did not say ..."

"Pfui. You unmistakably implied."

Cream fiddled with the regulation bowler hat on his lap. "Perhaps I have approached this matter in the wrong way."

"Indeed yes. The carrot is customarily dangled in plain view before any tactless allusion is made to the stick."

"I stand corrected. I've suffered through Committee B2 sessions for so long that I begin to forget how to deal with human beings. Sometimes it seems the thing will never end. You know how it is with the EC."

Foxe inclined his head politely.

With a visible effort, Cream started talking to the point about his outfit's problem, which had nothing to do with committees. It seemed there was this guy Xaos who might or might not be running a foolproof murder bureau. After a minute I let my attention slide a bit, thinking of a certain upcoming trip to Provence with Lila, a very good lady friend. Maybe when I got back Foxe would have seen sense about that antiquated typewriter that had caused all the coolness.

Clearly there was no chance at all of him accepting the DPR commission that was taking shape. A foregone conclusion. Foxe hates being a second choice, and part of the spiel was that the Yard's Odd Squad had already dead-ended on this one. He hates following orders, and Cream was issuing him a complete plan of action. He hates government work, and need I say more? Above all, he *really* loathes being coerced. No chance.

So it was a sudden cold shock when I heard him say distinctly, "Yes, I believe I shall be able to accept the case, at a fee to be determined by mutual agreement. Mr Goodman himself will be pleased to carry out the entrapment precisely as you suggest. I assure you that he is reliable, discreet and loyal ... indeed he will be giving up a long-planned holiday to work uncomplainingly on this very enquiry."

Cream was not visibly impressed. Me even less. As I said, a definite coolness.

This rift had started with the typewriter I use for all Foxe's reports and correspondence ... not to mention his damn plant records. Once upon a time an IBM Selectric 82c had been super-duper luxury; in 1992 it was a rattletrap and a pain.

"A great detective needs the best," I'd explained in courteous and reasonable tones, covering his desk with glossy brochures of word processors, laser printers. But Foxe had decided to get on a hobby horse.

"Charlie," he'd declared, opening his fifth bottle of beer that morning, "there is a high dignity in words. You well know that I employ them with ceaseless care and respect. I consciously choose not to have my sentences agitated in some electronic cocktail shaker or capriciously rearranged at – as you remark – the merest touch of a key. Call it obstinacy, call it Luddism ..."

I didn't call it anything, not out loud, but I'd privately opened up the Selectric and done things to the motor bearings. Now it made a noise like a two-stroke engine with asthma. I was planning to wear Foxe down.

After I'd showed Cream to the front door, I thought bitterly about the Provence trip and wondered if I'd worn him down too far. We discussed the case, very politely. I'll just pick out the highlights of the dossier.

Item: the corpse was a minor Parliamentary cog called Whittle, secretary to some Junior Minister's assistant.

Item: there was a villain, the man called Xaos who advertised a personal service for "removing obstacles" to a happy life, nudge nudge, know what I mean?

Item: there was a tearful confession, from Whittle's wife Diane, who had wanted a divorce, wanted it a whole lot. He hadn't. She closed out their joint account and went to pay a call on Xaos.

Item: there was no evidence. The Met had played pass-the-parcel with the affair. Forensic said flatly that there was nothing to show Whittle hadn't simply popped off from natural causes, immediate cause heart failure. Even the Odd Squad admitted that although the death was quote consistent with attack through psychic attrition unquote – the Evil Eye to you and me – the guy Xaos showed no sign of that Talent and anyway had apparently never got close enough to the victim. Maybe there was an accomplice, even if no one could trace one? But hey, this could well be something new and paranormal and therefore the DPR's pigeon. Pass the parcel. Exit Scotland Yard, chortling and washing their hands.

Item: I checked our file of current papers and found the *Eye* ad was still running. **OBSTACLES REMOVED.** *Clear the path to happiness. No satisfaction, no fee. Xaos, 071 022 3033.* Enough to set anyone thinking and wondering. Cream's dossier included the guy's address, a flat in Pimlico, but even this was no big secret. When I tapped in the number and made an appointment for 3pm, the chirpy voice at the other end told me just how to get there.

Foxe had further instructions. Our freelance colleague Paul Sanza, the best private operative outside Westbourne Terrace, was going to play the victim in this charade – the obstacle to be removed. "The bleating of the kid excites the tiger," Foxe murmured. And my part was to follow in the tracks of the embittered wife and consult Xaos.

"No doubt a circumstantial story will occur to you," said Foxe blandly. "For example, some attractive woman with whom you are besotted has chosen with the fickleness of all her sex to transfer her favours to Paul. Might this not constitute sufficient motivation?"

Paul is a skinny runt with an oversized nose and ears like satellite dishes. I have my own views of my personal attractions and was not best pleased.

"No," I said with feeling. "I thought I'd say he was a boss who'd stumbled into the kind of government work he never takes on, and totally screwed up my holiday with some attractive woman with whom I am besotted. And from whom I expect a sock in the eye tomorrow when I break it to her."

"Charlie. If I am to counter Mr Cream's grotesque implied threat of the temps register, I require leverage. It is necessary that we involve ourselves this once in their affairs."

I didn't believe a word of it and was composing a short, pointed speech, but then our chef Franz came in and announced lunch. His very own *beurre de cacahouettes avec confiture* is not a dish to keep waiting. Foxe demonstrated leverage and was out of the chair faster than you might think.

He allows no discussion of business at his table, and a week ago he'd decreed that all talk of typewriters and word processors counted as business. I wouldn't work for anyone else, but by God he could be trying. Today, between huge mouthfuls, it was language-lesson time. "Charlie, you will undoubtedly have recognized Xaos as a Greek name or pseudonym. The X is of course the letter *chi* and so the word corresponds to our term 'chaos'. A contemporary Greek translator would anglicize the name as Haos with an H, since ..."

Talk about respect for the dignity of words. He's never happier than when he's slamming them against the ropes.

The weather was fine. I decided to walk through Hyde Park and stretch my legs on the way to the appointment. It also gave me more time to practise the story I planned to hand out to Xaos.

His place turned out to be nothing impressive, a dump above a seedy grocer's. "Mr Xaos?" I said as he peered over the doorchain. "I'm Bill Durkin." That was a safety measure. Charlie Goodman, brilliant assistant to Caligula Foxe, was occasionally mentioned in newspapers.

"Just Xaos, Mr Durkin. Can I offer you some coffee?"

I said no thanks, sat down and looked him over. You couldn't call him striking or sinister: chubby, light-haired, thirtyish, about five-six. But something in his very pale eyes made me wonder whether he needed any accomplice for whatever games he got up to.

He said cheerfully, "The usual thing is for you to tell me what you think is getting in the way of the life you want to lead. Then I tell you whether it's something my personal Dyno-Rod service can clear. I turn down a lot of people I can't help."

That had been in the dossier too. The Yard had located and interviewed some of his rejects. A man who wanted Lord Heseltine offed for political reasons. Another with a grudge against the Warden of All Souls for trying to change his sex via laser beams from UFOs. A woman whose husband had cut and run, she didn't know where but she wanted to know for sure he wouldn't come back. Foxe had pushed his lips in and out and eventually said, "Suggestive."

My avowed problem was of course Paul Sanza. It's best to cram as much truth as you can into a story like this, so I told Xaos several warranted facts, at length: that Paul was a private snoop but had otherwise been a pretty good pal, that I played poker with him and the gang three times a week, that he won too often for my liking, and that he knew all about my lady friend Lila.

"But now the bastard fancies her himself," I lied. "He's good at ferreting things out, and he's dug up stuff about me. Never mind what. Just let me say she wouldn't like it one bit. So I'm to lay off Lila or he'll leak things to her, maybe even to the police. I should never have trusted a guy in his slimy line of work."

For the duration I believed in it enough to produce a light sweat on my forehead. Give the man an Oscar.

"Yes," said Xaos. "I can see that you must really hate this Sanza now. Him and no one else?"

I thought of asking whether he offered a wholesale discount, but just nodded.

"Now you might be thinking, how does the Xaos service work and why did I pick this name? And I'll gladly tell you. There is absolutely nothing up my sleeve. I don't even ask a fee in advance.

You pay only when fully satisfied. Of course, by then you'll also be satisfied about the measures I could take if you changed your mind ... but let's not go into that. Now: have you ever heard of chaos theory?"

"I read the colour supplements sometimes," I said cautiously.

"Then I expect you'll know the example they always give. The tiny beating of a butterfly's wing starts a chain of ripples which in the end affect the course of a hurricane on the far side of the world. A sensitive dependence on initial conditions. This is where I work, at a level that doesn't even register on instruments. A paranormal gift, you ask? No, I have no Talent in the usual sense...."

You and Foxe both, I thought. Me, I went and took the DPR tests like a good boy and was relieved when they classed me dead normal.

"But I do have an extraordinary sensitivity to the minute fluctuations of chaos. I see its patterns running through the world. Getting up in the morning, I might clearly sense that delaying one further instant in, say, pulling on a sock would set up a significant eddy in history. One that in the end could sway the political balance of Indo-China."

"What doesn't?" I said sourly. Was he just a common or garden loony after all? Were his successes just a few natural deaths that sort of happened by coincidence in a much longer roster of failures?

"I offered a deliberately far-out example, Mr Durkin. More to the point, if I choose to stay aware of some person's identity – someone such as your 'friend' Paul Sanza – then I can sense things about the flow of chaos as it relates to that person. By tiny choices I send out butterfly ripples. I turn the luck of the world against them. Perhaps it will be disease, perhaps accident. In all my waking hours when I'm on the job, I steer my actions with that in mind, and compel disaster. See, I twiddle this pencil *so*. Air currents move and propagate. Hours or days later it could mean the last straw for a particular party in Solihull or Dublin."

"Well, don't twiddle that thing at me." I usually manage a better class of repartee, but in his weird way Xaos was sort of impressive. His eyes got to you.

I offered him a Polaroid snap of Paul. He glanced at it and nodded. "Thanks. Since you've interacted with him so much in the past, my sensitivity has already picked up the feel of his pattern. It's important, by the way, that you don't deviate from your own routine. Keep going to those poker games with Sanza, and so on."

His casual attitude gave me a feeling of being somehow wrong-footed. Xaos didn't even seem specially interested in Paul's address. Foxe had been speculating after lunch about a repeat of the bluff someone had worked back in 1961, with witches and pentagrams and death spells as window-dressing to distract everyone from the strictly mundane planting of a lethal dose in the victim's larder. You needed an address for games like that. If there was any chance that he was on the level ... Those eyes!

"Well, Mr Durkin," said Xaos, "I'd be pleased to make a small bet with you. If this obstruction to your happiness has not disappeared in, let's say, two weeks, I'll gladly pay you five thousand pounds. And, of course, vice versa."

Of course it was okay and perfectly in character to agree with a tremor in my voice, but I wished it had been one hundred percent an act. We shook on it.

"But don't you get a lot of unwelcome attention?" I asked, hoping to start a crack somewhere. "The ad could mean anything, of course, but the rumour I heard was pretty clear about what you offer."

A thin, knowing smile. "Believe me, I'm safely beyond the reach of the law. I cannot be prosecuted. Goodbye."

Back at street level I signalled unobtrusively to Terry Carver, our second-best freelance after Paul himself. His job was to keep watch and tail Xaos if he took it into his head to go visiting. Then I located a Mercury callbox and keyed in the Sanza home number. He sounded cheerful enough.

"The curse has come upon you," I warned. "Have you got Sally Cole babysitting you there?"

"All according to plan, Charlie. She sends her best."

Sally was a reliable witch-smeller on loan from the Bonner agency, hired to blow the whistle if there really was any weirdo attack. Anyway, the textbooks insisted that while evil-eye merchants didn't need actual eye contact, they could operate only at fairly close range. Our other regular operatives were watching Paul's flat in Haringey, around the clock. Nothing could get to him without being spotted. Surely.

As usual between four o'clock and six, Foxe was pottering in the plant rooms at the top of the house when I got back. I climbed three floors to report as instructed, but he was in a cantankerous mood, blowing hot and cold: "I am not altogether happy with this involvement. I might yet reject the commission. Bah. Please type a full transcript of your conversation with the man Xaos, making three carbons. They may be required."

I pronounced a word under my breath and left him alone with his babies. Why any grown man should want to cultivate paranormal saprophytes ... They were no big thrill to look at, and you could spare only so much admiration for the way they rooted in weird surfaces. One grew on armourglass, another on teflon, a third sucked its nourishment somehow from hard vacuum. Foxe's star item was a sport from Nevada that made out quite happily on a polished slab of depleted uranium, which would personally worry me if I lived in Nevada.

Six and a half pages into the transcript, Foxe moved majestically across the office, settled in the one chair in the world he really loves, and rang for beer. After a pause, he looked hard at me. His index finger moved in tiny circles on the desktop, which is usually a sign that he's bottling something up.

"Charlie. Am I correct in believing that the infernal clatter of that machine is worse than customary?"

"Pardon, sir?"

His eyes narrowed. He picked up one of the completed sheets I'd laid on his desk, and felt it between finger and thumb. "To the best of my knowledge, the system of embossing print on paper was made obsolete by the six-dot alphabet published by Louis Braille in 1829 and elaborated in 1837."

"Gosh, it must be the dedicated energy I put into it, sir, struggling with weakening fingers against antique machinery."

"Pfui. It is an electric typewriter. You have turned up the impact setting with intent to annoy."

He had me there. You can't fool a detective genius. But I was still mad about the holiday, and escalated things by typing on for another paragraph as though I hadn't heard.

"Mr Goodman!" This time it was a full-throated bellow. My eardrums twanged. "Let it be known that I have not the slightest intention of investing in the puerile gadgetry to which you are so attracted." He inhaled deeply, resenting the effort of bellowing, and went on in whiny, sarcastic tones: "But what is this? It was four carbon copies that I required, and not three. You must have misheard me, Mr Goodman. You will need to retype the six, no, the seven pages already completed. I do hope it does not make you late for your *important* appointment to play poker tonight."

I pronounced another inaudible word, with feeling.

Dinner was not a happy meal. It was *doigts de poisson "oeil d'oiseau"*, another of Franz Brunner's great specialities, but Foxe was distinctly off his food. In spite of its impressive size, any little thing could turn his stomach. I made bright conversation about chaos theory and butterflies. It didn't seem to help.

Afterwards, Foxe conscientiously endured the racket of the typewriter as he dipped into a book, *Chaos* by James Gleick. Conceivably he was working. From his bilious expression and the way he dog-eared the pages, I deduced that he wasn't enjoying the style. In all the time before I finished he only said one word. Looking to and fro between a page of my transcript and something in the book, he stated: "Untenable."

Nor was the poker game at Paul's a wild success. I was late after all that retyping and took some chaff about devotion to duty. So did Terry, ringing in hourly to report that he was half frozen and Xaos still hadn't budged from home. The rest of the hired help were mightily pleased to be getting paid for attending their regular card session, but they didn't have a genius to live with. Paul came out ahead by forty pounds, most of it mine. I passed certain remarks about how it was hard to play and bodyguard at the same time, and how I preferred to go easy on a doomed man, but my heart wasn't in it.

Next morning, Foxe evidently felt the same. He declared a relapse.

Relapses take him in various ways. Sometimes he shuts himself in the plant rooms for a week, fiddling with unlikely cross-pollinations. Other times he shoves Franz out of the kitchen and camps there obsessively, cooking *lapin pays de Galles* in fifty different styles. This one, though, was just plain malingering in bed.

What it always means is that his brain is going on strike. Here we were in this damn stupid case, for no better reason than Foxe wanting to needle me, and with nothing to do but sit on our bottoms waiting to see if Paul toppled over and died. No dangerous errands for intrepid Goodman. No spicy little facts for the genius to work on. The closest he'd got to actual thought was claiming that my dialogue with Xaos contained "interesting and suggestive points". I couldn't see them myself.

Foxe was laying it on with a trowel today. At nine he skipped his regular two hours with the plants, and stayed in bed wallowing in self-pity. At ten he called Dr Wolmer, and I groaned at the thought of the cheque I'd have to draw because Foxe never chose to walk three doors along the road to the surgery. At eleven Wolmer came down from the bedroom, looking non-committal.

"Tell me straight, Doc," I asked earnestly as I showed him out. "Are they baffling symptoms of a kind unknown to science?"

"You could say that," he said. Of course he was too polite to suggest the great man might be, ahem, imagining it all.

Towards noon my desk phone buzzed. "Come to my room at once," said Foxe. Maybe now he wanted a lawyer and a priest.

He is an awesome sight in bed, a vast expanse of yellow silk pyjamas like the endless prairies of wherever it is they have endless prairies. Doc told me once that a human being eats his own weight of food every fifty days, and seeing Foxe like that makes you wonder how he can ever find the time. I studied him critically. He looked more unhappy than ill.

"Charlie, I am entertaining a conjecture. The possibility is remote, yet ... Since yesterday evening I have felt ... less and less well. I invariably distrust coincidence. Could the man Xaos have penetrated your deception in some fashion ... turned his weapon, whatever it might be, against not Paul but myself?"

"Anything's possible," I said, humouring him. "With funny eyes like that, he might do all sorts of odd things."

"You will proceed ... no. I may require you here. You will telephone Terry and instruct him to break cover. He is to enter the flat and render Xaos unconscious. Paul or one of the others will go to him with a syringe and a supply of pentothal, to keep him so. If Xaos is to be ... taken at his own face value, he cannot maintain his influence while kept insensible. The conjecture will be tested."

I have omitted the distracting grunts and gasps. Foxe was really hamming it up. It was pathetic. My own professional pride wouldn't let me believe for a moment that Xaos had seen through the story – he'd have had to be a telepath *and* a damn good actor. All the same, I disliked him on principle and approved of action, any action.

"I'm betting that you're wrong, sir, but here goes," I said, and sprinted downstairs, hoping Terry had remembered to pack his cellphone.

He had.

I cooled my heels for twenty-five minutes, flipping through much-thumbed brochures of Provence and once again growing increasingly irritated with Foxe. If I couldn't take my rightful holiday, why the hell couldn't it be me who burst in and socked Xaos on the jaw?

Then Terry called. He'd worked it better than that. "I just went up, told him a friend had recommended me to consult him, said yes to coffee and slipped him a Mickey Finn when his back was turned. Dead to the world. He was easy meat, Charlie."

"Right," I said. "Foxe will tell me to say 'satisfactory' and so I do. Be seeing you."

I buzzed the sickroom and passed on Terry's message. "And do you feel a sudden surge of relief and well-being, sir?"

"No," said the theatrically feeble voice.

Which was exactly what I'd expected. Imaginary illnesses are real toughies to treat, I thought to myself.

By now, I dare say you've guessed the secret of how Xaos really worked his tricks. You're probably thinking I'm dumb not to have deduced it for myself. Let me just say that I'm not the genius in this household, only the legman ... and puzzles are a million times harder to solve when you're close to them, living through them.

I lunched off a glass of milk. That didn't bother Franz, but he came down almost in tears when Foxe refused the tray carrying a light, eleven-course invalid snack. I had begun to get the creepy feeling that something was going on right under my nose, that I was missing the obvious.

Around then, Ron Cohen of the *Eye* rang to remark that according to the whispers of little birds in his ear, our favourite fatso was now pulling chestnuts out of the fire for the Department of the Preternaturally Ridiculous, and what about an inside story? I bandied words with him, not referring to small ads.

Seconds after I'd hung up, Paul reported in. Xaos continued to sleep like a babe, he reckoned they could keep him that way for another 24 hours solid, and to pass the time our gang had made a fine-tooth search of the dump. No voodoo props, no death rays, no written records of the obstacle-removing business. No news: of course the Yard had done the same and drawn a blank, though their dossier kept sort of quiet about it.

Mid-afternoon, and I heard the whir of Foxe's private lift. His idea of exercise is to go up and down twice. I wondered if he'd pulled out of his goddam relapse and started making plans for the new problem of our court appearance when citizen Xaos gave evidence on charges of assault, conspiracy, actual bodily harm with a hypodermic....

Then I saw something I'd never seen before. Foxe was standing in the office doorway in his vast yellow pyjamas, swaying ponderously, looking shrunken, greenish and three-quarters dead. Great drops of sweat stood out all over his big face. It was a hell of an impressive performance.

"Charlie. An alternative conjecture. Please ... obey me without question. I instruct you to order the word processing equipment of your choice, for immediate delivery. Use the agency credit card. I ... also wish to apologize for the cancellation of your holiday ... shall make amends. I ..." He closed his eyes and leaned hard against the door frame.

My God, I thought, he's actually delirious. He really was ill now, in such a state that I wouldn't have been surprised if he'd started splitting infinitives or using "contact" as a verb. It truly was sort of touching to think our little rift had been so much on his mind that he'd staggered down like this for a deathbed repentance scene.

"You should be in bed, sir," I said, and sincerely meant it.

"Mr Goodman. Kindly carry out my instructions at once." There was enough of the old snap in his voice that my hand dived straight for the telephone.

"Black Mountain Systems? I have an urgent order." I knew by heart what I wanted, of course. I mean, what the office wanted.

When I turned, Foxe was sitting behind the big desk in his pyjamas, mopping his face with the wrong handkerchief (it was a souvenir of the Ballard case and still had the original bloodstains) and breathing heavily. His colour was a little better now.

"Kindly fetch Mr Cream at once. I will instruct Paul to bring the man Xaos here. My alternative hypothesis has been fully confirmed. Thank heavens."

I have to confess I still hadn't the faintest idea what he meant.

By the time I'd hauled a strongly protesting Cream from his Ministry (lucky he wasn't off committeeing in Brussels again), Paul had arrived and decanted Xaos into one of the yellow leather chairs. He looked thoroughly groggy, and so would you. Foxe had dressed, shaved and – I'd bet – eaten his head off. I steered our client to the red chair.

Foxe looked at him with satisfaction. "Mr Cream, I would like to introduce you to Mr Xaos."

"Just Xaos. No Mr. And you won't believe the lawsuit I'm going to hit you with when I get clear of your goons."

"Be silent, sir. I shall be brief. As we agreed, Mr Cream, my operatives carried out a decoy manoeuvre. Mr Goodman approached the gentleman sitting there, who in effect undertook to ensure for a consideration that a certain man died within a fortnight. Several points about the reported conversation struck me, such as the nonsensical smokescreen of part-digested chaos theory, the seeming lack of interest in personal details of the proposed victim, and the emphatic remark that Mr Xaos himself was safe from prosecution. Indeed he is."

"If they can't prosecute, then you haven't earned your fee," said Cream sharply.

"We shall see. May I continue? Frankly, I know little of the pesky ways of paranormal Talent, but nevertheless I formed an interesting conjecture to account for this assurance of immunity. The Yard searched in vain for a murderous accomplice. What occurred to me was the notion of an unknowing accomplice."

Cream said: "That sounds like a contradiction in terms." Xaos chuckled uneasily.

"Mr Xaos, I speculated, is the possessor of an interesting Talent. He cannot himself wield, but can temporarily confer, a power of malignity akin to what is commonly known as the Evil Eye. To test this conjecture after visiting him," Foxe said through his teeth, "Mr Goodman undertook to act out spurious feelings of resentment and dislike towards myself, pretending for the purpose to be discommoded by an obsolete typewriter. A small and seemingly a childish pretext, but Mr Goodman's powers of theatrical self-deception are remarkable. The result ..."

A cold shock like a bucket of ice-water had hit me in the stomach. If I'd been any madder with Foxe ... My eyes were popping with sheer rage at what Xaos had so goddam nearly made me do. The bastard, the absolute bastard. For a moment I couldn't speak, only glare.

"Charlie!"

Xaos had slumped sideways in the yellow chair. Paul Sanza was at his side straight away. "Heart, I think. My God, he's gone. No, he seems to be picking up again.... That's odd. Pulse went and came back again. Yes, he should pull through now. I think."

"Which would tend to confirm my hypothesis," Foxe said silkily. "Have Franz bring brandy. Charlie, my apologies. I inadvertently goaded you into anger, forgetting the extent of your loyalty and devotion."

He takes a lot for granted, does Caligula Foxe. I fought for calm and worked away at swallowing the lump I'd never admit was in my throat.

Foxe's shoulders lifted a tenth of a millimetre, which for him was an expansive shrug. "You see, Mr Cream? Of course in the Whittle case it was the wife Diane after all. Following Mr Xaos's treatment, a period of serious hating at close range would have put paid to anyone. (One sees, does one not, why he refused customers who wished the deaths of people in remote or unknown locations?) You can't prosecute him: he didn't do it. You can't prosecute her: she acted unknowingly and the evil gift will have faded away, leaving no evidence. I deduce that it must fade because, otherwise, even the Yard would have detected her unwitting Talent."

No wonder Xaos had insisted I should carry on playing poker with Paul. Good grief. That, if only I'd had a real grudge, would have handed him the black spot for sure.

"H'mm," said Cream, scratching his jaw and pointedly ignoring the weak, catarrhal noises from the body in the yellow chair.

"I am pleased to release the man Xaos into your custody. In all justice the DPR should lock him away as a social disease, but no doubt you will prefer to place him on a meagre stipend and make some dubious use of his ability. Meanwhile, I shall ask no fee but require an assurance that your pestilent Committee B2 will in future regard deductive and intuitive genius as falling outside the scope of the paranormal."

"Nonsense. How the devil can I commit the Department to a stance like that?"

"Consider the alternative," said Foxe dreamily, wiggling a finger at him. "Mr Goodman occasionally publishes records of my cruder and more sensational cases. If the Xaos affair were made public, then so likewise would be the hitherto unremarked fact that temporary Talents can be induced. I rather imagine this would mean starting again, *de novo*, on Committee B2's legalistic definition of the paranormal. Eighteen months' work, do I recall your saying, and a million words of draft regulations?"

Cream had gone twice as pale as his name. "Jesus," he said. "I mean, how extremely inconvenient that would be. I ... Very well. On behalf of the Department, I accept your terms."

"Satisfactory. Would you care for beer?" Foxe rang the bell.

"No, thank you." The civil servant issued a constipated little smile. "I suppose the DPR is getting off lightly. I've heard a great deal about your exorbitant fees and, frankly, am somewhat surprised that you don't want money as well."

"But I do," murmured Foxe, indicating the chair where, under Paul's and my tender care, Xaos was groaning and spluttering into his brandy. "A certain bet was made with an authorized representative of this agency. Assuming that Mr Sanza can contrive not to die before the end of the stipulated fortnight, Mr Xaos will owe me the sum of five thousand pounds. I intend to collect."

The ex-obstacle remover snarled feebly at Foxe. If looks could kill ... But of course *his* couldn't.

Later, I struggled hard to master the new word processor as Foxe pretended to read his evening paper and gave me the occasional cynical look. It was a damn sight more complicated than the ads had claimed. Don't let him say anything, I thought as for the umpteenth time the machine beeped rudely and flashed *ERROR*. In five or six days, according to Xaos, the curse would wear off and I'd be able to risk getting mad at people again. For now, just don't let him *say* anything.

He said: "Tonight, at my request, Franz is preparing *crapaud*

dans le trou Anglais in a sauce of his own invention. A most satisfactory conclusion to the case."

It was a recipe he knew very well I could get along without. "I'll
try my best to enjoy it, sir," I said with false eagerness, "but of
course it could discommode me in some small and seemingly childish way. I might have to struggle to control my temper, you know,
as brutal feelings of hatred rise up in me at each fresh mouthful ..."

Foxe's eyes narrowed dangerously. I felt a huge, death-cold
wave of sickening weakness crash through me and realized that
Xaos had left him with a parting gift. By gum, for the next whole
week we'd *both* have to be incredibly calm and polite. Somehow.

We discussed it.

Acknowledgements

Some of these stories and skits have appeared elsewhere, in slightly or even greatly different form. The original publications were as follows. Thanks to all the editors for their indulgence.

Part One – The Dragonhiker's Guide to Battlefield Covenant at Dune's Edge: Odyssey Two

The As*m*v opening to the Introduction is based on part of my review of Isaac Asimov's *Quasar, Quasar, Burning Bright* in *Vector 95*, October 1979. Much of the other inset skit material appeared as "Play It Again, Frodo" in *White Dwarf 79*, July 1986.

"Duel of Words": *Sfinx 2:2*, 1983.

"Lost Event Horizon": *Imagine 12*, March 1984.

"The Distressing Damsel": *Amazing SF*, July 1984.

"The Mad Gods' Omelette": *White Dwarf 59*, November 1984.

"The Thing in the Bedroom": *Knave 16:11*, November 1984.

"Jellyfish": *Knave 17:5*, May 1985.

"Look At It This Way": *Amazing SF*, July 1985.

"Outbreak": *A Novacon Garland* published by the Birmingham SF Group, November 1985. (Hence the unsubtle use of the BSFG acronym, allusion to the group's annual SF convention Novacon, etc.)

"The Gutting" is a adapted extract from *Guts!* by myself and John Grant; this horror spoof was eventually published by Cosmos Books in 2001.

The rest of Part One appeared for the first time in the 1998 *Dragonhiker*. An earlier version of "Spawn of Non-Q" was written in collaboration with Allan Scott, who had not actually read *The World of Null-A* and was hugely relieved to find all his episodes omitted ... with the exception of a single gag. The resulting jerkiness seems on the whole to increase the van-Vogtian flavour.

Part Two – 2

"The Case of Jack the Clipper": *Interzone 126*, December 1997

"The Case That Never Was": *Weird Tales 326*, Winter 2001-2002

"Christmas Games": *Christmas Forever* ed. David G. Hartwell, 1993

"If Looks Could Kill": *Eurotemps* ed. Alex Stewart, 1992

"The Last Robot Story": *3SF 2*, 2002

"The Net of Babel": *Interzone 92*, February 1995

"Not Ours To See": *The Fortune Teller* ed. Lawrence Schimel and Martin H. Greenberg, 1997

"Out of Space, Out of Time": *Science Fiction Age*, 1998

"The Repulsive Story of the Red Leech": *The Mammoth Book of New Sherlock Holmes Adventures* ed. Mike Ashley, 1997

"Sex Pirates of the Blood Asteroid": *Aries 1* ed. John Grant, 1979

"The Spear of the Sun": *Interzone 112*, October 1996. Initially written for the anthology *Alternate Skiffy* ed. Mike Resnick and Patrick Nielsen Hayden, whose theme was alternate histories of science fiction itself, but whose publication was delayed to 1998.

"The Thing From Inner Space": *BSFA Newsletter 6* (*Matrix*), May 1976

Printed in August 2023
by Rotomail Italia S.p.A., Vignate (MI) - Italy